the
TASTE
of AIR

Gail Cleare

Unlocking New Worlds

The Taste of Air
Copyright © 2016 by Gail Cleare All rights reserved.
First Print Edition: August 2016

Print ISBN-13: 978-1-940215-81-5
Print ISBN-10: 1-940215-81-1

Red Adept Publishing, LLC
104 Bugenfield Court
Garner, NC 27529
http://RedAdeptPublishing.com/

Cover and Formatting: Streetlight Graphics

For Bruce, my soul mate and astral twin, who gave me the courage to roar.

CHAPTER 1

Nell ~ 2014

HER DAY BEGAN WITH REASSURING rituals. *Make the beds, start a load of laundry, empty the dishwasher.* After lining up shiny crystal tumblers inside the glass-fronted cabinets, she filled the upper shelves with neatly nested plates, bowls, and cups. Her finger found a chipped edge, and she tossed the imperfect saucer into the garbage. It was expensive china, but she would order a replacement. The house always looked fresh, with cut flowers on the dining room table. It smelled of roses and sandalwood. When Nell walked through her beautiful, decluttered, well-organized home, balance and serenity followed.

She had pulled on a jacket and was typing a grocery list on her cell phone when it rang. Nell didn't recognize the caller ID but answered just in case, as she knew good mothers did.

"Eleanor Williams?"

Not the school. They never call me that.

"Yes?" She didn't feel like being patient with a telemarketer and reached for the off button.

"Mrs. Williams, I'm calling about your mother, Mary Ellen Reilly." An elevator bell sounded in the background, and a voice was talking over an intercom.

Nell frowned and put the phone back to her ear. "What about her?"

"This is Hartland General Hospital in Vermont. Sorry to call with bad news, but your mother is in our intensive care unit."

This had to be some kind of weird mistake.

"You must have the wrong person. My mother lives in Massachusetts. I just talked to her yesterday." Nell paced in front of the kitchen island.

"She gave us your number." The woman sounded impatient, then her voice softened. "This morning, Mrs. Reilly named you her legal health care proxy."

Nell steadied herself against the spotless granite countertop and sat down on a barstool. Mom was supposed to be safely tucked into her apartment at the Maplewood Community, not three or four hours away in some hospital. *Can this be for real?*

"Is she okay? What happened?" Nell threaded her fingers through her cropped hair and tugged.

"Your mother was admitted early this morning with a respiratory infection. Her condition is listed as serious."

That was familiar territory. Every year, Mom caught a nasty cold and had a terrible time getting rid of the cough. She'd been diagnosed with walking pneumonia the previous winter and recovered at home, but this time, she'd been hospitalized. At her age, it could be a disaster. Nell reached for the notepad and pen and noticed her hand was shaking.

What was Mom doing in Vermont? She hadn't mentioned a trip.

"Is someone with her?" Mom used to go on little weekend jaunts with her girlfriends from the senior center until Nell and Bridget convinced her to stop driving.

"Not that I've heard." The woman's tone was insistent. "Can you get here soon? The doctors want to see you."

"Okay," Nell said, her voice faltering. "Where are you located exactly?"

Her usually perfect script looked nearly incoherent when she scribbled the address with the letters and numbers staggered across the page. She stared at the note while a trickle of panic washed over her. Mom was counting on her to take charge. She'd asked for Nell, not Bridget, which was flattering, but now she had to live up to it.

The past few years, they'd been nearing the point where their mother-daughter roles would reverse. When Nell turned forty the previous year, the term *middle-aged* developed a new meaning. She was literally in the middle, between her children and her remaining parent, caring for both the younger generation and the older one. Bridget didn't have kids and worked full-time, so it was different for her.

Nell pictured her mother three months before, when everyone was together on vacation in Florida. Out on the golf course, playing a slow but sociable eighteen holes, silver-haired and slender, Mary Reilly was still beautiful at seventy-five. Except for the annual chest cold, Mom was in good health.

Grabbing the phone again, Nell dialed her mother's cell number. It seemed worth a try. The call went directly to voicemail, so Nell speed-dialed Bridget.

"Good morning, sister dear. What's up?" Her older sister's musical voice answered the telephone with a slight Southern drawl, something acquired since she'd moved to the suburbs of Washington, DC. The loud bubbling in the background meant Bridget was enjoying her usual morning soak in the hot tub.

"Not good. We've got trouble." Nell shouted into the phone to be heard.

"Trouble? Honey, trouble is my middle name," Bridget sang out.

"Bridget. Pay attention, this is important." Nell raised her voice again. "Turn off the jets so you can hear me."

The bubbling stopped.

"What's got you all riled up so early in the morning?"

Nell told her what had happened. There was a moment's silence.

"This is *our* mother you're talking about? For sure?" Bridget's playful tone had disappeared, as had her faux Southern accent.

"Apparently so. She gave them my number. How did she get so sick all the sudden? And what is she doing way up in Vermont?" Nell calmed herself with a deep breath, waiting for the inevitable commands that would come next.

"I can't even guess. This is totally bizarre. You'd better get up there fast since she asked for you this time. I'll call Maplewood and give them hell." Bridget jumped into crisis-management mode and took charge as she had always done since the day Nell learned to walk and started to follow her around. Then her voice faltered. "Okay, Nell? I can cancel my client meetings and be ready to hop on a plane whenever you need me."

"I'll go see what's happening," Nell said. "Call you this afternoon."

"Love you. Talk soon."

Nell headed into David's study to go online and buy a ticket on the noon flight to Vermont from nearby Newark Airport. She tried not to think about the terrible things that might be about to happen and focused on getting herself out the door. After calling her husband, she spoke to the housekeeper and the babysitter and emailed the other parents in the carpool. Then she went upstairs to throw some things in a bag, all the time wondering what in the world her mother was doing in Vermont all by herself.

At one o'clock, Nell's plane landed in Burlington. Lake Champlain glittered beyond the city center, stretching wide along the western horizon with the misty mountains of upper New York State behind it in the distance. She rented an economy car, bought a map, and turned south, leaving the urban area behind.

Her mind was caught in a repeating loop of worry about Mom, but eventually, the fantastic landscape penetrated her consciousness. Softly rounded bright-green mountains filled the view in all directions, row upon row of them, receding into the pale distance. Weaving her way through valleys, where black-and-white cows grazed in vast, grassy fields, Nell felt as if she'd entered a fantasy world. It reinforced the eerie sensation that the whole day had been nothing but a dream.

The bright blue sky soared overhead, a gigantic bubble of pure clean air. It invited her to roll down the windows and breathe deep. Back home in New Jersey, the air was yellow and gritty, the colors dull. Here, the palette was almost fluorescent. The planet seemed alive, wild, and pulsing in a way that the concrete hive where Nell lived never did.

When she turned off at the exit for Hartland, a winding country road led past farms and houses toward the village center. The iconic white spire of a Congregational church appeared, then the cluster of Colonial-era buildings that surrounded the town green. She parked in the hospital lot at the far end of the green.

Nell caught a glimpse of her tense eyes in the rearview mirror. She gave her short, blond hair an efficient tousling then locked the car and followed signs to enter the lobby with a whoosh of revolving glass doors. A woman in a pink uniform sat at the reception desk, talking on the phone. Nell glanced at her name tag. VOLUNTEER – Doris Barton.

Doris ended the call and looked up at Nell with a friendly smile. "Can I help you?"

"I'm here to see Mary Reilly." The lobby was deserted. Nell wondered how many beds the small building could possibly accommodate. She might have to move Mom someplace where they had the latest technology and more expertise.

"Are you her daughter?" There was too much sympathy in the woman's eyes.

Nell nodded as a nervous throb tightened her stomach.

"Could I see some identification?"

Nell passed over her driver's license and picked lint off her black jacket while the woman made copies. She balled up all the little bits of fluff and stuffed them into her pocket before Doris turned around.

"Here's a copy of the health-care proxy she signed, for your records." She handed Nell a document.

Mom had listed Nell's legal name, Eleanor Reilly Williams, with her address and cell phone number. It was definitely Mom's handwriting. In that moment, Nell surrendered to the reality of the situation. She folded the paper and slipped it into her purse.

"She's in Intensive Care." The woman pointed to a doorway. "I'll call and say you're on the way. Down that hall. Just follow the signs."

Walking through long corridors, Nell found her way deeper into the building. The walls turned from sage green to pale blue to dusty rose. The hallways became dim and hushed, with the citrus scent of cleaning solution in the air. When she pushed open the door to Intensive Care, two nurses wearing scrubs pointed her toward one of the white-curtained doorways.

In the middle of a nest of stainless-steel machines, blinking LEDs, and electrical cords, Mom lay on a metal bed that looked like a giant praying mantis. Her eyes were closed. She looked so pale that she virtually disappeared into the sheets, and only the blue veins showed. Her limp white hair blended in with the pillowcase. She seemed frail and paper-thin, a ghost woman.

A fat gray tube fastened onto her open mouth like a huge parasitic worm. Rhythmically blowing air into her lungs from a nearby machine, it looked like some kind of torture, and tears streamed down Nell's cheeks as she picked her way across the room to stand by the bed. The situation was much worse than she'd imagined. Someone she hardly recognized had replaced the strong, vibrant woman who'd raised her.

She laid her hand over her mother's, trying not to disturb the IV line held in place with bloodstained tape. Nell listened to the machine breathe. Her mother's face looked serene, as though she were miles and years away. Her chest moved up and down.

A young nurse wearing purple scrubs entered the cubicle. "I'm Jennifer. I've been taking care of Mary since about seven this morning." She smiled at Nell. "We gave her some medication to help her rest. It should last for several more hours." She reached up to adjust one of the tubes. Their eyes met, and the woman silently commanded Nell not to get hysterical.

Thinking again that her mother was counting on her, she suppressed the impulse to panic and tried to focus on practical matters. She cleared her throat and straightened her back. "How is she? Where's the doctor? Can I talk to him?"

"The pulmonologist was here a while ago. She'll be back later," Jennifer said. "The hospital's doctor on duty came by this morning, and he'll be back at the end of the day. A chest X-ray confirmed Mary has pneumonia. She's on antibiotics through the IV. Her heartbeat is slow and steady, CAT scan normal, blood pressure good, and she's stable. Her general health seems fine. The machine is breathing for her, so she can rest and fight the pneumonia."

Nell blinked, absorbing the information. "That thing." She pointed at the ventilator. "How long will she need to have it inside her?"

"We try not to keep them on the machine for more than a couple of days, so they don't get too dependent. It can be hard to wean them off. We may have to put in a feeding tube later if the doctor decides to continue with the ventilator. She needs nourishment to stay strong." The nurse reached up and adjusted the line running to Mom's arm.

Nell pictured a tube running down her mother's throat and into her stomach, and she shuddered.

"You can sit here and wait or get something to eat. Maybe some coffee?" Jennifer said.

"I could definitely use some caffeine." Nell rubbed the back of her neck, where a sore muscle twinged. "Are you sure she won't wake up?"

"The cafeteria is right downstairs. Here's the ICU number. Give me your cell number, and I'll call you if anything changes."

"All right, I'll go in a little while." Nell took the business card Jennifer offered and wrote her number on the nurse's clipboard. She got a tissue out

6

of her pocketbook to swab the tears from her face. "First, I need to know how Mom got here. Can you tell me what happened?"

"She came in early this morning through the Emergency Room. Somebody must have called 9-1-1. Don't worry. I'll be in to check on her every few minutes." The nurse put her hand on Nell's shoulder and smiled encouragement.

Nell sat in the chair by Mom's bed and watched her sleep. She started to calm down as the sense of urgency faded. Her mother seemed to be resting in comfort, not in any pain. While she sat, Nell reorganized the contents of her purse and tossed all the day's crumpled tissues into a trash can. Everything fit after that, which made her feel much better. So did the steady sound of the machine breathing and the peaceful expression on Mom's delicate face. It looked as if she was dreaming about something happy. Nell wondered what thoughts had smoothed the worry lines on her mother's brow.

She'd been up before dawn to get the kids ready for school and felt so tense the muscles in her shoulders quivered. Nell stood up and tried to stretch the kinks out of her back. Then she went in search of coffee, wandering out the way she had come in. Mom's care seemed logical and under control for the moment, though it would be good to talk to a doctor soon and find out more.

She looked at her watch. Back at home, the kids would be getting out of school about now. The housekeeper should be finishing chores and starting to cook dinner. Nell would call in a little while to check on everyone, but she wasn't worried. Things ran smoothly at Nell's house even when she wasn't there in person to supervise. It was all about building a system, a routine. Everyone knew what was expected of them.

When she was a child, it hadn't been so simple. Mom's behavior was loving and consistent, but Daddy's approval had come and gone for no apparent reason. That was probably why she always needed to please people. When Mom felt better and found out how well Nell had managed, she would be impressed. As soon as the doctor came back, Nell could get all the facts and start making decisions. But she might as well get a few things out of the way while she was waiting. She needed a place to stay and something to eat.

Nell ended up back at the front desk where Doris sat. The bright light in the lobby sent a spike of pain flashing through her left temple, a sign that a migraine was on the way.

Nell asked Doris to recommend a nearby motel or bed-and-breakfast, figuring she could quickly check in and grab some coffee while she waited for Mom to wake up. She received a blank look in response. The receptionist clicked a button on her computer and looked at the screen.

"Thought so. Don't you want to stay at your mother's place? It's just a few minutes from here."

Nell stared at her, dazed. "My mother's place?"

The woman clicked another button, and a page began to emerge from the printer behind her desk. It was Mary's registration form. The address line read, "27 Lakeshore Road, Hartland, VT." A phone number with the local area code was listed.

"Beautiful old cottages down by the lake. She must love it there. Need directions?" Without waiting for an answer, the woman printed out a map and pushed it across the desk. She pointed out how to get to the lake, while Nell's mind raced to the most logical conclusion. Mom must have rented a place on the water. The owners might know something about what happened to her. Nell would drive over for a quick snoop and see if anyone was around.

Going outside with the map clutched in her hand, Nell fumbled with her keys and got into the car. Half a mile away was Lakeshore Road, which as she expected, followed the banks of a small lake. Rocky beaches were studded with mica that sparkled in the sunlight. A few sailboats tacked back and forth across the dark-blue water—another beautiful landscape painted in those glowing colors. A pair of cardinals darted across the road in front of her, the male a scarlet flash against the pines.

Nell pulled up at number twenty-seven, which was across the street from the lake. The white cottage had a small yard in front, neatly mowed, and an attached one-car garage. The front door was fire-engine red, just like the one on the house where Nell and Bridget had grown up. Black shutters framed the windows too. Looking at the oddly familiar house brought the scent of cinnamon to mind along with a memory of getting off the school bus to find Mom in her apron and warm applesauce cake waiting on the kitchen counter.

Parking in the driveway, she waited for someone to appear. Maybe the cottage belonged to friends and Mom had been visiting. Nobody seemed to be around. It was silent except for birdcalls and the barking of a small dog.

Nell got out of her car and walked up the path. Leaning forward to push the doorbell, she tried to peek into the windows without being obvious. For some reason, the place was making her feel odd. *Funny coincidence that it looks so much like our old house.* The memory blurred and shifted in her mind like a dream from long ago. Nell's brain began to tingle, anxiety building up in her chest. She looked around more carefully and saw her mother's favorite flowering annuals, salmon-colored New Guinea impatiens, planted between the shrubs across the front of the house. Mom always planted them in early spring so they'd be in full bloom for the parade on Memorial Day.

All the shades were positioned exactly the same across the front of the cottage, lined up like soldiers. Mom had always been a stickler for that, saying it was a habit she'd picked up in the army, where she'd been a nurse before she and Daddy were married.

Nell leaned forward and rang the doorbell again then knocked. The sound echoed through the quiet neighborhood. There were no signs of movement inside the cottage.

Almost without thinking, in a strange, dreamy state of mind, she stepped into the flowerbed to the right of the door and reached behind the shutter. A key hung from a small hook, exactly where it should be. Her hand found it with a certainty gained from years of experience.

Whatever was going on, Nell didn't like it. The place was a trip back to her teen years. It was as though she had slipped into a time warp.

She looked at the key in her hand as if it was a bug that might bite her. Then she walked up the steps, put the key in the lock, and turned it. The red door swung open.

She entered a narrow living room that stretched the full depth of the house. A clock ticked like a slow, sure heartbeat. Standing in the middle of the room, she turned full circle and examined the place carefully. The unremarkable furniture was old but looked comfortable. A worn Oriental carpet covered the floor in shades of blue and gold. There were silk flowers on the table by the window and shelves filled with cheerful ceramic tea sets. Over the fireplace hung a framed print of Mary Cassatt's painting of two little girls playing at the beach, one of her mother's favorite images. She'd always said it reminded her of Nell and Bridget. Nell had bought her a print at the Louvre Museum when she and David went to Paris on their honeymoon.

Nothing else looked familiar, though, and Nell started to relax. It was a vacation rental, of course. Why would she recognize it? *The key was just a fluke. It was a great hiding place, that's all.* Hopefully, the landlord wouldn't walk in and catch her roaming around. Well, if Mom had rented the place, then it wouldn't matter anyhow. She just needed to confirm that her mother had really been staying there, so she turned and continued to explore.

Walking through to the adjoining kitchen at the back of the house, she found it clean and tidy with nothing on the counters or table. The room smelled faintly of toast. *Probably from yesterday, unless somebody else was here.*

Passing a cozy den, she climbed up the stairs. Nell tried the bathroom first, looking for prescriptions, but the medicine cabinet only held some over-the-counter drugs. Her neck muscles crackled with tension, and her temple throbbed, so she took two painkillers and swallowed them with water from her cupped hand. The front bedroom looked like a guest room, an empty stage waiting for the next actor to appear. The larger bedroom, which looked out on the backyard, seemed inhabited. She noticed books and reading glasses on the bedside table and a white sweater hanging on a hook.

Opening the dresser drawers, she found a woman's nightgowns and underwear, size small, and then the kind of bra Mom liked, the brand Nell herself had recommended. She noticed a familiar scent floating up out of the drawers. Baby powder and lavender, the same fragrance she smelled whenever she put her arms around Mom's neck for a hug. Touching the clothes reverently, she stroked the wrinkles flat and put everything away.

Nell took off her jacket and hung it on the back of a chair. She looked over at the door of what must be a closet. Her throat ached with anxiety, and she hesitated, but then she stepped forward, swung the door open, and reached to pull the dangling light chain.

Hanging right on the back of the closet door, a long garment glowed a bright hot red, spotlighted by the bare bulb.

She blinked, but the uneven topstitching on one cuff was unmistakable. It was the red flannel bathrobe Nell had made for her mother in sewing class in high school. It looked as though Mom had just taken it off and would be right back inside it again that night for popcorn and TV.

The robe smelled like Mom too. Nell pressed the fabric to her face and inhaled, tears leaking from her eyes. She felt stretched as thin as the skin of an overripe tomato, ready to split at the slightest touch.

The closet was full of her mother's clothes, way too many for a short visit. There were winter sweaters and summer shorts, parkas and snow boots along with T-shirts and sandals. The clothes were definitely Mom's. Nell recognized them. It looked as if her mother had been living there for a long time.

How could this be happening? Mom lived at Maplewood, where people looked in on her every day. They would have noticed if she was gone. And why hadn't she told Nell or Bridget about this house? Nell's calm dissolved, and the insecurity that was right around the corner most of the time came rushing into the place in her stomach where she held her fear.

Her world had transformed from the orderly refuge where she always felt safe into a chaotic state of confusion. Nell's head buzzed with a strange sense of betrayal. The hurt child inside cried out for life to return to normal, but she had a feeling nothing would ever be that way again.

Standing in front of her mother's closet, she tried to imagine Mom sneaking off to Vermont. It wasn't easy to picture. A wave of resentment swept through her, then she gasped for breath and clutched the left side of her head, where a steady pain burned. She took a deep breath and swallowed hard, trying to accept the truth. The combination of worry and shock had left Nell stunned, the migraine blazing out of control.

Shoulders sagging, Nell shuffled to the narrow bed that stood against the far wall and turned the white coverlet back from the pillow. A double window looked down on a lush garden filled with purple lupines and pink daylilies, which looked watery and Impressionistic through the aura of the headache. It hurt to look at the light, so she pulled down the shades.

She checked her cell to confirm no calls or texts had come in, set the alarm for half an hour, and put the phone on the bedside table. Lying down to stretch out, Nell let her head melt into the pillow as it released a wisp of that same reassuring powdery scent. A rosy glow of nostalgia hung in her mind when she closed her eyes and drifted. The throbbing in her head began to dull as she let her muscles loosen.

This was Mom's cottage. She stayed here on and off for some unknown period of time, Lying in this bed with her head on this lavender-scented pillow. Napping in the long summer afternoons, with the hum of bees flowing across the smooth green lawn.

And doing God knew what the rest of the time. That was a question to pursue later. But first, just a few minutes of blissful oblivion.

Nell fell asleep, comforted by the scent of home.

CHAPTER 2

Nell ~ 2014

EVERY SUNDAY WHEN NELL AND Bridget were growing up, the whole family got up early, dressed in their best clothes, and went to church. The Reilly clan was Catholic, and the sisters' father, Thomas Reilly, had never missed a Sunday morning service in his life except during the time he served in Vietnam. Nell's family sat in the same pew every week, and the highlight of the service for the girls was communion, when everyone took turns walking up to the rail in front of the altar, and they could see what their friends were wearing. Then the sisters could kneel in the pew and pretend to pray while they whispered to one another.

Thomas always wore a suit and tie and Mary a dress with pearls, stockings, and pumps. The two girls wore the dresses their mother had made for them on her Singer sewing machine. Mom had learned to sew from her mother and had used the skill ever since to look stylish on a budget. Mom and her sister, Kate, prided themselves on their beautiful handwork. Their sheer blouses featured fine embroidery, pleated smocking, and tiny little hemstitches. They'd been the fashion leaders of their sorority house at the state university.

But Bridget and Nell were different. They wanted to look like the other girls in their school, who wore only certain brands of ready-to-wear clothes. When the sisters described an outfit to Mom and she adapted a pattern to make it for them, the result was never the same. They were secretly ashamed to be seen in it.

Mom had tried to teach Bridget how to sew, giving up after the first argument. Three years later, Nell surprised everyone by signing up for a high-school sewing class in Home Economics. Her mother did her best to keep out of it, and Nell persevered.

That Christmas, a big box from Nell to her mother dwarfed the other gifts under the tree. Inside was the red flannel bathrobe. It was too big and too long, the seams wavered in and out, and the patterned white topstitching on the left sleeve was crooked.

Mom loved it. She rolled up the sleeves and wore it every night that winter, dragging the ragged hem behind her on the floor.

Despite the encouragement, Nell never sewed again after that semester. When the weather turned too warm for flannel, the red bathrobe disappeared into the back of her mother's closet, never to be seen again.

Until she walked into Mary Reilly's secret house in Vermont.

Nell lay on her mother's bed and looked out the window at the garden, wondering if her father had known about this place. Perhaps her parents bought the cottage together. Or had Mom found it after his death? There were no signs of his clothing or belongings in the house so far.

She dialed the number for Intensive Care, and while waiting for the connection, Nell went into the front bedroom and opened the closet door. It contained a few of her mother's old winter coats, and the drawers of the dresser were empty.

When the ICU answered, Nell learned that her mother was still sleeping. Checking the time, she saw only a little over an hour had passed since she'd left the hospital. She asked for the doctor's phone number.

Nell needed answers and was prepared to demand them. If she couldn't immediately find out everything she wanted to know about the cottage, at least she would get all the details of her mother's medical condition.

For a moment, she thought of calling her husband and asking him to intervene—people always seemed to pay more attention to David—but Nell quickly dismissed the notion. Mom had asked for her, so Nell would be the one to protect her.

Flashes of her mother lying in her hospital bed with the tube taped into her mouth flickered through Nell's mind. She cringed as the horrible images registered, and her adrenaline began to pump. Then came a flood of anger and the need to blame someone. She was itching for a fight.

Scowling, Nell thought of the administrators at Maplewood, who had been so reassuring when she and Bridget went on a tour before signing the contracts. They were paying plenty for the expertise and support the place claimed to provide. She would definitely discuss the matter with Bridget.

But first, she dialed home. The connection got fuzzy and died, so she tried again. After a couple of rings, her son Ben answered the phone.

"Hi, sweetie, it's Mom."

"Hi, Mom. How's Grandma?" At fifteen, Ben's voice squeaked at unexpected moments.

"She's pretty sick, but they're taking good care of her."

"I hope she gets well soon. We're making her some funny cards to send to the hospital." Ben was addicted to the Comedy Network and had memorized a wide assortment of jokes for all occasions. His grandmother was always a receptive audience for his stand-up routine.

"I'll tell her, honey. How was school?" If he had a test coming up, she needed to remind him. Nell tried to remember what was going on with his school projects that week, but her mind was suddenly blank. Maybe she'd have to let him practice being independent.

"Lacrosse practice was cool. I scored a couple times."

"Great! No TV until homework is done, Ben." She decided a generic warning would be good enough for the moment.

"I know, Mom. Chill." He sounded annoyed. Nell realized she had crossed the line again as she seemed to so often now that Ben was a full-fledged teenager. "Here," he growled. "Talk to Lauren."

"Love you, honey," Nell said as the phone clattered onto the table. She could hear the housekeeper's voice and the vacuum cleaner. It was a relief to know that life at home seemed to be going on as usual despite her absence.

"Mommy? Is that you?" Her daughter, ten years old, was still unabashedly a little girl and thought teenagers were dumb. Nell prayed she would stay that way for as long as possible.

"Hello, Punkin," Nell said. "How's it going?"

"I'm good, Mommy. Mademoiselle Blanchette brought some cool CDs to class, and we listened to this weird French music, and everybody danced." She laughed, her voice crackling into a giggle. "She said I was good."

"You are a very good dancer, sweetie. I hope you're good at learning French too. But ballet lessons are more fun, right?"

"Where are you, Mommy? When are you coming home?"

"Probably in a couple of days. Grandma is sick, and I need to help her."

15

"Did you give her some tea with honey?"

Nell smiled at the sweet, caring suggestion. "Not yet, Lauren, but that's a great idea. I have to go now, but you be a good girl for Daddy and Mrs. Shelby, okay? Kiss Daddy for me."

They said good-bye, and Nell pushed the red off button as she pictured the small face on the other end of the connection. She loved her kids so much, more than anything in the world. The little details of their lives were the focus of her days. But honestly, getting away from them for a little while was a blessing, especially at the moment. There were just too many other things for her to worry about.

She wanted to call David and Bridget too, but hunger pangs rumbled in her stomach. The headache was gone, but Nell realized she hadn't eaten since breakfast. A little food would help her cope with everything better, then she would call her husband and sister. She slipped her cell phone into her pocket and went down to the kitchen.

Mom's favorite coffee, hazelnut flavored, was in the fridge. There was also fresh milk, a loaf of bread, some vegetables, and a freezer full of meat and packaged dinners. Some of them looked ancient, coated by a furry layer of ice crystals.

How long has Mom been coming here? Curiosity overwhelmed her thoughts. She started a pot of coffee, made a quick sandwich, and explored the kitchen while she ate, opening drawers and cupboards. She looked for a pile of mail or receipts that might have names and dates on them but found only dishes and kitchen utensils.

She noticed a wooden key rack on the wall next to the door to the garage. From one of the hooks dangled a silver keychain with two keys on it. One of them looked like a house key, and the other had FORD written on it.

Her mind flashing with suspicion, Nell opened the door. Sure enough, there sat the white Ford Taurus that Mom had supposedly sold a year ago. She walked around to the rear end of the car. It sported a green-and-white Vermont license plate.

Mom had apparently been a very naughty girl, running away from home and driving when she had promised not to ever get behind the wheel of a car again. Nell wondered what else her mother had been up to.

She was seeing her mother in a whole new light. No longer the perfectly open, perfectly innocent, perfectly honest woman who'd taught Nell and Bridget to always do the right thing, she had transformed in Nell's mind into… what?

Nell frowned and shook her head, hearing the final loud gurgles of the coffeemaker as it finished its cycle. As she walked back into the kitchen, a faint scratching came from across the room. Imagining raccoons under the porch or squirrels in the walls, she froze and listened. The noise came again, accompanied by a faint whine.

She went to the back door to see a small white dog outside, staring up at her with a worried expression. He twitched when she caught his eye, and he ran over to the bushes to lift his leg, looking at her all the while. Then he ran back and sat down again. He raised his paw as if to knock and scratched the screen.

Nell unlocked the kitchen door and opened it. The dog stood up and wagged his tail, reaching out to snag the edge of the screen door with his paw. Flipping it open with a practiced gesture, he trotted into the kitchen, a distinguished senior stiffness in his gait. He headed around the end of the counter, where Nell noticed a small bowl of water sitting on the floor.

"Hey, boy, who are you?" Nell spoke to him in soothing tones as he drank, crouching to let him sniff her hand. It was a Westie, the white version of Toto from *The Wizard of Oz*, Mom's favorite movie. Nell turned his collar around to catch hold of the tag, which read, "WINSTON. I belong to: M.E. Reilly, 27 Lakeshore Drive, Hartland, VT."

"Winston?" Nell said, and he sat, looking up at her. She stroked the dog's head, and he smiled, revealing his canines. "Looks like you're my long-lost baby brother, eh?"

He raised one paw and offered it to her, a trick Mom had taught to all their dogs. Nell shook his paw then followed the meaningful look he sent toward a cookie jar on the counter, which turned out to contain dog biscuits. Breaking one in half, she discovered he knew how to sit up as well.

"Have you been shut outside all this time, since last night?" Nell stroked his silky head. "Poor fella. You must be starved."

How on earth had Mom taken care of a dog? What had she done with him when she was away? Her pet-sitting bills must have been astronomical.

Nell stood up to search the cupboards for dog food, but when she found it and turned back around, the dog was gone. Calling his name and whistling, she looked into the living room and then went on down the hallway to the den. He was curled up on the couch, lying on a fleece pad. A footstool was drawn up nearby, and a pair of reading glasses sat on the lamp table. A bag with knitting needles sticking out of it was tucked next to the couch on the floor.

This must be where they snuggled. Nell sat down in her mother's seat next to Winston and petted him. When she lifted her eyes, she discovered why there hadn't been any photos in the other rooms. Her mother's gallery of loved ones covered the wall behind the television. Nell stared at the images with an odd mixture of reassurance and resentment.

Framed pictures of Nell and Bridget as children, pictures of Daddy, of Grandma and Grandpa, and of Mom and Aunt Kate in matching dresses. Pictures of Nell's kids, lots of them, at all ages. Bridget with her second husband, wearing a beret and standing in front of the Eiffel Tower. Nell's wedding portrait, yellowing, and a shot of her with David on their tenth anniversary. Their entire family history was spread out before her.

The sight of those familiar faces shocked Nell, as though they didn't belong in the house. Or as though she didn't. The confusion and anxiety returned, and she felt her throat tighten.

Then she noticed two unfamiliar pictures. The first was a black-and-white photo of Mom and Dad at a bar with some of his navy buddies, circa 1960s. Mom looked great in her army nurse's uniform, and Dad was young and handsome in his pilot's uniform. The shot had obviously been taken when they both served with the armed forces during the Vietnam War. Everyone was holding up their glasses in a toast and smiling at the camera. A neon sign on the wall behind the bar said, Honey's.

The second photo was more mysterious. Directly above the TV, in a central place of honor, hung a faded color photo of Mom standing on a dock by a sailboat with some people whom Nell had never seen before, a man and a woman.

The man stood in the middle with an arm around each woman, a shock of silvered dark hair above the sunglasses and full, shaggy moustache. He looked tall, strong, and handsome and had a big white smile. The other woman was about Mom's size, with a sweet expression and curly brown hair. The unknown couple appeared to be in their fifties or so, and Mom looked slightly older. Her blond hair was already mostly white.

Who are these people? Nell got up to take the picture off the wall and examined it. She could make out the red front door of the cottage in the distance behind the entrance to the dock and noticed a furry white face peeking out from under her mother's arm.

"It's you, Winston, isn't it? When you were a puppy." She sat down again to stroke the dog. He flipped over onto his back, begging for a tummy rub.

They appeared to be at the lake across the street from Mom's cottage. Maybe they were neighbors, friends. Maybe they still lived here and could tell her what was going on. Nell slid the cardboard backing off the picture and pulled the photo out of the frame. On the back was a time-and-date stamp. The photo had been printed fourteen years earlier.

Mom was here fourteen years ago. How could that be?

Daddy was still alive then, struggling with Alzheimer's. He was living at home, and Mom was still caring for him by herself. She had to feed him, dress him, bathe him, and help him go to the bathroom. He was anxious all the time, and Mom was exhausted. It was a hard time for everyone. Soon afterwards, Daddy had a stroke and moved into hospice care.

She remembered bringing her family for Christmas that last holiday. He hadn't known their names or who Nell was. Ben was on his knees scooting little cars around on the kitchen floor while she and Mom made dinner, and David was absorbed in the news on television. Daddy sat at the table, watching from the quiet end of the room.

"Hey you, girl," he called to Nell. "You... with the pretty face." He smiled at her lovingly, struggling to find the lost words.

"Yes, Dad. It's me, Nell. Your daughter." She went over to give him a hug.

He looked startled but smiled.

"Your little boy..." he whispered. "He's just, just... great."

"Thanks, Dad." She patted his shoulder.

He winced as though it hurt. She pulled her hand back, upset. He looked angry for a moment, then he gazed at her blankly as though she were a total stranger.

"Don't worry," Mom had said from across the room, where she was peeling carrots at the sink. "He still loves us." She was leaning against the edge of the counter as if too tired to stand without support, her hands at work under the running water. "He can't remember what he was trying to say. It makes him grouchy. Must feel like hell."

Nell nodded but still felt unhappy.

Thomas watched Ben play and caught Nell's eye. Awareness flashed in his expression again for a moment.

"Pretty face…" he whispered, smiling.

Then he was gone again, and there was nobody home inside. Nobody was behind those sparkling blue eyes that used to light up whenever she entered the room. She'd been his favorite, the one who always did was she was told. The one who tried so hard to be perfect.

That was one of many times during his illness when Nell caught a glimpse of the man who'd raised her, only to lose him again moments later. A living death had snuck in and stolen his true self away, leaving behind an empty body that looked like her father. The real man popped in and out, appearing less and less often as time passed. The family had to mourn his loss over and over again.

By the time her father left his body permanently, Nell could understand why people sometimes said that death came as a blessing. In his case, the actual person had died long since, though his husk withered ever so slowly.

Thomas Reilly had been laid to rest on a cloudy day in November when a Canadian cold front filled the cemetery with swirling snow flurries that unhooked his spirit from the flesh at last, blowing it free to find the next adventure.

Nell sat on the sofa, stroking Winston, and reached for a fresh tissue in the lamp table drawer, where she knew the box would be. She tried to put everything together in her mind but couldn't make sense of it. Should she call David? Bridget? What she really wanted was to talk to her mother, but that was impossible.

Her temples throbbed as the headache began to return. Checking her watch, she figured there was at least another hour before Mom would be awake. Maybe a shot of caffeine would help.

She poured herself a mug of coffee and poured kibble for Winston. The dog munched slowly, not ravenously as she'd expected. Going to the back door, Nell looked into the yard, thinking he might have a doghouse out there.

That was when she noticed the little path. A rose arbor adorned the back of the lawn, an archway leading out through the perennial border. A slight thinning of the grass between the arbor and the back door revealed that feet, or paws, had traveled the route many times.

Nell went out the screen door and let it swing shut behind her. As she lingered on the stoop, sipping her coffee, and peered to see what was beyond the arbor, the door slammed again. Winston trotted out from behind her and headed straight across the lawn, stopping at the arbor to look back over his shoulder as if to say, "Aren't you coming?" Then he went through the arch and disappeared into the woods.

"Winston. Come," Nell called, putting down her cup to run across the lawn. Having rescued him, she didn't want him to run off even if he seemed to know where he was going.

On the other side of the rose arbor, the path led into the woods. The dog was heading along it fast, tail up and full of confidence. Nell ran after him. It was dark and gloomy under the trees, and the way was slippery with fallen pine needles. She wondered if she ought to leave a trail of breadcrumbs behind just in case. Did they have wolves or bears or coyotes in the mountains? Probably so. She called Winston again, but he hurried into the thick bushes with his white tail waving like a flag.

As she came around a big maple tree, the woods opened up into a wide clearing. A rickety old shed, a partially stacked woodpile, and the tumbledown back porch of a peeling old white farmhouse came into view.

Winston was obviously familiar with the neighbors. He ran right up onto the back porch and barked outside the door. Nell realized that was the sound she had heard earlier in the day. He'd been asking to be let in since nobody was home at Mom's house. Apparently, nobody had been home here either.

A filthy old blue truck sat in the driveway, and the kitchen door stood open. Nell could see a red Boston Red Sox baseball cap and some bags of groceries sitting on the kitchen counter. A radio blasted music out into the yard. She walked boldly up the back steps, dodged a stinky garbage can filled with empty beer bottles and buzzing flies, and knocked on the screen door.

"Hello? Anyone home?"

Nell and Winston waited, the dog panting. She straightened her shirt and tucked her hair behind her ears.

A tall man with shaggy white hair appeared at the door. Rugged, with a barrel-chested build, he appeared to be in his sixties. He needed a shave, and the plaid flannel shirt had a torn pocket. Its ragged tails hung down over stained, greasy jeans. Despite all that, he was still handsome enough to give her a glimpse of what he'd been like as a young man.

He frowned when he saw her, and he opened the screen door to let the dog in but closed it again quickly with Nell still outside. He looked at her through the transparent wire mesh that protected them from one another. His eyes were wide and wild, like a scared animal.

"You must be Nell," he said in a gruff voice. "Saw your picture over at Ellie's house."

Nell wondered who this "Ellie" was and thought she might have seen the man's picture too. He looked like an older version of the guy standing in front of the sailboat, with a whiter moustache.

"Yes, I'm Nell Williams." She shaded her eyes with her hand. "I don't know your name?"

"Jake Bascomb." He still frowned.

"Winston ran over here. I was trying to get him back."

"He's okay." Jake started to turn away.

"I was just… that is, I wonder if I could ask you a few questions."

"About what?" He looked at her with eyes flashing, like a horse about to bolt.

"I had no idea that Mom was… up here." Nell smiled in what she hoped was a charming way. "She's very sick, you know. I'm worried about her."

"Yeah." His expression softened.

"Can you tell me what happened?"

He hesitated but held the door open. "Come on in."

Nell looked up as she passed him, intimidated by his size. At least six foot four inches tall, he towered over her. With that powerful chest and those thick, muscular arms, he could easily have tossed her across the room. She scooted into the kitchen and turned to face him.

"Who is Ellie? Another neighbor?"

"Ellie? That's your mother, you know, Mary *Ellen*. That's what we call her."

So Mom even has a special name up here at her secret getaway spot. Nobody ever calls her Ellie. It's always Mary, or Mary Ellen. Nell suppressed an annoyed grimace. *Wasn't Mom's real life good enough? Why did she need to get away from it? Why did she have to change her name?*

The feelings Nell had experienced earlier surged again, making her palms sweat and her chest tingle. She pushed them deeper inside.

Jake waved her over toward the kitchen table, where Winston watched from a wicker dog bed underneath. He seemed equally comfortable in Jake's house as he had at Mom's. His home away from home. That explained who had been caring for him when Mom was out of town. No kennels or pet sitters required. He had two lives, too, just like *Ellie.*

Nell clenched her jaw and heard her teeth grind.

"Got to stow these provisions." Jake turned his back on her and reached for one of the grocery bags. "Give me a minute."

She sat down at the table, which was littered with magazines, newspapers, piles of unopened mail, and dirty dishes. The whole room was a mess. A fly buzzed at the window, and a puddle of something brown, sticky, and disgusting had spilled on the table. Across the room, the trash can was piled high with several empty liquor bottles poking up out of the detritus. The nauseating smell of rotten vegetables, wet cigarette butts, and Scotch wafted over to her. Noticing the sharp contrast between Jake's style of housekeeping and her mother's immaculate cottage, Nell doubted whether Mom could possibly have spent much time over here. Not recently, anyhow.

A faintly nautical theme dominated the furnishings of the room, with a large oil painting of a sailboat hanging on the wall by the door. Jake himself looked tanned and windswept, and she guessed he must spend a lot of time out on the lake, perhaps fishing and probably drinking. She watched as he put the groceries away, turning to scrutinize her every few seconds as though she might be doing something depraved behind his back. His bloodshot blue eyes were ringed with downturned creases that looked as if he'd spent many days squinting into the sun and many nights crying into his beer.

Jake got two glasses out of a cupboard and filled them with cold water from the tap. He placed one in front of her and sat down across the table.

"Drink some water. Stress dehydrates you. How is she? I haven't checked in a few hours."

Nell did not like the look of her glass and decided she wasn't thirsty. She pulled her cell phone out of her pocket and checked to make sure she hadn't missed any calls. She set it on the table between them to keep an eye on it.

"Last I heard, she was asleep. They're supposed to call me."

"Sorry… this happened." He spoke, and when their eyes connected, she noticed a flash of kinship. He might be a charismatic man when he wanted to be. She caught a glimpse of what he must have been like back in the day.

"Me too," Nell said, her voice cracking. She tried to swallow, tears choking her.

She decided the glass didn't look so bad after all, and they both picked up their waters and drank.

Nell cleared her throat. "Do you know how she got so sick?"

He looked down at his big hands, and so did she. His fingernails were broken and stained with dirt.

"I guess it was my fault."

"How do you mean?"

"If it weren't for my stupid mistakes," Jake said, running his fingers through his hair and pushing it back with a nervous gesture, "Ellie would be sitting here right now. And I wouldn't be responsible for almost killing both of the women I've loved most in the world." He shook his head with his mouth turned down and a worried crease between his brows.

Nell stared at him in disbelief, but before she could think or react, her cell phone rang. The caller ID showed it was the hospital.

"This is the ICU at Hartland General, Mrs. Williams. We wondered if you could come back over here as soon as possible," a voice said.

"Is there news?" Nell held her breath to hear the answer.

"Mary is awake, and she wants to see you."

CHAPTER 3

Mary ~ 1967

MARY SULLIVAN AND HER FRIEND Charlotte, US Army nurses in Honolulu awaiting transport to Vietnam, were going to meet their friends for a drink and to say good-bye. They'd been getting ready for this moment a long time, and now that it was nearly time to ship out, Mary was so twitchy she could barely sit still.

She had been working in the emergency room at Mass General Hospital in Boston, a registered nurse and college graduate, when the urge to enlist struck. The television news films of those boys lying in the jungle, in pain and bleeding, made her want to help. Mary had entered the US Army Nurse Corps as an officer, a first lieutenant. She'd seen plenty of severe trauma cases in the ER, so they weren't daunting to her.

The next morning, she and Charlotte would board a plane headed to Long Binh, the US base near Saigon.

"I'm a little nervous now that it's really happening." Charlotte twisted a Kleenex in her fingers.

"Me too. Scared shitless, to tell the truth." Mary groaned as the taxi lurched over a pothole in the road.

The girls rode through the city's glamorous Waikiki Beach area, which buzzed with nightlife. People in military uniforms were everywhere, crossing the street and strolling down the sidewalks. Clubs and restaurants flashed neon signs, and off to the northwest, the lights of the airport and Pearl Harbor glowed in the night sky.

"That damn recruiting officer was so cute. Where is he now?" Charlotte joked, but neither of them laughed.

Mary and Charlotte had trained together at Fort Sam Houston in Texas.

Several other friends from there had ended up in Hawaii too, on the way to Guam and then on to Vietnam. One young man in particular, a navy pilot slated for duty on an aircraft carrier, had completely charmed Mary. Fit and handsome, Lieutenant Thomas Reilly had a sly sense of humor. Whenever he was in the group, people laughed, which helped cut the tension. They were all trying not to think about fear.

Mary was attracted to Thomas at first sight. They had been together nearly every night for a month, and the intimacy between them had deepened. There was a lot of kissing and touching, but Mary drew the line at having actual sex. She didn't want to risk getting pregnant, especially when heading into a war zone. Pregnant military personnel would be sent home immediately.

The best solution was to avoid sex entirely for her one-year tour of duty, Mary had decided. They were on their way into a dangerous situation, and the future was unknown, so it was a bad time to start something serious. Mary tried to hold her emotions in check. Falling in love with Thomas would have been easy if things were different.

Mary hoped they would meet again someday. It was going to be hard to say good-bye.

"The boys better have saved a table, or we're out of luck." Charlotte looked at the queue of people waiting outside the bar.

"Are you kidding? Two babes like us? We can get a seat anywhere we want." Mary laughed as she freshened her frosted pink lipstick.

"I'd rather have my own chair, though, not some GI's lap."

They paid the cab driver and stepped out onto the sidewalk. A crowd of servicemen surged around the entrance to the bar. Mary and Charlotte elbowed their way inside, where colored lights glistened and the word HONEY'S in bright neon script decorated the wall behind the long bar.

The jukebox played Mary's current favorite, "Come See About Me" by the Supremes. She sang along, looking around the room for their friends. The music and chatter were so loud she couldn't even hear herself, then the tall Irishman from Massachusetts stood up near the dance floor and waved to her. She mouthed, "There they are," to Charlotte. The two women weaved their way through the crowd to where their friends were sitting.

Thomas held a chair out, and she slid by to take the seat, brushing against him. She looked into his eyes, and Thomas pulled her close for a slow kiss. Dazzled, she reached to hang onto his shoulders. His buddies immediately chimed in with hoots and catcalls.

"Hey. Will you two get a room?"

"Yeah, Tom, quit corrupting Nelson here with your X-rated behavior. He's still a virgin, you know."

"Reilly, how come you always have to get the girl?"

"This girl is the only one who ever mattered," Thomas said quietly, raising Mary's hand to his lips.

Mary felt the blush creep up to her cheeks, but she didn't pull away.

A girl selling flowers went from table to table with her bucket of blossoms, and Thomas called her over. He chose a dark-red rose and offered it to Mary. She sniffed the delicate petals, and the scent reminded her of home, of her mother's garden. The music and the volume of conversation offered a strange kind of privacy. Nobody else could hear what the two of them said to one another.

"Mary, you know I love you, right?" Thomas touched her cheek. "I hate to let you go tomorrow." His expression changed, a glimmer of fear showing.

"But Thomas, you'll be leaving soon, too. We need to be brave. It's too late for anything else."

"Yes. We'll come back and be together then." He pressed her hand to his lips again, turning it over to kiss the tender inside of her wrist.

Her arm began to tremble as the sensation shot through her, a strange tight feeling in her stomach. "I hope so."

He hesitated. "Will you marry me, then?"

Mary laughed. "We'll live happily ever after." Lots of soldiers had been proposing to her lately, most of them total strangers.

"I mean it, Mary." He looked at her with a serious expression. "A house, babies, the whole nine yards? Will you be my girl forever?"

She stared at him as he reached into his breast pocket and pulled out a small white box.

"Thomas, what are you doing?" she said, guessing the answer.

He smiled and opened the box to show her the ring.

Mary tried to speak and couldn't. All her cautious rationalizations disintegrated as she gave in to the thrill of knowing he returned her feelings. She swallowed. "Yes," she mouthed, all sound lost in the noise of the club. She nodded enthusiastically, grinning. "YES."

"Good." Tom smiled and slid the ring onto her finger. "Not a bad fit."

He spoke directly into her ear, his lips tickling. "A future for us together. That's worth staying alive for, isn't it?"

She shivered and nodded, looking down at her left hand. The little diamond solitaire sparkled, a promise of hope. Mary threw her arms around Thomas, and they kissed, sealing the vow. Their friends at the table started teasing again until she flashed them the ring, then they went wild with clapping and congratulations.

When Charlotte beckoned a little while later, Mary went with her to the ladies' room. She showed her friend the ring up close, and they both cried. After three mai tais, champagne, and a serious marriage proposal, Mary was floating on a pink cloud. When she tried to find her way through the crowd back to the table, she tripped. A tall soldier reached out to catch her just in time.

"Whoa there, sweet thing." He laughed as he pulled her back upright. "Guess I shouldn't ask you to dance, eh? Not too steady on your feet."

"Oh, that's okay. I'm saving all my dances for my fiancé anyhow." Her words slurred, and she realized how drunk she was. "But thanks for saving me, kind sir."

"Your fiancé, is it? Lucky dog."

"No, no… he's a pilot."

The young man looked at her with admiration and grinned. "All right, Lieutenant, lucky pilot it is. And good luck to you too. We all need it."

He tipped an imaginary cap to her and stepped back to fade into the crowd.

The club's photographer stopped to capture their group as everyone leaned in close and toasted Mary and Thomas. When they paid the bill, Mary asked the girl to send the photo prints to her parents' address. Nobody knew how much mail was getting through at the front.

Late that night, Mary lay in her bunk worrying about the future as she listened to sounds in the barracks. The soft murmur of female voices on one side soothed her while quiet sobbing came from behind the opposite wall. She wondered whether she would ever see Thomas Reilly again.

Drifting off to sleep in a half-conscious vision, she saw bullets hail down from the sky while men screamed, their bodies gushing red and their eyes filled with terror. *But not Thomas, dear God*, Mary begged. Not her Thomas. Let them both come through the war in one piece, and then their future together would be perfect.

CHAPTER 4

Nell ~ 2014

WHEN NELL GOT BACK TO the hospital, the sun was going down. Lights were blinking on all over town. But inside the ICU, the shades were always drawn, the lights and voices dimmed. It was a world where time stood still.

Trying not to make a sound, Nell entered her mother's cubicle and sat down in the chair next to the bed. Once again, Mom's eyes were closed, but when Nell gently laid a hand over hers, they flickered open. The horrible tube was still fastened into her mouth, but her eyes smiled when she recognized her daughter.

"I love you, Mom." Nell's bottom lip trembled. She wanted to grab her mother by the shoulders, both to hug her and to shake her and demand an explanation. The woman she was looking at seemed almost like a stranger. A bubble of agitation began to swell in her chest.

Mom slowly pointed at herself then held up two fingers. *Me too*, she had said.

"Mary Ellen Reilly," Nell scolded, pretending to tease though she really meant every word. "How did you get yourself into a predicament like this?"

Mom shrugged her shoulders and blinked her eyes, then she gave Nell's hand a weak squeeze.

"Everything okay in here, girls?" The nurse came in to check the tubes and monitors, making notes on the patient chart. "Glad to see your daughter, Mary?" She smoothed Mom's hair back from her brow with an affectionate pat.

Mom's eyes smiled back, and she nodded.

The nurse pointed toward the bedside table, where there was a pad of paper and a pen. "She can't talk, but she can write if you hold the pad for her. That's how we've been communicating. Don't tire her out, please. She needs to rest."

The nurse left them alone again.

"Mom." Nell hesitated. "I don't know what to think about... all this." Seeing her mother so frail and ill made it hard to talk about her feelings.

Mary gazed at Nell, her eyes full of unspoken words. She gestured toward the writing tools. Nell put the pen in her hand and balanced the pad on the mattress.

Mary wrote slowly, her hand trembling. "COTTAGE."

"Yes." Nell nodded. "I've been there. They gave me the address. It's... very nice."

"WINSTON," Mary wrote, raising her eyebrows questioningly.

"I let him in and fed him." Nell smiled, relieved her mother had brought up something easier to talk about. "I'm not sure how long he was outside, but he's fine now. Very cute. Adorable, in fact."

Mary closed her eyes for a moment. Then she opened them again and wrote on the pad, "JAKE."

"Yes, we've met. Briefly."

Mary's throat contracted as though she were trying to speak. Then she struggled to write something else on the pad. "HE DIDN'T," the shaky letters said.

Nell read them aloud and leaned closer. "He didn't what, Mom? Don't worry. I fed Winston, and he's fine."

Mary's eyes filled with tears, which began to roll down her pale cheeks. Nell reached over to blot them with a tissue, making soothing noises.

"No, no, hush now," she said softly. "Don't cry, Mom. It's okay, really."

Mom's anxious eyes pleaded, and she moved the pen again.

"DO IT," she wrote underneath the other lines.

Nell looked down at the pad, trying to make sense of the message. "I'll do anything you want, Mom, whatever you want me to do, of course. Hush, now, you just rest. We can talk some more later, and you can tell me then. It's all okay."

She patted her mother's arm and stroked her forehead. Mom's eyes smiled at her wearily then fluttered shut as she relaxed and drifted off again.

She looked peaceful. Nell could see her chest moving up and down, and the monitors continued to blink steadily.

Looking down at the pad when she put it back on the bedside table, Nell realized what Mom had actually been writing. "JAKE. HE DIDN'T DO IT."

Nell stared at the letters as the dread she had been feeling all day swept over her again. Hadn't Jake said something about making mistakes? Did he do something that put Mom in danger? Why was Mom defending him? She seemed to assume that Nell would accuse him of some wrongdoing.

Jake had also mentioned "both" women. Nell wondered who the other one was and what had happened to her. Perhaps it was the sweet-faced woman in the photo with Mom and Jake. What was her connection with Mom? Where was she now, fourteen years later?

Nell had so many questions. What Mom had written about Jake didn't answer anything at all. In fact, it opened the door to a whole new mystery. Nell's instincts told her there was much more to the story and Jake Bascomb was at the heart of it. If he was somehow responsible for hurting her mother, Nell would make sure he never got near Mom again.

It was bad enough that this strange man was so involved with Mom that she'd deceived her own family to become his "Ellie" but even worse to think he might have taken advantage of Mom's generous nature to harm her in some way. Nell didn't believe for a minute that he was innocent, though she didn't yet know what the crime was supposed to be.

Nell looked down at her mother's sleeping face, at her closed eyes, blue shadows in the deep hollows. So sweet and beautiful and so full of secrets.

CHAPTER 5

Bridget ~ 2014

BRIDGET WAVED AT THE SECURITY guard and drove through the gate, stopping to empty the mailbox at the foot of her driveway. She gazed approvingly at the smooth green lawns and manicured flower beds in this beautiful community in McLean, Virginia, just outside Washington, DC. Her professional image demanded a home address equal in prestige with those of her interior-design clients. No house in the area was worth less than a million dollars, and some were valued at more than ten times that much.

She parked her white Mercedes sedan in the three-car garage at the back of the house, noticing her stepdaughter Heather's baby-blue BMW convertible as she pulled in. Admiring the new manicure on her long fingernails, Bridget pushed the button to close the garage door and went through the entry to the kitchen-slash-great room, a beautiful open space that looked out on a flagstone patio and swimming pool.

But the first thing Bridget saw was her fabulous brown leather jacket lying in a wrinkled pile on the floor next to the marble-topped island. Walking over to pick it up, she found Heather's backpack and shoes dumped nearby.

Bridget's eyes narrowed, and she clenched her jaw, but she counted slowly to three and managed to avoid an explosion.

In her mid-forties and with no kids of her own to raise, Bridget had at first welcomed the chance to take on her husband's daughter. But Heather was totally self-absorbed and showed no interest in her stepmother other than as a source of cash and clothes. Lucky for Heather, they wore the same size, and there were plenty of outfits to share.

Bridget put her things down on the counter and greeted her little black poodle, Lulubelle. Tucking the dog under one arm, Bridget flipped her artfully streaked blond hair behind her shoulder and went through the envelopes and magazines with one hand, throwing the junk mail into the trash. One letter stood out from the rest, neatly typed with the return address reading "Confidential Services, LLP." She snatched it up, dropping Lulu gently back onto the floor. Ripping the envelope open, she scanned the single page inside. Maybe this would be it, the news she had been waiting to hear.

"Dear Ms. Reilly," it began. "We are sorry to inform you that the adoption records you requested were lost when a fire destroyed…"

She shoved the letter back into the envelope. Another dead end. *Is this really worth it?* Should she keep looking, or was it a waste of time and money? Some people didn't deserve a second chance. She must be one of them.

Bridget picked up her things and went upstairs. She would file the letter, with all the other reports, in the folder taped to the underside of her sweater drawer. Her husband would never guess there were secrets from the past that could be used against her.

Eric would be home soon. Time to get dressed for the evening. And the next day, she'd be off to Vermont. *I should pack now so everything will be ready.*

Down the hallway, the sound of rock music pounded behind the closed door of Heather's bedroom. Bridget lifted her hand to knock but hesitated when she heard two girls laughing. Heather had a friend over. Rather than face the scornful tolerance that would doubtless greet her, Bridget decided to wait until Eric came home. Heather knew better than to be rude in front of her father. His punishments could be ruthless.

Bridget headed for her dressing room and picked out what she would need for the trip. She packed a couple of small bags and hid them behind her bathrobes. Thinking about Nell and their mother way up north, Bridget dialed her sister's cell phone and listened to it ring and ring. Voicemail picked up, so she left a message.

"Hey, Nell, it's me. We're going to a business dinner tonight, but I'll have my phone. Please, please call and tell me what's happening. How's Mom? Call me."

Turning her thoughts to her new Dior gown, Bridget stood in front of the rack that held her evening wear and ran one hand along the beautiful dresses, making them swing. She tried to put all the bad news out of her mind, but it still floated in her memory, and the shining colors before her blurred into a rainbow.

Sometimes things happen, and we never guess where it's all going. We make mistakes, and then we have to pay.

The glamorous life she led might not have seemed difficult to others, but Bridget knew better. Her teenage years and first two marriages had left her heart crazed with little cracks where it had shattered and been glued back together, over and over again. At any moment, the fragile mask of sophisticated indifference could totally disintegrate. *All the more reason for a fresh coat of makeup and a push-up bra.* Hiding her vulnerability was essential when going out for an evening with her husband. He homed in on weakness like a hound on a scent.

She ran her eye down the row of gowns. Catching a glimpse of herself in the long mirror on the wall, she flinched. Those frown lines between her eyebrows, the tension around the mouth—they would definitely have to go. Forcing her face to relax, she showed her beautiful teeth in a model's smile. But in her eyes there was still a flutter of darkness behind the blue.

She heard the garage door and knew Eric was home. She straightened her shoulders and deliberately radiated confidence. Time to enter the battlefield.

She could still play the game, though it was beginning to wear her down. Tomorrow, Bridget promised herself, she would call her divorce attorney and see what could be done about the money. Once upon a time, she had made Eric fall in love with her, and for the right incentives, she could probably make him glad to see her go. Best if she left town while her lawyer served the papers and negotiated.

This little trip to Vermont was coming at a perfect time. Plus, she was dying to find out the story behind Mom's strange adventure. Bridget guessed there was a man involved, though romantic liaisons were not normally her mother's thing. Whatever was wrong with Mom's health, Bridget felt sure it would soon be mended. Her mother had always been very strong and fit. It was impossible to imagine her in serious danger.

Bridget was much more worried about her own health once Eric caught wind of what she was about to do.

CHAPTER 6

Nell ~ 2014

NELL WATCHED HER MOTHER SLEEP for another hour or so. The nurse came in and beckoned her into the hallway. "The hospital's doctor on duty is here. He'd like to speak with you."

A tall, slim man wearing golf clothes under his white lab coat, Dr. Hicks had a soft way with words. Nell's frustration evaporated. She liked him.

"She's doing as well as we can expect." He led Nell to a nook at the end of the hallway where they could speak privately. "When she came in early this morning, she had a high fever and her air passages were nearly closed. We're lucky she made it through the night. She's in great shape for her age, remarkable really, but it's a good thing she called for help."

He showed Nell an X-ray of her mother's lungs on his laptop and pointed out the infected areas. He mentioned the name of the bacteria that had invaded Mom's body, *streptococcus pneumoniae.*

"What happened to her? How did it get so bad?"

"We don't know. She could barely talk when the EMTs brought her in," Dr. Hicks said. "I imagine she was probably sick for a day or more before seeking medical care."

Nell thought of her phone call with Mom on the previous morning. She must have already been ill, though she didn't say anything. Obviously, Mom had been in Vermont then, not at Maplewood. How strange to think of her mother telling an outright lie. Nell couldn't remember that ever happening before. Why hadn't Mom trusted her?

"How long will she need to recover from this?" Nell asked.

"It's too soon to predict," Dr. Hicks said. "I'm concerned about her being quite a bit underweight. How do you feel about putting her on a feeding tube until she's off the respirator?"

Nell reluctantly agreed to it. The doctor assured her that soon as possible, they would wean Mom off the machines and all the tubes could go away.

"She needs complete rest and nothing to worry about," he said emphatically. "Seeing you here will work wonders. You need to keep her spirits up. Be cheerful, and let her rest. Read to her. Show her pictures of your kids. No heavy discussions. Okay?"

Nell nodded, relieved. He seemed to know what he was doing.

"I can do that. Should I sit with her tonight?"

"Stay as long as you want, but then go get a good night's sleep." He walked her back to the nurses' station. "She's sedated now, so she won't be awake much. It's important for her healing. Tomorrow morning, she'll have been on the antibiotics for twenty-four hours, and we'll be one step closer to recovery. No reason why she shouldn't come all the way back to where she was before, despite her age. She's a strong woman, and she's responding to the treatment."

Nell looked in on Mom, who was sleeping again. After sitting for an hour or so, watching her mother breathe, she said good night to the nurses and made sure they still had her cell-phone number. Once outside, she sat on a bench to try and make some calls. The cell-phone service was spotty up in the mountains, and her texts and phone messages seemed to get stuck for a while then all come through at once. She noticed there were several new messages, and first, she listened to her sister's. When she returned the call, Bridget didn't pick up, and it went through to voicemail. Nell left a short message and condensed all the news about Mom's health.

Then she called David and told him about her meeting with the doctor. She heard the kids squabbling in the background and the sound of the TV.

"That sounds terrible." His voice was sharp and worried. "I feel so bad for her and for you too."

"It's pretty scary. I miss you."

That seemed to cheer him up. "I miss you too, baby. Wish I could be there with you to hold your hand and Mary's. Do you want me to fly up? Can I help?"

Nell pictured his dark hair and eyes, square jaw, and seductive mouth.

She almost caught a whiff of his scent as the image sharpened in her mind and multiplied into thousands of images of loving moments between them, streaming back through time. For a moment, she missed him so much her chest ached. She wanted to tell him about the cottage and how she'd found it and about Jake. David would know how to handle all that.

Her lips pulled into a smile. "No, it's good that you're in charge of the kids so I don't have to worry about them. But thanks for the offer. Sorry it's a pain for you to take care of everything at home by yourself."

"Don't worry, I'll handle it." Then his voice changed as he scolded the kids. "Hey, keep it down, will you? I'm on the phone here."

Nell heard her daughter whine and the sound of glass breaking.

"God damn it. Hurry home, Nell. I'm not very good at this."

"I will. But I'm sure you'll do fine, David." Distracted from what she'd meant to say, she ground her teeth and considered that a top-level executive really ought to be able to manage two sweet kids without any trouble. And she couldn't exactly hurry home. She wasn't on some spa weekend with the girls. "It's going to be a while, you know. I'm not sure how long. Mom is in really bad shape, and she needs me a lot more than you do right now." Fatigue pushed her down like a weight on her shoulders.

"Of course, of course, sorry," David mumbled. In the background, the dog started barking, and the kids were shouting at each other. "Take care, Nell. I love you." He sounded angry.

"Love you too. Kiss the kids."

He hung up, and the sounds of uncontrolled family chaos were suddenly cut off.

Nell pushed the red button on her phone. Glad that David had to be the parent for a change, she decided it was good for him to experience the family from Nell's point of view. If she'd been home, he would have just walked into the study and closed the door.

Nell drove back to the cottage. It was dark out in the country, and the black sky that floated over the lake was full of stars. She'd brought Winston back home and left the porch light on before leaving for the hospital, and the house looked warm and welcoming. Relieved at the prospect of a night alone with no kids or husband to make demands, she got her luggage out of the backseat of the rental car and saw the dog's face at the living room window.

He greeted her with much tail wagging. Nell fed him and put a frozen dinner in the oven, setting the timer. After opening a bottle of red wine from the liquor cabinet, she brought a glass into the den and joined Winston on the couch. She switched on the television, kicking off her shoes.

It had been a hell of a day. Her brain couldn't absorb another thing. Mom's care seemed to be on the right track. *Nothing more to be done about that tonight.* Trying to empty her overloaded mind, Nell sipped her wine and stared at the talking heads on the screen.

While the voices droned on, Nell found herself gazing once again at the gallery of photos on the wall. A smile curled her lips when she came to the shots of her kids when they were babies. Then her eyes arrived at the photo of Mary, Jake, and the mystery woman, and Nell wondered again who the woman was and where she was now.

Nell noticed a cupboard door set into the wainscoted wall underneath the photos, behind the TV. After getting up to wheel the TV stand aside, Nell pulled open double doors, revealing a deep space fitted with shelves. There were jigsaw puzzles and board games along with stacks of books and some boxes. Pulling a carton out of the cupboard, Nell looked inside and caught her breath with excitement. She lifted out a photo album, bringing it back to the couch to hold in her lap.

Some of the answers must be here. Sure enough, the images were of people and places she had never seen before. It seemed to be a visual history of Mary's life at the cottage.

The album began with a series of shots taken at a picnic. The lake was visible in the background, and people were wearing summer clothes. One photo showed Mary Reilly with a group of women, posed in front of a picnic table. Mary had short blond hair like Nell's and looked to be around the same age. The resemblance between them was startling.

Nell frowned and slipped the photo out of the corner holders to look at the back. Sure enough, the date was stamped there… but it was nine years prior to the date on the framed photo hanging on the wall. That was nearly twenty-three years ago. Mom would have been a few years older than Bridget, though she didn't look it.

So it seemed that Mom had actually been sneaking up to the cottage for over twenty years. Fourteen years had sounded like a lot, but this was amazing. That was just before Daddy was diagnosed with Alzheimer's. Nell and Bridget were both in college but still living at home during school vacations. She thought carefully, counting backward in her mind. The picture was taken soon after Grandma died, she figured.

Maybe Mom used the money she'd inherited to buy this place. But why secretly, and how had she pulled it off?

Everything had seemed fine back then. They were all sad about Grandma, sure, but Nell's parents were affectionate toward each other. Daddy was grouchy sometimes, as always, and he fought a lot with Bridget, which was unusual. Then the summer before she left for college, Bridget went away to have her baby, and Daddy more or less stopped talking to her. He and Nell still got along great. She never disobeyed him, and he approved of her strong work ethic. She didn't remember Mom going off by herself for more than a few days except for little trips to the "outlet malls" with her friends. Nell and Bridget would go to their friends' houses when Mom was away. Now Nell had discovered that her mother had really been escaping to her little getaway in Vermont for some time to herself.

Turning the page, Nell saw a picture of a big cake with WELCOME written on it and another of a man pouring wine into champagne glasses. Looking closer, she thought it might be Jake Bascomb, with short dark-brown hair and a neatly trimmed brown moustache. Those big hands and muscular forearms looked familiar. And yes, there she was too—the mystery woman, sweet and smiling with her arm around Mom's shoulders and their heads tipped together, cheeks touching.

Nell went through the album page by page, scrutinizing every photo. It spanned the time right up to about five years ago and then stopped, the last pages blank and a few loose photos tucked inside the back cover. She reasoned that Mom had started taking pictures on her new cell phone at that point and probably stopped making prints. Nell and David had bought her an iPhone for Christmas that year, and Ben made her a Facebook page so she could keep in touch with them online.

Jake and the other woman appeared many times in the album, as eventually did Winston and several children and adults Nell did not know. She didn't recognize any of the people in a winter shot taken outside the church in the town center. A woman stood in the middle of the group, holding a baby in a long christening gown. Most of the pictures were summertime shots, though a few showed fall foliage, spring green, and stark expanses of incredibly deep snow. Many of the pictures were taken in a sailboat out on the lake. One person who did not appear, conspicuous in his absence, was Nell's father.

So Thomas Reilly had never been to the lake house. Had he even known about it?

Nell heard the timer buzz and went to pull her dinner out of the oven and poke at it with a fork. She didn't feel hungry anymore. A bleak state of mind had come over her. Even though her father had been gone for years, her impression of the past had suddenly changed, and she questioned all her previous assumptions. What had her father done to deserve this betrayal? Or perhaps she and Bridget had done something to make their mother lead a double life. It was horrible.

Unless there was something Nell had not yet discovered, some kind of a justification. It was hard to imagine her mother, always the model of gracious behavior, ever being hurtful or dishonorable. The whole thing didn't make any sense, and it made her head hurt. She dumped the rest of her wine into the kitchen sink and washed it down the drain.

Nell locked up, turned out the lights, and dragged her luggage upstairs to the front bedroom. Winston watched from the doorway as she unpacked her clothes, found sheets for the bed, and made it up then got into her pajamas. The dog was curled up next to the pillow when she returned from the bathroom, his eyes pleading with her not to make him leave.

"Okay, boy, we can share the bed tonight." She stroked his head. "We both need a friend about now."

Looking for something to read, she went into her mother's bedroom where she remembered noticing a book on the bedside table. With the room dark and the window shades up, she could see the backyard lit by the swelling moon. Through the dark woods beyond the arbor, lights twinkled. *That must be Jake's house, seen straight through the trees.* When she'd taken the path that curved around, it had seemed farther away.

A shape moved, catching her eye. Something big in the shadows. It looked like a person standing there, just inside the edge of the lawn.

Nell felt a jolt of fear and quickly stepped back from the window.

Ducking behind the curtain, she peered out, careful not to stand where the light from the hallway would reveal her silhouette.

Now that she knew where to look, she could see him clearly. Moonlight glinted off his eye, and his shoulder obscured the pale roses on the arbor. The man shape seemed to radiate animosity, and she shivered. He stood watching the cottage for a minute then reached up to adjust his baseball cap. Turning on his heel, he disappeared into the woods.

Nell let out a breath. "Spying on me, Jake?" she whispered. "Or keeping an eye on things for *Ellie*?"

She watched the yard for a few minutes, but nothing else moved. Maybe she was being too critical, but she just didn't trust that man.

Nell sprinted back to her room and ducked under the covers with Winston. Cuddling the little dog against her stomach, she whispered to him as he licked her nose, and eventually, they both fell asleep.

CHAPTER 7

Mary ~ 1990

"OF COURSE YOU'LL GIVE UP the baby. Don't be ridiculous. Haven't you embarrassed the family enough?" Thomas Reilly wore a dark scowl, and he growled the words.

Mary and Bridget sat across from him on the sofa in the living room. Mary's arm was around her daughter's shoulders, which heaved as the girl wept. Mary's eyes burned with suppressed anger. Things were bad enough already. He didn't need to make it worse by torturing Bridget. The poor girl would suffer plenty without his punishing lack of sympathy. She adored her father and needed his love at a time like this.

"But, Daddy." Bridget struggled to speak. "What if this was meant to be… my chance to do the right thing? What if my baby…?"

"No," Thomas said firmly. "It's totally out of the question, stupid girl. You'll ruin your life and ours too. I'm not helping raise an illegitimate child. If you do this"—he pointed in her face—"you'll be one hundred percent on your own."

Mary squeezed Bridget tighter. "No you won't, honey. You'll have me." Mary tipped up her chin and glared at her husband.

"What the hell?" Thomas sputtered. His face was flushed with anger.

"You heard me." Mary's tone was adamant. She locked eyes with Thomas, daring him to challenge her. "It's Bridget's decision to make, and I'll support her either way."

Bridget sat up a little straighter and wiped her eyes though her lower lip still trembled. "Yes, Daddy. It's my body and my decision."

A storm of rage broke across his face. "And how are you going to survive," Thomas sneered, "with no education, no job, and a brat to support? You don't think Wellesley will let you bring a baby to college with you next fall, do you?"

"Well, not exactly, but…"

Thomas stood up and paced. "You won't be bringing it here to this house, either. And those fancy friends of yours, do you think they'll want to come around when it looks like you're hiding a basketball under your shirt?" He shot her a nasty grin. "Have you thought about what those girls will be whispering behind their hands?"

Bridget froze, an expression of horror on her face. She burst into tears again.

"Thomas, stop it immediately." Power swelled up from deep inside Mary and made her voice strong. "I want you to leave this house now, and don't come back until you're ready to behave like a patient, loving father. If that means never, then so be it."

He stood up, stumbling, his face red and ugly. "You can't do that, Mary. This is my house, my home. I say what happens here." His fists clenched and eyes squinted, he kicked the coffee table, knocking it over and spilling all the magazines and half-filled cups onto the floor.

"The days of wives and children being considered chattel in this country are long gone, Thomas Reilly." Mary was calm and strong, in command. "You take your temper and march it right out the door. We don't need your drama here. If you don't go, I'll call for help. Everyone in town will find out about it before the day is done." She picked up the telephone and poised her finger over the buttons. "What will it be?"

He swept out of the room like a tornado, sucking all the air out with him.

Mary took Bridget in her arms, and they rocked.

"I don't know what to do, Mom. Don't even know what my choices are."

"It's okay, honey. We'll find out."

"I don't think I can… abort. It just doesn't feel right to me. And what if something went wrong?" Bridget began to weep again, silently this time.

"I'm glad you said that, sweetie. I don't feel comfortable with that idea either. Want to hear a suggestion?"

Bridget blotted her face with a tissue and nodded, waiting.

"What if we go talk to Father Benedict? He'll know what the Church might be able to do to help." Mary stroked her daughter's hair, soothing her with love.

"But how could that help? Won't he just be mad at me for, you know… sinning?"

Mary smiled. "He'll probably tell you to make your confession, but he won't be mad. The church has always helped take care of mothers like you, and the babies. Catholic Charities helps with adoptions too. Let's find out what they offer, okay?"

Bridget nodded, reaching for her mother again to wrap her arms around Mary's waist.

"Guess Daddy's right," she said, her voice muffled as her face pressed again Mary's chest. "I really messed things up. Such an idiot."

"Honey, you're not the first eighteen-year-old to find herself in this predicament, and you won't be the last."

"Mom, I got an A in biology. You'd think I would have the brains not to get swept away by some supposed romance without thinking first."

"Love is love, Bridget. It's a powerful force."

Bridget looked up at her mother curiously. "Was it like that for you when you met Daddy?"

"In a way, yes." Mary thought about the night Thomas proposed, when they were both so happy. Then she thought of the long days without him afterwards. "Let's just say I know what you're talking about."

"Guess Daddy's right about something else too. I can't raise a baby and go to college next fall. I'll lose my scholarship and can forget about ever graduating from a top school. It would be community college or nothing. I'd probably end up waiting tables for the rest of my life."

"Bridget, you're an amazing, talented young woman. I believe you can do whatever you want to with your life. No matter what."

"Really, Mom?"

Mary heard the gratitude and hope in Bridget's voice. "For sure, honey. Now, what do you say we dry our eyes and go stop by the parish hall? I think Father B. will be just getting finished with his confirmation classes about now."

"Okay, Mom. I love you."

"Me too, sweet pea. Me too."

While Bridget went to wash her face and brush her hair, Mary sat and remembered. She tried to control her anger toward Thomas, but every time she pressed it down inside her, it bubbled back up again. He was totally inflexible, so unbending with his strict rules and rigid values that he couldn't see the harm he did to his family and to himself. She didn't have a chance to recognize that trait when they first got together—everything had happened so fast. And now, to be honest, she regretted not taking more time to get to know the man.

She had her two beautiful girls and a lovely home, but still, she was forced to deal with his bullying every day. Thomas wasn't physically abusive, but he sure was a bossy grouch—nothing like what she'd expected from knowing him before the war. He wasn't fun anymore. The charismatic man who had entertained everyone popped out from time to time in public, but at home, he was tense and defensive. Some nights when she finally lay her head down on the pillow, Mary wondered whether she would have the energy to pick it up again in the morning.

And now this new trouble. He would drive their daughter away or damage her self-esteem forever if Mary didn't stop him.

Mary cradled her head in her hands.

Then Bridget came back into the room, and Mary lifted her head and smiled, sending a brilliant beam of love straight from the heart. All her spirit was focused on lifting her daughter up above the insecurity that Thomas's words had created. She hoped it would be enough but knew it was probably too late.

CHAPTER 8

Bridget ~ 2014

BRIDGET GOT NELL'S MESSAGE LATE that evening in the car on the way home from the fundraiser. Relieved to learn that things seemed to be under control, she decided to return her sister's call first thing in the morning. She leaned back in her seat and squeezed the armrests with clawed hands as Eric whipped along the Capital Beltway, weaving in and out of lanes. They might get home two or three minutes sooner but no more than that.

That isn't why he does it. He likes the danger and doesn't care if I'm uncomfortable.

She hated the daredevil part of his personality. It had attracted her at first, along with his commanding physical strength, which made her feel protected and secure even while she squirmed from being so firmly under his thumb. She looked at Eric's hand on the mahogany gearshift and pictured it fisted in the back of her hair as he positioned her mouth where he wanted it. A shiver trickled through her, and she sighed.

When Eric had first shown an interest in her, she was so anxious to please that she changed her hair, clothes, music, diet, hobbies, reading, ideas, politics, work schedule, and even her address, all to accommodate him. But just like her two previous husbands, after a while he disdained her for giving in so easily. That night at the banquet, she'd watched him exchange meaningful glances with a female colleague, and when they both disappeared at the same time, Bridget guessed what was probably going on in the men's bathroom. She had been there herself a few years back.

Good marriages don't happen to bad people. What did I expect?

If only she could go back in time and choose a different path... but it was too late, and her destiny was sealed. She was doomed to have her heart broken again and again. It was what she deserved.

Finding it more and more difficult to hide her vulnerability, she had begun a delicate dance with Eric, spinning and dodging to protect herself. Never one to pass up an opportunity to take advantage of weakness, he had shifted the dynamic between them so that she obeyed him without question rather than risk another fight.

"The girls are still up," Bridget said as they pulled into the driveway. The house was ablaze with lights, and music throbbed, way too loud.

"Lucky the neighbors didn't call security." She looked up at Heather's windows on the second floor, where dancing forms could be glimpsed through the sheer curtains.

"I'll take care of it." Eric parked his black Porsche next to the Mercedes. "You go on ahead and warm up the bed."

"Okay." She turned her face toward him with a smile.

He bent closer, taking her into his arms and slipping one hand into the low décolletage of her dress to squeeze her breast as they kissed. Then Eric reached across her to flip the door handle and let her out of the car, the lazy gentleman's gesture. She forgave him that because when it came to more important things, he wasn't lazy at all. And he wasn't much of a gentleman, either.

Bridget always fell for the bad boys. But that could change. Maybe there was something to be said for the kind of marriage her sister had, with a few modifications of course—more sex, more excitement, and a lot less housework.

As she climbed the stairs to the second floor, she wondered what her parents' marriage had really been like. Mom had money from her career as a nurse and a modest inheritance from Grandma. Financially, she'd been relatively independent. She'd gone off antiquing with her girlfriends now and then and always came home on Sunday night with penny candy for the girls and something special for Daddy. But Mom always gave in if she and Daddy disagreed. He'd raise his voice and get that look on his face, and the discussion would be over.

Bridget went into her closet and kicked off her strappy heels, dutifully putting them into their special box. She unzipped her dress and stepped out of it, slipping it onto a padded hanger. Sitting down at her dressing table in her slip, she started to remove her makeup.

Daddy was incredibly strict and controlling, but he never hit us. That was a huge point in his favor.

Bridget's hand went to the spot on her cheek, hidden under the expert makeup, which still hurt when she pressed. Yes, it was time to make a move. It was a shame about the sex, but nothing else was working for her anymore. Best to get out before things got any worse.

CHAPTER 9

Nell ~ 2014

NELL OPENED HER WINDOW SHADE to see a rose-and-gold dawn painting the sky over the lake. The water looked smooth, a shining mirror that reflected the circle of pine trees that rimmed the shore, a puddle of pink cupped inside the green lip. Winston put his paws up on the windowsill next to her.

"Need to go out?"

He licked her face.

"Okay." She laughed as he kissed her. "I guess we're up."

She pulled on a terrycloth robe over her pajamas, followed Winston downstairs, and let him out into the backyard, then made herself some coffee. Bringing it out to the back porch, she sat on the steps.

A flock of tiny goldfinches swooped down from the trees to visit the bird feeder that hung from a wrought-iron shepherd's crook in the perennial border. At some point during the night, it had rained. Fat, shiny drops of water fell from the branches when the birds landed or took flight. It was perfect and beautiful, a storybook moment, and she was beginning to understand why her mother had been so drawn to this place. Perhaps Nell could even relate to wanting to keep it all to herself, a private sanctuary.

There was magic in Mary Reilly's garden, a place filled with fragrant blossoms, shifting light, and the flutter of feathers. A mockingbird sang a long chain of intricate variations, notes tumbling through the air, each phrase repeated three times. Nell closed her eyes and felt the hot sun on her face. She inhaled the delicious air.

It wouldn't be bad to have her own place, where she could escape by herself from time to time with no obligations. The cottage was so peaceful. The usual tension in the back of her neck was somehow... lighter.

Why hadn't she ever gotten away for a few days before? She knew the answer: because of feeling guilty for wanting to escape. This journey had been justified since it was an emergency. The absence of shame made the air taste even sweeter.

Mom must have experienced tons of guilt, Nell thought. Was the reward worth the emotional cost?

Nell realized that she hadn't told anyone yet about Mom's secret life. Not David, not Bridget. It gave her an exciting sense of power to realize that at the moment, nobody even knew where she was staying. For the moment, the cottage was her private haven. She sighed and stretched out her legs in the grass, which was full of sparkles from the rain.

She closed her eyes and tipped her face up to the sun, and her husband's face shimmered in her thoughts. David didn't mean to be so demanding. He was respectful, wise, collaborative—the perfect family man. Unlike Mom, Nell had no good reason to crave an escape. The idea was ridiculous. Yet there she was, enjoying her time at the cottage alone even though Mom was terribly sick and David was scrambling to keep up with everything at home.

Back in New Jersey, her personal space consisted of a little nook in the kitchen where she kept her laptop. If she wanted to be alone to write in her journal, she had to lock herself in the bathroom. It was hard not to be jealous, but while David had a man cave, a home office, and a constant supply of food and clean clothes, he still had to endure the insane stress of the ultra-competitive corporate world. She honestly wasn't sure which was worse, her job or his. Life swept them all along as one day led to the next in a fast-forward blur. Nell's plans and dreams for her life were melting into mist like last night's rain on the maple leaves.

Nell called Winston back inside and went upstairs to dress in jeans, a white shirt, and sneakers. The small diamond studs and the plain platinum wedding band with its matching square-cut diamond were the only jewelry she ever wore. The next day, she would go for her usual morning run, but at the moment she wanted to see Mom as soon as possible.

Preparing for a long day at the hospital, Nell rummaged in the kitchen until she found a shopping bag and tossed everything that might be useful inside it. Granola bars, apples, bottled water, and magazines. Then she remembered what the doctor had suggested and went back upstairs to get the book she had seen in the back bedroom. Maybe Mom would enjoy taking up the story where she'd left off.

Finding the book on the nightstand, Nell noticed that it wore a clear plastic wrapper and a sticker saying it belonged to the local public library. A bookmark was sticking up out of the pages. Flipping to the inside back cover, she found the due date, which was a few days away. Making a mental note to get it renewed, she put the book in the bag with the other things.

Winston watched her with a worried expression.

"Can't leave you here alone all day, can I? Well, come on, then. Let's find out if your other parent is at home. We'll see what Mom's spooky neighbor does when I ask him if he was lurking outside last night."

In the broad light of day, Nell felt secure enough to pull the tiger's tail. She led Winston out the back door and across the yard, taking the path through the woods.

As she approached Jake's farmhouse, she heard a thudding noise. Coming around the big maple tree, she saw he was engrossed in splitting firewood, his back turned to her. He flung the axe high over his head, waited for it to begin to fall, and then pulled it down hard and fast, letting gravity add to the power of each stroke. His broad shoulders bunched when the axe went up, and the rolled-up sleeves of his plaid flannel shirt revealed those muscular forearms, the big hands firmly gripping the axe handle. He looked young and fit, moving in a rhythmic routine. Now his Red Sox cap was blue, and he wore it turned backwards.

Impressed by the skill and brute strength it must take to hit the wood hard enough to split it neatly in half, Nell hesitated on the edge of the yard to watch. She hoped his aim was good. That vicious falling blade could easily take off a toe or two if it fell in the wrong place.

A man that strong could be dangerous, she thought, and a trickle of last night's fear ran through her. Best to stay out of the way and not be too provoking.

Winston raced across the grass, yipping with joy. He circled the pile of freshly split wood to jump on his friend, tail wagging frantically. Throwing down the axe, the man knelt to greet the dog, who licked his face and squeaked with excitement.

Nell continued into the yard but stopped in her tracks when she realized with a flash of confusion that the face under the baseball cap was not Jake's. Though he undeniably resembled Mom's neighbor, this man looked to be just a few years older than Bridget and was a total stranger.

"Um... hi. G-Good morning," Nell stammered as Winston ran back to her and the man looked up, breaking into a dazzling smile when he spotted her. Their eyes connected, and she felt her heart speed up for a moment.

"Hey, you must be Nell, right?" he said, his big hand engulfing hers in a warm grasp. He stepped toward her. "Dad told me you were here. I'm Adam Bascomb."

He had thick brown hair with a sprinkle of gray at the temples and the same sky-blue eyes as his father. Like his father, he towered over her, at least six foot three. *If you pinned a mustache on him, he'd look exactly like the early photos of Jake in the den.*

With one big difference: Adam's old jeans and flannel work shirt were spotless and carefully mended. His shirt was tucked in, and his leather steel-toed boots looked new. His hair was neatly trimmed, and he had shaved.

"It's good to meet you." Nell smiled back at him. Well, he was certainly friendlier than his father. A lot less scary too. Her hand was still in his, and they both seemed to be fine with that. Then Nell remembered she had a husband and kids and took a quick step backward.

"How's your mom? I want to get over to see her today." He held the axe by its handle with the heavy metal head resting on the ground near his foot. She thought again about the power it must take to bring it down with enough force to pop the dense rock maple open like a peanut shell.

"I'm on my way back to the hospital. As of last night, she was still really sick. She's not allowed many visitors." Nell smoothed her hair, wondering if there was lipstick on her front teeth.

"Sure am sorry. She's one terrific lady. Is there anything I can do... you know, to help out? Anything you need, groceries or... whatever?" He raised one eyebrow.

"Well, I do need some help with the dog." Nell saw that Winston was watching their exchange. "Can he hang out with you while I'm at the hospital? I hate to leave him shut up inside all day."

"Sure, no problem. We're old pals. He lives over here half the time anyhow. I'll bring him back to Ellie's place later. Here's my number." Adam handed her a business card that said, "J. Bascomb & Son, Antiques."

Nell thanked him and turned to walk back to the cottage, wondering whether he was still watching. She hadn't noticed whether he was wearing a wedding ring. Not that it mattered, really. But wow, that was certainly one attractive man. Just as Adam's father must have been at that age. It made Nell wonder again about her mother's relationship with Jake Bascomb. Maybe it was more than a neighborly friendship after all.

Nell headed to the hospital. It was only seven thirty in the morning, so she didn't call Bridget. Her sister was not the early-riser type. The best chance to catch her was later when she hit the hot tub.

Nell wondered what Maplewood had told Bridget about letting Mom go off to Vermont on her own. There was no excuse for it, however clever Mom had been at making her escape. She had her own apartment and lived independently, but someone was supposed to visit her every day to help with chores and make sure she was okay. What did they think had happened to her when she disappeared? Their negligence was infuriating.

Nell was sure her sister would get to the bottom of this. Bridget was indomitable when it came to confrontations. The only time Nell had known her to cave in was when the conflict involved one of her husbands. And when Bridget succumbed to Daddy's relentless bullying and agreed to give up her baby for adoption. Her resolve seemed to melt.

Nell dialed David on his cell phone, hoping she would catch him on the commuter train to New York City.

"Hi, baby, how are you? How's Mom?" David said.

She could hear the rattle of the train in the background, men's voices, laughter.

"Good morning, Mr. Williams. I'm okay but missing my man." She drove slowly along Lakeshore Drive with one hand on the wheel and the other holding her phone.

"Dave. Come on, partner." A loud voice called from near her husband's phone. The words "hearts" and "no trump" were discernable amid the background chatter.

"Are you playing bridge? Is this a bad time to talk?"

"It's never a bad time to talk to you, sweetie," David said absentmindedly.

Then he laughed. "Okay, you caught me. Could I call you back in a while? Is everything all right there?"

"Everything is fine. I'm on my way to see her again now."

"Great, great… kiss her for me, will you? And text me the address where you're staying. Did you find out what she was doing way up there?" His voice faded, and the rhythmic clacking of the train swelled for a moment.

"Sort of but not completely. It's kind of a long story…"

The connection buzzed, and his answer was swallowed by the distortion. She heard a man's voice calling David's name.

"Okay, talk to you soon," Nell said, raising her voice.

"Bye, love you…" Static sizzled on the line, and the call was cut off.

"You too," she answered though the connection had already ended.

Nell pictured her good-looking husband and children and their clean, uncluttered home. Everything in its place and easy to maintain. Totally under control, the way Nell preferred her life. No fighting or yelling, everything calm and everybody happy. Not like her teen years, when the sound of angry voices at home had been only too familiar.

When Bridget and Daddy went at it, Nell shut herself in her bedroom and played her Madonna album as loud as she could. The arguing didn't seem to bother them, but it certainly bothered Nell. She loved her dad, and she loved Bridget. She didn't want to have to take sides. Right then, she vowed to make a different kind of life when she had her own family.

She remembered the night her sister came home and described peeing on the pregnancy test in the McDonald's bathroom. Bridget pulled the white stick out of her purse and showed it to Nell. It had a big plus sign on it, which meant there was a baby coming. The girls held hands as they sat on Nell's bed, facing each other.

"What will Daddy say?" Nell always worried about his temper. Sometimes she got mad at Bridget for setting him off.

"I don't care," Bridget said, her chin tipped up.

"Will you get married?" Nell wondered what Bridget's boyfriend thought.

"No way. I'm going to college next year. Anyhow, he's a jerk."

"The boy knows?"

Bridget lifted her head, a determined look in her eyes. "Showed him the plus sign."

"And he didn't want to… you're right, he is a jerk." Nell squeezed

Bridget's hands, on the verge of crying. At fourteen, Nell had major fantasies about romance and love. The thought of that kind of betrayal broke her heart.

"Never mind." Bridget had given Nell a hug. "I don't even like him anymore. Why would I want to marry him? I'll find someone much better, and we'll live happily ever after and have three kids. Two boys and a girl. That's it, you'll see."

So Bridget's plans hadn't worked out either. It occurred to Nell that both their lives were defined by regrets and the things that were out of reach. No matter how perfect her life might seem on the surface, Nell still missed the boundless future of possibilities she had pictured when she was a girl.

As she turned toward the center of town, Nell let herself daydream once again about winning a grant to go off and write somewhere, all alone. She had sent away for an application to the Iowa Writers' Workshop once and got halfway through filling it out before she'd stopped and ripped it to shreds.

Nell could imagine the conversation with David if she had been accepted:

"Um… but who's going to drive the carpool next week, honey?"

"Not me. I'll be in Iowa City drafting a Pulitzer Prize winning novel."

"But… won't we run out of clean clothes?"

"I guess the housekeeper could do the laundry, David."

"Yes, that might work. Good suggestion. Will you be home in time to make artichoke dip for the poker game next week? I promised to bring it."

"No, I don't think so. I'll only be on chapter one by then."

"Oh. Well. That will be a big disappointment. You know how the guys love your dip."

"Gosh, maybe I shouldn't go, then. Wouldn't want to let them down."

"No, no… I want you to be happy, Nell. If you really want to go, you should do it. We'll get by somehow. It's just a few weeks, isn't it?"

"Actually, it's two years. It's an MFA program."

Silence.

"Two years? Really? Well, I suppose Lauren might still recognize you when you come home. Ben will be off to college by then, though."

"Would you like a divorce, David, so you can find someone else to have sex with on the weekends?"

"Sounds terrific. Just send the bills, I'll take care of them and you can pay me back later. The Pulitzer pays quite well, doesn't it?"

"I think it's ten thousand dollars."

"Is that all? Does this plan seem wise, Nell? Wouldn't your time be better spent here at home, cleaning the pool and power washing the house?"

A chuckle escaping her throat, Nell turned by the town green and drove into the hospital parking lot. Her shoulders relaxed, and she realized how tense they had been. It wasn't fair to fantasize about David that way. He was a very sweet guy. Nell was the one with the problem, not him. She had stepped onto this path long ago, and she had to follow it. Running off to live by herself was a ridiculous thought. She wondered what Mom would say about it. Maybe Nell would ask her when she recovered.

Taking in a deep breath and letting it out slowly, Nell flipped on the radio and listened to the news. The local weather forecast was for rain that night and the following day. But for the moment, the sky was still blue.

CHAPTER 10

Mary ~ 1998

MARY AND HER BEST FRIEND sat on the swinging bench by the rose arbor and sipped their tea. Ginnie had brought a cake, and they each held a slice on a paper napkin.

"It's not that he's a bad man," Mary said. "In fact, he was a leader in our community and a deacon at the church. It's not the Alzheimer's, either, though that part is awful. It's something more personal. I don't even know how to talk about it."

"You don't have to tell me if you don't want to. I didn't mean to pry." Ginnie reached down and squeezed her hand. "We're just so glad to have you here whenever you can get away. I hope you believe that."

"Oh yes." Mary smiled. "And I'm glad to be here too. I want to tell you everything—it's just hard. It has to do with his attitude toward me all these years and the way he's treated our daughter... it's shameful. There's no excuse for it."

Ginnie kept a discreet silence, raising her eyebrows and waiting.

"Oh, you know men." Mary laughed and rolled her eyes. "They always have to be the boss, and they always know best about everything. Even when they're one hundred percent wrong."

They both laughed. Mary thought how good it was to have a friend to talk to about her secrets. It made carrying them around so much easier.

"I can relate," Ginnie said. "Jake is the same way sometimes. But then others, he drives me crazy by expecting me to make all the decisions while he just floats along. If by some unlucky chance I make the wrong choice, God forbid, then watch out. He'll raise a ruckus they can hear all over the neighborhood."

"Which is worse, I wonder?" Mary sipped her tea. "Micromanaging all the time or making us take the responsibility then criticizing our decisions?"

"I know with Jake it has a lot to do with his mood. He has a dark side, you know."

"Yes. So does Thomas."

"I can picture two women back in caveman days, having this same conversation. 'Wolf Tooth in bad mood today, sister, ugh, watch out for club on head.'" Ginnie grinned.

"I think you're right. It's a peculiarity of the sex. They just can't work things out without howling and bashing trees for a while first, like gorillas." Mary made a monkey sound, and both women burst out laughing.

Mary's smile faded first. "Actually, it's been building up to this for a long time. We got engaged before we shipped out, and I didn't really know what I was getting into. I was in love."

"Does any woman ever really know what she's getting into?" Ginnie raised one eyebrow.

"Good point," Mary said, thinking of her sister's failed marriages. "Somebody must, I assume. Or where did all the happily-ever-after stories come from?"

"Dreams? Wishful thinking? Lies their mothers told them?"

"Or lies their fathers told them, more likely." Mary looked up over the rim of her mug at Ginnie.

"Well," Ginnie said, finishing the last of her cake, "at least we aren't considered our husbands' possessions anymore, and you wouldn't be ostracized from society for getting a divorce if you want one."

"True. But my daughters might ostracize me from their hearts, I'm afraid." Mary's voice tightened and cracked as she held back the sudden urge to cry. She held her breath for a moment, eyes closed, then opened them again to see her friend watching and waiting.

"You haven't told them how things are?"

"Not yet." Mary leaned over to put her empty mug on the little wicker table next to the swing. She wondered how that sounded. It was so dishonest, shameful.

"That's a hard one. You must be terrified."

"I'm having trouble knowing how to start the conversation at this point."

"Yes, I can see why." Ginnie put her hand on Mary's and squeezed.

58

"There's a lot to tell. It's been going on for a long time. And you have to be so careful what you say."

They sat in silence, listening to the birds and watching the light move in the trees.

"Ginnie, I'll never say a word about you and Jake and the baby. You know that, don't you? Please don't ever worry about that." Mary looked her friend deep in the eyes.

"Well, that's good to hear." Ginnie's voice sounded a little shaky too. "It's all wrapped up together, you know. And it could fall apart fast if someone were to pull the wrong string."

"I don't want to hurt you or Jake. You've both been so kind to me. Beyond kind, really. I'm so grateful." Mary realized how true that was, how indebted she was to them. They had made her feel at home in Hartland and helped her withstand the torment of caring for a dying man she didn't love anymore.

Ginnie put her arm around Mary shoulders. "I know you are, and don't worry, I trust you. Just go slow and careful, and it will all work out. You can invite the girls up here to visit when you're ready, and we'll all get along like one big happy family."

"I thought we decided that happy families are a myth."

"No, happy housewives are a myth," Ginnie said. "The men and kids are deliriously happy as long as supper is ready on time and there are plenty of clean socks in the drawers."

"Nell sort of fits the happy-housewife description, but Bridget doesn't at all. I still see signs of misery in her."

"She needed her father's approval, don't you think?" Ginnie spoke straight to the point.

"The nasty old fool destroyed her self-confidence just when she needed it most." Mary felt her face flush as she clenched her fists.

"Well then, let him have it. Bonk him on the head with your saber-tooth club. Fight for cavewomen's rights."

"Ginnie, I can't fight him. I'm a nurse, sworn to take care of the poor sick man." Mary set the swing rocking with her foot. "I made another promise when we married. 'In sickness and in health...'"

"Right. Sorry about that."

"But that doesn't mean I can't whine about it a bit, especially when I'm sitting in a safe place with my best friend in the world."

"Venting is highly underrated by men, don't you think?" Ginnie had a serious tone, but her face looked mischievous. "They always feel compelled to jump up and fix everything."

"Yes, there's nothing like a good whine to make me feel much better." Mary played along, making it sound like a joke even though it was true.

They swung for a while in peaceful silence. The only sounds were the sputter of feathers in the trees and buzzing in the roses as the sun slowly shifted across the sky.

CHAPTER 11

Nell ~ 2014

NELL PARKED IN THE HOSPITAL lot and carried her bag of goodies inside. She saw Jake had beaten her to it. He sat in the chair next to the bed, his head bowed and resting on his hands. Mom was awake, looking at him. The ugly gray breathing tube was still attached to her mouth. She stroked Jake's hair gently, her hand barely moving.

Watching them, Nell felt like an outsider. Should she knock? Clear her throat? Just walk right in? Her foot tapped the floor as she hesitated.

The same nurse Nell had met the day before was on duty. Jennifer came out from behind the desk and put her hand on Nell's shoulder. When Nell turned to respond, the woman's eyes were wary.

"I won't make a fuss." Nell spoke quietly. "But should he be in there? He's not family, you know. Doesn't she need to rest?"

"Her fever is down, and her blood work looks a little better. I've had my eye on him. He's been behaving himself."

Nell felt her face pull into a sullen pout. "But it's my turn now."

The nurse smiled, patting Nell's arm. "All right, I'll get rid of him for you." Jennifer went inside the cubicle and said something in a low voice, hustling about to check on the machines and tubes, taking her patient's vital signs and writing them on the chart.

Jake gave Mom's hand a final squeeze and wiped his face. Nell saw he had been crying. He stood up and unfolded to his full height, making the woman in the white bed look tiny as a child. The room suddenly seemed crowded. Ducking his head as though to make himself smaller, Jake sidled out the door and into the hallway. He raised his eyes and noticed Nell standing there. She pinched her mouth tight. Glaring at her fiercely, he nodded in her direction and strode off without a word.

Nell's mouth fell open in indignant surprise. *Grouchy as always.* What was his problem, anyhow? Maybe he was being defensive, afraid she blamed him for what had happened to her mother.

But if anyone had a reason to be mad, it was Nell. Jake had obviously been neglecting his darling "Ellie" recently, or she wouldn't have gotten so sick and ended up in the hospital. What kind of a friend was that? Nell did blame him.

Jennifer came out of the cubicle and waved Nell inside. Mom's eyes were closed, and the ventilator was moving her chest up and down. Nell made a small sound as she settled into the bedside chair, and her mother's eyes fluttered open, filling with love. Nell reached for Mom's hand and stroked the fingers gently.

"Good morning," she said in a cheery voice. "I saw a beautiful sunrise this morning."

Mom's eyes smiled.

"Winston is spending the day with Adam." Nell reached into her bag to unpack the magazines and books she'd brought.

Mom's brow furrowed, and her eyes looked curious.

"Oh yes, I've met him too. Very nice and extremely handsome. Tall, like his father. But a lot friendlier."

Her mother's eyes smiled again.

"I love the cottage, Mom. It's a magical place. The lake is gorgeous, and so is your yard."

Mom tried to nod, but the ventilator was in the way.

"I can certainly see why you are so attracted to this place. It has a relaxing atmosphere." She looked her mother straight in the eye and couldn't resist adding, "I can *almost* understand why you kept it a secret from us… for all this time."

Mom's eyes began to tear up. She motioned toward the pad and pen on the bedside table. Nell held it for her while she wrote, "SORRY," and then in a shakier hand, "LOVE."

"I love you too, Mom. Don't worry. It's okay. I just wish I knew what was going on." She leaned over and gently stroked her mother's forehead. She started to hug her, but all the tubes and wires kept them apart.

Mom lay mute, her eyes stricken. She struggled with the pencil uselessly, her hand shaking.

"Don't worry, just rest now. We can talk about it later."

Nell took out the novel she'd brought and read aloud for an hour or so. Mom lay peacefully and listened. Eventually, the nurse came to beckon Nell out to the hallway.

"She's due for her medication now," Jennifer said. "That should make her sleep for a few hours. Why don't you take a walk, get some lunch? You can bring it back in here if you like."

Nell got directions to the library, which was at the other end of the town green next to the church. Between the hospital and the library was a strip of commercial buildings with a little market and café. Park benches and picnic tables edged the perimeter of the rectangular, grassy park. A cluster of playground equipment was arranged on the far end, where she was headed. Nell walked down the sidewalk, swinging her bag and feeling a bit giddy in the crisp green Vermont air.

The library was a beautifully restored antique building with a modern addition on the back. Landscaped with bright flowerbeds, brick walkways, and wrought-iron light fixtures, it invited exploration. She entered through the front door of the older section and walked down the center hallway toward the addition, where a modern kiosk housed the librarians.

Nell recognized one of them immediately as the pink lady from the hospital. She wore a gray skirt and blue sweater and little reading glasses balanced on the end of her nose. Her name tag said, Doris Barton, Assistant Librarian.

"Well, hi there, honey," Doris said in a soft voice as Nell approached. "How's your mother doing?"

Her assistant, who looked like a high-school girl, was stacking books onto a trolley. She smiled at Nell and wheeled it away. A mother with two youngsters waved at Doris and went out the swinging doors to the parking lot.

"She's better, thanks." Nell took Mom's novel out of her bag and put it on the counter, saw the sign that said QUIET PLEASE, and lowered her voice. "I've been reading to her. She really enjoys it. This needs to be renewed. Can you help?"

"Sure," Doris said, flipping the back cover open to stamp the reminder card. Then her fingers flew over the computer keyboard for a moment. "All set. Two more weeks." She flipped the book cover closed. "So," she said quietly and pulled down her glasses to peer at Nell over them. "Did you get settled in down by the lake?"

"Yes, I love the cottage."

"How about the neighbors?" Doris raised her eyebrows.

"Um, well, they're fine, I mean... oh. You mean Jake, don't you?" Nell interpreted the look the woman was sending her. "Jake Bascomb?"

Doris nodded. "He's not bothering you, is he?"

Nell remembered the figure in the backyard the previous night. She shivered, still spooked. "Why would he be bothering me?"

"There's a lot of people around here who are put off by that man," Doris said, her voice nearly a whisper. "Especially after what happened to his wife."

Nell whispered back. "What did happen to her? He started to say something about it, but we were interrupted."

"She was found dead, drowned in the lake. He was taken in for questioning, but they let him go. Lots of people thought the police should have done more to find out what really happened." Doris reached over to pat Nell's hand. "You watch out, honey. I heard he had your mother out in his sailboat a few days ago, and she went overboard. The water's cold even this time of year. She was probably in shock when she got so sick."

"Oh my God." Nell's mouth fell open, and her eyes went wide with shock. Her intuitions about Jake seemed to be right on target. "I can't believe he would endanger her." Nell's voice got louder and heated. "No wonder he acted so uncomfortable with me. He must have known I'd be furious when I found out."

Doris nodded. "Just don't you be alone with that man. They say he has quite a temper." She lowered her voice and leaned toward Nell. "He drinks sometimes. More than he should."

Nell put the book back into her bag, said good-bye to Doris, and went outside to walk down the sidewalk in a daze. She stopped at the little café and ordered a sandwich to go, sitting at a table outside with a cup of coffee while she waited. Contemplating what she'd learned, she took out her cell phone and called Bridget.

Her sister answered on the second ring. "Hi, Nell, how's Mom?"

Nell filled her in on the situation, answering questions about the medications and prognosis.

"What did Maplewood say?" she asked Bridget.

"You won't believe it. They actually made up some cock-and-bull story about Mom being picked up by our cousin."

"Our what?"

"They say Mom was picked up, and not for the first time, by a man who she told them is her nephew. Some guy named Adam. They said he was very polite, and Mom seemed totally comfortable leaving with him. Do you think she was kidnapped?"

"I just met someone here named Adam."

"A big tall guy, forties? Brown hair? That was their description," Bridget said.

Nell frowned. "Yes, it must be him."

Adam Bascomb was the explanation for how Mary had gotten back and forth from Maplewood to Vermont since she'd surrendered her driver's license. He'd been giving her rides.

Inside the café, a woman called out Nell's name. Her sandwich was ready.

"Let me call you back. I need to investigate this," she said to Bridget. "We have a lot to talk about. Don't do anything until you hear from me, okay?"

"I'm catching a plane to Vermont in a few hours. We can talk in person then."

"That's great news. I'll text you the address."

The picture was starting to fill in, Nell thought as she picked up her lunch and walked back to the hospital. Mom was even more deeply involved with these two men than Nell had originally guessed. Resolved to uncover the whole story, she pulled Adam's business card out of her pocket and read the address more carefully.

CHAPTER 12

Bridget ~ 2014

BRIDGET STEPPED OUT OF THE shower and inspected her body in the full-length mirror as she toweled off. Everything still seemed to be holding up reasonably well, thank goodness. She slipped into a robe, sat down at the makeup table, and towel dried her hair. Shaping it with a round brush, she blew it dry and clipped it back from her face to work on her makeup. There it was, the little bruise on her jaw. She frowned and reached for the concealer stick to blot it out.

Eric had grabbed her by the chin again. He had gone too far this time. A little bit rough was okay, but his attitude was out of line. There was a sneer in his voice lately. Her eyes hardened as she gazed at herself, the usual insecurities erased by anger.

Bridget hated it when people underestimated her intelligence because she was a fluffy, beautiful blonde and her favorite color was pink. She'd been feeling for quite a while that Eric thought she was stupid.

Well, she wasn't. And if he didn't know that by now, then Eric was the one with a problem in the IQ department. Bridget knew more than Eric realized about lots of things, their financial situation being one of them. When money first started to disappear from their joint accounts, she'd gone on alert like a cat who heard a rustle in the bushes. They had bought the house together with cash, but now there was a mortgage bill being sent to Eric's office. Bridget had spotted it in a pile of mail when she met him there one day. He must have forged her signature on the papers.

Bridget patted powder over the makeup on her jaw, hiding the bruise. She frowned at her perfect peaches-and-cream complexion. Her eyes brimmed with tears, and the mascara was a tiny bit smeared, so she reached for a tissue and carefully fixed it.

There she was, ideally cast to be the beautiful princess in the fairy-tale castle, longing for love and happiness and ending up with the goblin instead of the prince—over and over again. When would she fall in love with the hero for a change?

She sighed and straightened her shoulders. There was really no question at all about what to do next. Bridget carried a lot of guilt around, but she was a survivor. She could move out of the house and leave Eric with his secret mortgage, have her own life, maybe even be single for a while.

After this trouble is all over, maybe I'll try to find my daughter one more time. Check the online adoption directories, see if any new listings have turned up.

Several times, Bridget had typed in her baby's birthplace and date and hit the search button, waiting with her breath held while the arrow symbol on the screen twisted round and round. Time and again, the results had come up empty.

Maybe she should speak to the adoption-agency people in person. Be persuasive. Bridget was good at being persuasive. She could read her audience and give them what they wanted. Yes, even manipulate them. Not appreciating that was Eric's biggest mistake. He believed she was weak, but she was really just expressing her genius for adaptation, her chameleon nature. He felt satisfied and victorious while she subtly steered things her way.

Soon, all of their secrets would be out in the open. His and hers.

Bridget's secret was personal, a secret of the heart that she'd be happy to reveal to the world if she ever had the chance. Her intuition told her that Eric's secrets were another kind entirely.

It was time to get dressed and go to Georgetown, where she owned an adorable townhouse. That property was in her own name, thank goodness. Downstairs were her interior-design offices, and upstairs was the small but elegant apartment into which she had been gradually moving her most essential personal belongings. Bridget had learned something from her previous divorces. She was ready for whatever might happen.

Bridget chose a deep-eggplant silk dress and jacket with matching soft leather pumps. Her long strand of perfect, creamy pearls and dangling pearl-and-diamond earrings completed the polished look. She had packed a wide assortment of comfortable, casual clothes for her trip, figuring she wouldn't need much else up in the woods. Her good jewelry went into a soft padded fabric envelope that fit into the bottom of her purse.

She probably wouldn't be coming back to this house for quite some time, if ever, so she filled garment bags with formal evening wear and coats to bring over to the townhouse in Georgetown. Making several trips up and down the stairs, she filled up her Mercedes until there was barely enough room to see out the back.

Lulubelle sat on her favorite window seat in the kitchen and watched this activity with growing concern. She knew what suitcases meant.

"Want to come with Mama, baby?" Bridget crooned, and Lulu raised her front legs like a dancer, begging to be picked up. Bridget snapped on a leash, zipped the dog into her pet carrier, and looked around the house one last time. She went out the door to the garage and pulled it shut behind her.

As she drove through the immaculate streets toward the security gate, Bridget thought about the years she had spent in this community. She realized with surprise that she had never met most of her neighbors. She'd seen their names on the mailboxes, but she didn't know where they worked, how the couples had met, or what their hobbies were.

When she and Eric had first moved in, they were invited to a holiday party across the street, but he needed to work that night. The rare times Bridget went outside, she usually stayed within the tall redwood fence that surrounded their backyard pool.

It all looked so perfect, so cozy. So desirable. The great American dream. But what secrets lurked inside those fabulous homes? Maybe they were just as dark and miserable as the ones in Eric and Bridget's house.

Bridget's left eye began to twitch. She put on her sunglasses and smiled at the handsome guard who waved her through the gate. Accelerating toward the entrance to the Beltway, she left her old life behind in the swirling dust.

Bridget worked at her desk for most of the day, wrapping up as much paperwork as she could before her trip. Her office was littered with bright paint swatches, tile and carpet samples, and display boards with samples of moldings and brass hardware. The space had a busy, creative atmosphere.

The sunny room felt successful, designed to impress clients when they came in for a private meeting. The furniture was antique, in perfect condition and upholstered in beautiful pale colors. Triple-swagged window curtains in rose and gold, with embroidered tapestry tiebacks, adorned the tall windows. A pink floral eighteenth-century Aubusson carpet covered the floor. Comfortable chairs flanked a tufted pale-peach silk-covered sofa that featured an ornate hand-carved frame with a pierced-grape motif. Soft brocade pillows were arranged artfully in its corners.

Lulubelle waited patiently in a gilded wicker dog bed on a pink velvet pillow, posed as though for a magazine spread. She lifted her head every time someone came in or went out, on the alert for Bridget's next move.

Bridget met with each of her assistants and doled out assignments so that things would run smoothly in her absence. Her employees were all dedicated and talented. Anyhow, she would be in touch by phone and laptop. There was nothing to worry about.

Nothing to do with work, anyway. One thing was nagging her, though. It was odd, considering how shallow and unpleasant their relationship had always been, but Bridget found herself worrying about Eric's daughter, Heather.

They had never gotten along. But there it was, annoyingly persistent: maternal concern.

Bridget looked at her watch and made a decision. The exclusive private school that Heather attended would soon be getting out for the day. There was just enough time for her to stop by before everyone went home. She could go straight to the airport from there. Putting Lulu's pet carrier in the backseat with her luggage, Bridget drove to the dignified mansion that housed the school and parked in front of the entrance.

When the bell rang and a horde of uniform-clad teenagers began to pour out of the building, Bridget was leaning against the elaborate wrought-iron fence that edged the sidewalk. A Hermes scarf and big Jackie-O sunglasses covered most of her face and hair. She hoped not to be recognized by any of the other mothers at the moment. That might complicate things. There was just enough time for a quick chat, then she would go.

Heather came bouncing down the steps with her two best friends, all of them chattering at the same time. When she first saw Bridget, she looked right past, not recognizing her. Then her eyes turned back, and she focused, a suspicious frown on her face. After saying a few words to her friends, who moved on to wait in the parking lot, she approached her stepmother warily.

"What do *you* want?" Heather spoke in a hostile voice, her face screwed up in disgust.

Bridget wondered for a second why she had come but told herself it was something she wanted to do for herself, not for anybody else. "We need to talk for a minute."

"Why?"

"Come over to the car with me, and I'll tell you."

"Can't we talk at home? I'm busy," the girl whined, looking back at her friends, who giggled and beckoned.

"No. Now."

"Am I... in trouble?" Heather seemed to be afraid Bridget might have discovered one of her escapades.

"Just come on. It won't take long." Bridget took the girl's arm and led her across to the Mercedes.

Heather followed, apparently hesitant to resist when she might need her stepmother's good will to get out of whatever punishment was about to be leveled on her. They got into the car, and Bridget took off her sunglasses. She looked at the teenager's smooth, unblemished face, so sweet and pretty. So different from the ugly viper that dwelled within. *What a waste*, she thought, deciding what to say.

Bridget reached out to brush a strand of hair away from Heather's eyes. The girl flinched, pulling back. Bridget smiled gently, feeling melancholy.

"What is *wrong* with you?" Heather demanded, pouting. "What's going on?"

"I'm going away, Heather. I came to say good-bye."

"You mean, on a trip? Somewhere cool? No fair. I never get to go anywhere."

"No."

"Huh? Where are you going, then? Somewhere boring for work? Is Dad going too?" Heather grinned, and Bridget guessed she was already planning the huge, illicit party she would have the next day, when she hoped to have the whole house to herself.

"No, I'm going alone. And I'm not coming back. Not to the house."

"Why? What do you mean?" Starting to suspect the truth, Heather raised her eyebrows in surprise.

"I'm leaving your father, Heather."

"No," Heather shouted, reaching out to clutch Bridget's hand. "No, you can't do that."

"Why? Why do you care?"

"You can't leave me... alone with him. You just can't." The girl seemed to panic, tears welling up in her eyes.

"Why not, honey? He's your dad. He'll take good care of you." Surprised at Heather's reaction, Bridget patted her hand.

"No he won't, no he won't." Heather sobbed, the tears running freely down her face. "He doesn't care about me. He never really wanted me, either. It was just to get back at Mom. And she let him do it." She peered at Bridget through her tears, her lips turned down in a trembling mask of despair. "Nobody wants me. You don't, either."

"Sweetie, it always felt like the other way around to me."

Heather swallowed and looked at Bridget with a flash of guilt in her eyes. "No, I always thought... um... you were cool. You have all those great clothes and all and a great job. You're, like, a really good person." Heather looked down and picked at a loose thread on her plaid skirt.

Bridget smiled, recognizing that the master tale spinner was at work, though there did seem to be a seed of truth in what the girl was saying.

"Heather, I'm leaving Eric, not you. There are some problems I can't talk about right now... they're just between him and me. Do you understand?"

Heather nodded her head though her face was still pouty. She had stopped crying and wiped her cheeks with her hand. With her red nose and puffy eyes, she looked younger somehow, more innocent. She chewed on her lower lip.

"But I can't live there alone with Daddy. He's never home. Who will take me shopping and do the school stuff?"

"I'll be back in town after a few weeks, and we'll work something out. Maybe your mom will help. Don't worry about it. I promise everything will be okay."

"I guess. Whatever." Heather frowned at her, not convinced.

"And for now, what if you go to stay with one of your friends for a few days? Don't you think Julie or Grayson would invite you over? Their mothers are always glad to have you."

Heather started to perk up, tempted by the prospect of a fun time with her girlfriends. "Yeah, I guess that would work."

"Check in with your dad about setting that up. He's in charge. I'm sure he'll say it's okay. You have my cell number. We'll keep in touch, right? You can call me anytime, day or night."

"Okay." Heather gave her a genuine smile. "Well, I'd better go now. Thanks, Bridget. You really are, you know, what I said… a good person." She opened the car door to get out.

"Why, thanks, honey," Bridget said, surprised.

"You would have been a good mom," Heather said as an afterthought. She slammed the car door behind her and ran across the street to join her friends.

Bridget's face crumpled into a grimace of sadness. She quickly put the sunglasses back on, her hand shaking.

A good mother. Yes, she could have been. If only she could time travel and change her decision. If only things had been different.

It might be too late to rewrite the past, but maybe she was just in time to change the future.

CHAPTER 13

Mary ~ 1992

MARY'S NEW NEIGHBOR DROVE DOWN the road next to the lake in his blue truck, creeping along as the furniture, piled high in the back, rattled. His business name was painted on the driver's door: Jacob Bascomb, Antiques. She considered running out to flag him down, but she was pinned between the door frame and the mattress, so she just waved instead. Wearing little pink shorts and a halter top, she must have looked as if the mattress could easily crush her. She wriggled helplessly to encourage the impression. Playing the damsel in distress had always worked for her back in the day.

It worked again.

The man pulled over and stopped. "Need some help, sweet thing?"

"Oh brother, do I." She looked back over her shoulder and gave him a wide smile.

Getting out of the truck to walk across the lawn, he stroked his thick moustache as he surveyed the situation, unsuccessfully trying to hide the grin behind his hand.

"Get ready." He took hold of the mattress to pull, popping it and Mary out of the doorway. She tumbled halfway down the front steps and caught herself against the railing. He burst out laughing.

"Why don't you go on ahead?" He pointed, picking up the mattress by the side strap with the other hand as though lifting a suitcase. He carried it easily into the empty living room while Mary held the screen door open.

"Oh." She stared up at the long length of him. "That was simple. For you, that is."

"Where do you want it?" He looked down at her, and a wave of heat rose from her chest and neck into her cheeks. She suddenly felt underdressed.

"Upstairs, the back bedroom please." She backed away a few steps. "Thank you so much."

Mary pulled on a cotton sweater, and when he returned, she was buttoned up and sitting on the front steps with two cold beers. She handed one to him and pointed at the truck, where an armchair was balanced on top of the pile.

"That wouldn't be for sale, would it? Looks like a good chair. I could use it."

"It's all for sale. What do you need?"

"Pretty much everything. I only brought my clothes, some kitchen stuff, and the bed."

"Will your husband be coming along with a moving van?" He glanced at the wedding ring that was still on her finger.

"No," Mary answered calmly. "He won't."

There was a beat of silence.

"Okay." He took a breath and smiled. "Pick whatever you want. There's a nice kitchen table, too, and a chest of drawers."

"How much do you want for all of it?" When he told her, she laughed, getting her purse to write him a check from her new personal account. "A bargain." Mary placed it into his outstretched hand, which was double the size of hers. "It must be my lucky day." She gave him her most dazzling smile.

"Nope, it's ours." He glanced at the check. "Welcome to the neighborhood, Mary Ellen Reilly. Ginnie and Adam and I'd be pleased if you came over for dinner tonight."

"Well, I'd be delighted. Can't contribute much to the meal, though. Haven't gone shopping yet."

He gestured toward the truck. "I'll bring this stuff inside if you tell me where to put it."

She hadn't been flirting with him before, not really. It was just friendly conversation—he must know that. They would be good neighbors. The lake was the right place for her at this moment in her life. Both girls were off to college. No reason to keep up the act. In a couple of weeks, she'd call and invite them up. Then they'd talk as three adult women. The girls would understand when they heard the whole story. And what a relief it would be to come clean about everything without fear of Thomas's reaction. First, she just had to finish setting up and get the last of her things from home.

Mary watched her new neighbor unloading the truck. He carried all the furniture into the empty cottage, barely breaking a sweat. A kitchen table and chairs, a loveseat and armchair for the living room, a bedside table for upstairs—all of it was hers and hers alone. *Freedom, for a change. My own place, where I can be whoever I want to be.*

"Thanks very much! Lucky you were passing by," she called, waving farewell.

He cranked the ignition and turned, smiling. "I'll tell Ginnie to call you with dinner details." The truck drove down the street, turning left at the corner by the town beach.

Mary leaned out the front doorway, watching a sunset reflecting off the lake, bright rays of inspiration shooting into a pink sky. For the first time in many years, she felt a hint of real happiness.

CHAPTER 14

Nell ~ 2014

NELL SAT WITH HER MOTHER until Mary fell asleep again, then she asked the nurse for directions to the address listed on Adam Bascomb's business card.

A couple of blocks from the town green stood a huge old barn with a carved wooden sign out front. "J. Bascomb & Son Antiques." Pulling into the driveway, she saw a truck parked inside the double doors. It was filled with a dining table and chairs, and the tailgate was down.

Shrill barking echoed inside the barn, and Winston came racing out. He went crazy with wriggles and yips of joy when he realized it was Nell. She patted him, and he flipped over, offering his belly.

"You've sure got him charmed, don't you?" Adam's voice came from overhead, where the door to the barn's hayloft was hooked open. Nell looked up and saw him watching her.

He smiled, and she felt a little flash go off in her brain, a sense of déjà vu.

"Hi," she said, unable to remember for a second what she was doing there.

"Hi. Be right down." Adam hesitated for a second, looking at her as though he might have something more to add, but then he pulled back and disappeared inside.

Nell shook her head and took a deep breath. What had just happened? She remembered she had come to confront him and tried to pull herself together. When he walked out of the barn, smoothing down his hair with one hand, she fixed a stern expression on her face.

"Something wrong?" Adam's grin disappeared. "Is Ellie doing okay?"

"She's fine. No thanks to you, *Cousin Adam*." Nell tapped her foot and waited, glaring at him.

"Um… what do you mean?" He avoided her eyes.

"You know, as in, my supposed cousin who's been checking Mom out of Maplewood and giving her rides back and forth to Vermont for… how long, Adam? How long is it now?" As she spoke, Nell moved toward him, invading his personal space.

He winced and pulled away, his eyes wide. "Well, it's been a few years now, but… Nell, she wanted me to, she begged me. She said you and Bridget didn't want her driving anymore and you'd be glad I was keeping her safe. Shit. Don't hate me. I'm sorry." Adam looked at her with concern. "I love your mother. I'd never do anything to hurt her, truly."

"Yeah, we did make her give up her license." Nell's anger deflated, and her shoulders slumped. "We thought she sold the car."

"She drove it up here that one last time and switched the registration to Vermont. After that, she had me drive it down to Maplewood to pick her up. I brought her back there again when she was ready to go." He put his hand on Nell's arm, and her skin tingled. "I always take good care of her, Nell. It's not my fault she got sick, you know."

"Yes." Nell's anger was softening. "I hear we can thank somebody else named Bascomb for that, right?" Without thinking, she leaned toward him. Adam seemed like such a nice guy. He had really just been trying to help Mom out, doing her a neighborly favor?

"I wasn't around, but there was some kind of accident out in the sailboat, and my dad feels… just awful about it," he mumbled. "Especially after what happened when… um… my mother…"

"Your mother?" Nell saw the pain flash across his face. They stood in the barn doorway with the little dog sitting at their feet, staring up with his head cocked.

"Mom fell overboard when Dad was at the tiller too. The boom hit her in the head. She… died." Adam spoke quietly. His face had turned pale, solemn.

Concern swelled inside Nell. She almost reached out to stroke his hair as she would have with her husband or kids, then she realized what was happening and stepped back.

"I'm so sorry." She stuffed her hand into her pocket. "That must have been awful for all of you."

"Yeah. It was worst for my dad. But Ellie helped him through it."

"She seems very fond of both of you."

"They were best friends, you know. Your mom and mine."

"What was her name?"

"Virginia. Ginnie for short."

"Ginnie." Nell had finally learned the name of the smiling woman in all the photos of Mom and Jake. Mom's best friend. Who Nell had never met and never would. The woman Jake Bascomb had said he killed, because of… what had he called it? His "stubborn pride."

"And what about you?" Adam said. "You have a husband somewhere, right? Family?"

"Happily married, great husband, great kids."

"Thought so." He smiled his approval. "I bet you're a wonderful mom."

"You? Wife, kids?"

"Nope. Divorced. Got my own little place in town." Something in his eyes closed like shutters. She wondered what the story of Adam's life was.

Nell realized she didn't care as much about his part in Mom's secret getaways. She had noticed a sense of kindred spirit as they talked. She'd been handling all this strange craziness alone, and he seemed so kind. Maybe his friendship could help her face the situation with more courage.

"I'd better get back to the hospital." Nell took a few reluctant steps toward her car.

He nodded, but his eyes held hers. "Okay, I'll drop off Winston at your house later. See you then."

Backing away, she nearly stumbled over a little rock in the driveway as she tried to work out why he looked familiar. Maybe she'd seen him in the pictures at Mom's house. That must be it.

Nell got into her car and started it, pulling away with a wave.

She glanced in the rearview mirror when she stopped at the corner to turn. He was still standing, motionless, watching her go.

That afternoon, Mom seemed a little better. There was some color in her cheeks, and her eyes had a touch of their old vitality. When the doctor came by to examine her, he seemed encouraged and told Nell they might consider weaning her mother off the respirator the next day.

Nell was dying to ask her mother a million questions, but she held off patiently and let Mom rest. When her mother could actually speak, it would be easier to learn all the details.

Nell read aloud for a while, and they watched talk shows together. Mom snoozed during the commercials. Nell sent David and Bridget a group text message, giving them the street address of the cottage and a summary of Mom's medical condition. As the afternoon waned, she thought about what had happened at the antiques barn. It had been so bizarre. Sort of like being hypnotized. She'd almost reached out and touched his hair. They'd never even met before that morning, yet he seemed so familiar. David would have an absolute fit.

Except David didn't know anything about it. He didn't know about Mom's cottage or that any of these people even existed. Strange how that had worked out by accident. She hadn't had a chance to talk to him for more than a second. The cell reception up in the mountains was terrible, and they were playing phone tag. It was too long a story to text, so it would have to wait until they connected.

She frowned, realizing that David had never called her back that morning after they spoke while he was on the train. Walking outside the ICU to use her phone, she saw there were several missed calls. There was only one bar on the service indicator, and when she dialed her voicemail, the messages sounded fuzzy until she went over and stood by the window. She had a brief message David had left as he walked from the train station to the office, and a more recent one from Bridget.

Bridget's voice sounded anxious. "Hey, baby sister. Just checking in. Hope things are going better up there than they are down here. Call me."

Nell went outside to the hospital parking lot to try for better reception. First, she called home and spoke to the housekeeper, who confirmed everything was going smoothly and the kids were still at their after-school activities. Then she dialed her sister's mobile phone.

Bridget answered on the first ring. "Hi, Nell, sweetie pie, how are you? How's Mom?"

"Fine. Mom's a little better. Got your message. What did you mean about things not going well?"

Bridget's voice faded in and out as though she was driving. There were voices in the background, like a radio playing. "I did it again, sugar. I picked the wrong guy. Amazing, isn't it?"

"Oh no," Nell moaned, biting her lip. Not again. She rolled her eyes and prepared for the mandatory comfort-Bridget's-broken-heart routine. "You poor thing. What happened? And where are you?"

"On my way to the airport. He hurt me, Nell. A little too much. Last night."

Nell's stomach clenched, and she gasped. She had no experience with that kind of abuse, but for her, that would be a deal breaker too. Her mocking attitude evaporated.

"Plus, he's been stealing my money." Bridget's tone hardened. "I've actually known about that for a little while, but I hadn't decided what to do."

Nell had thought they'd been through Bridget's breakups so many times before there could be no surprises left. Yet there she was, feeling sorry for Bridget and wanting to protect her as usual.

"You should get away from him," Nell blurted. "You should come here and stay for a good long while. There's plenty of room. It's the perfect hideout. Tell him you're visiting Mom, but don't tell him where you're going."

"Okay." Bridget sounded relieved. "Where am I going?"

"To Mom's place. She's… unlisted."

"Um… what?"

"Mom's place—you heard me right."

"Really…?"

"Tell you the whole story when you get here," Nell said. "Don't say anything to anybody in the meantime. Now, go get on that plane, okay?"

"All right, if you say so. Sounds very intriguing, I must say."

"Oh, you have no idea."

"Fascinating, I can't wait to hear the rest."

"You will. Just get yourself up here."

"Any good-looking men in this story?" Bridget's voice had become lighter, more playful. The Southern accent was creeping back in again too. Nell could tell she was covering up her emotions with this familiar disguise, the flirtatious party girl. It was like putting on armor.

"Bridget. My God, let's get rid of the last one before you start that again."

"Just asking. Sorry. I can't help it. Well, are there?"

"Yes. Father and son, both apparently single."

"You don't say. Well then, I'll be up on the next flight." Bridget laughed. "Text you when I land."

Nell pushed the off button and smiled at the phone.

Well, it was about time Bridget knew what was going on. Finding out about Mom's secret life would be a shocker for her too. Nell wanted to share the worry. She hadn't seen much of her sister in the past decade or so, but their bond was as strong as ever. The gap between visits was Nell's doing. The drama that followed Bridget around like a shadow just didn't belong in Nell's world, and she didn't want her family upset by too much exposure to the hysterical side of the Reilly clan.

Still, for all that Bridget made her nuts, she also comforted Nell as no one else could. Almost like another mother. Being hugged by Bridget was like coming home and plugging in for an emotional recharge of unconditional love. Nell hadn't had that feeling in a long time. She missed her sister.

Her eyes teared up, and her throat tightened. She pulled out one of the tissues she'd taken to keeping stuffed up her sleeve and wiped her eyes.

It would be good for Bridget to be safe and have a chance to work out her plans. And not a bad idea for Nell to have someone else in the house that night when Adam Bascomb brought Winston home. For the first time in memory, Nell was the sister who might need a chaperone, alone with a strange man.

Mixed with her relief was just a little disappointment.

CHAPTER 15

Bridget ~ 2014

BRIDGET TURNED ONTO THE GEORGE Washington Memorial Parkway and drove south along the Potomac River toward National Airport. She had plenty of time before her plane boarded. The radio said flights were being delayed by a hurricane heading toward the coast, so she might even be stuck for a while. When she saw the exit for Arlington, she turned off without questioning the impulse and took the turns that led to her husband's office. The least she owed Eric was a farewell. According to her lawyer, he owed her a lot more.

It seemed smart to end their relationship with a power move. That kind of thing impressed him. Bridget wanted to confront him in person. A clean parting of the ways, with as little emotion as possible, would be ideal. When she came back home to live her life in Georgetown after however long, she didn't want him to hassle her. But if he did give her any trouble, she would go after him for stealing her share of mutual assets and forging her signature on the mortgage papers. She knew a good bodyguard in case the dispute got ugly. But Eric was just a bully, a coward at heart. At the moment, the element of surprise was hopefully on her side.

Bridget parked outside the sleek glass-and-steel cube where Eric's offices were located on the top floor. Leaving her jacket in the car, she smoothed the dark-purple silk sheath over her hips, putting Lulu into a big handbag with her head peeking out the top. Bridget smiled at the doorman and took the elevator up. The doors opened on a sleek chrome-and-glass lobby with a large reception area and a mahogany corridor leading to the executive offices.

Eric's secretary, Barbara, adored the poodle and always made a huge fuss over her. As Bridget and Lulu entered the office, she rose from her desk, cooing and making kissing sounds.

"Is he in?" Bridget motioned toward Eric's door with a nod. She handed Lulu to Barbara, who barely restrained a squeal of joy.

"Yes, and he's alone. Why don't I play with this little cutie while you talk? We like to play chase the paper ball. Don't we?" Barbara talked to Lulu in a high baby voice, and the dog loved it.

"Thanks. I'll just show myself in. A little surprise." Bridget went over to her husband's office door.

The secretary nodded, already totally distracted. Bridget hesitated for a second then put her hand on the knob and walked inside without knocking.

Eric clearly wasn't expecting that. He stood in the adjoining bathroom with the door ajar and in plain sight, bent over in the process of snorting some kind of white powder off the countertop. Probably cocaine, his current go-to anesthesia.

She took advantage of the chance to slip behind his chrome-and-glass desk and sit in his big leather chair. She leaned back and propped up her feet, which looked fabulous in the sexy dark-purple strappy heels. Her legs looked great too. *Eat your heart out, you fool.* She sent psychic daggers in his direction. Crossing her arms, Bridget waited.

When Eric came out of the bathroom, wiping his nose, he saw her and jumped, swearing. He glared at her suspiciously, but she just laughed.

"What're you doing here?" He was staring at her legs, probably trying to look up her skirt. That was good. He was distracted. Score one point for Bridget.

"Thought I'd stop in for a visit. Why, something wrong with that?"

His eyes narrowed, and he began to circle around the desk like a wolf stalking a rabbit. "I heard from my daughter a few minutes ago. She told me the most ridiculous story." Score one point for Eric. She'd been hoping Heather hadn't called him right away.

"Oh?" Bridget held very still as he walked behind her, out of her range of vision. Then he reappeared on her other side, coming close to lean against the edge of the desk. His large, muscular presence loomed over her. Second point for Eric.

"Are you leaving me, Bridget? Is that what you're here to say?"

She raised her eyes and looked straight at him. "Right now, I'm going to take care of my mother and Nell. When I come back, I'll be living in Georgetown. Alone. You know as well as I do that it's over, Eric."

He stared at her. "No discussion? No counseling, no working things out?" His face started getting red, as anger edged into his tone. Eric rubbed his fists together, cracking the knuckles. The sound made her cringe.

"If you wanted to work things out," she said, "you should have asked me to sign the mortgage papers instead of forging my signature. Did you get one of your buddies to notarize it? Did you pay him with coke?"

He raised his eyebrows then quickly hid his reaction. So he hadn't thought she knew about the mortgage. Another point for Bridget.

"And if you wanted a discussion"—Bridget stood up to meet him eye to eye—"we should have talked about what you were going to do with all the money you took out of our accounts, don't you think?"

Eric glared at her, his face surly and hands fisted. "So you know about it. So what? You're just a stupid bitch anyhow, Bridget. What are you going to do about it, go cry to your decrepit old mother and your OCD sister? You're pathetic, you know that?"

She went around the desk and walked to the door, feeling more confident with every step and happy to know that he was checking out her ass. She stopped and turned for her parting shot. She had earned it.

"I was going to kiss you good-bye." Bridget blew him a kiss. "But I wouldn't want to catch something nasty."

Before he could answer, she whipped out the door and closed it, stealing the last word—for that round, anyhow.

She picked up Lulu from her enthusiastic babysitter and hotfooted it out to the car, hoping Eric wouldn't pursue her. *Probably shouldn't have let loose with that last shot*, she thought while driving back to the parkway. Getting him too angry could have dire consequences. She just couldn't help it, though. Life didn't offer many chances to send off a zinger and make a clean exit.

Bridget turned up the radio and sang along with it. An exhilarating sense of freedom expanded within her. The fear she had been denying began to relax its clenched vigilance, and with that came the urge to tremble. Her hands shook as she grasped the steering wheel and watched for signs to the airport exit.

She pulled into long-term parking and found a good spot near the terminal entrance. Tears were rolling down her cheeks and the hysterical giggles had turned to sobs as she grabbed a handful of tissues and filled them with a tiny percentage of her pain and disappointment. Her marriages all started out well, but she couldn't seem to sustain them over the long haul. She always picked the wrong guy. It wasn't their fault—it was hers. There was something wrong with the way she related to men, and that fact kept coming back to haunt her. The shrink she went to after her second divorce said it had to do with feeling rejected by her father. She realized that was probably true, but knowing it didn't interrupt the pattern.

When she was done crying, she felt much better. Bridget fixed her makeup and gathered her things, locking the car. She rolled her suitcase into the terminal, carrying Lulu in her purse. When they got to the correct terminal, she went straight to the ladies' room and changed into jeans, T-shirt, boots, and a leather jacket. She gave Lulu some water and checked to make sure her ticket confirmation said she was traveling with a pet. Small enough to fit under the seat, Lulu's carrier qualified as carry-on luggage, and she could ride in the cabin.

"Beautiful dress." A dark-haired woman with a melodic foreign accent was waiting with a bucket and sponges to clean the sinks. She motioned toward the eggplant silk, lying in a heap on top of Bridget's suitcase.

"You want it? I'll never wear it again. I was going to throw it in the trash," Bridget said.

"You sure? No, is too good for trash. Very pretty." The woman picked up the dress and held it against herself. It looked like a reasonable fit.

"Definitely." Bridget handed her the matching jacket and shoes. "That dress is bad juju for me. Bad memories."

The woman nodded, sage and sure. "A man?"

Bridget met her eyes, and they connected. The impromptu meeting of the Global Sisterhood came to order.

"Yes. A bad man."

"I will take dress. Maybe it get new lover for me. Then something happy will break the bad *destino*."

"I certainly hope so." Bridget smiled at her. Then she shivered, crossed herself, and wheeled her bag out into the hallway to find the gate that would lead to whatever was coming next.

CHAPTER 16

Mary ~ 2002

MARY REILLY CAREFULLY UNPINNED THE wide-brimmed black hat. She lifted it off her head and laid it in the tissue paper that lined the waiting hatbox. Her "funeral hat," Thomas used to call it. For ten years, she had nursed him through the ravages and indignity of Alzheimer's disease, and that day, she had worn the black hat to her husband's funeral.

Appropriate headgear for the solemn occasion, it was made of heavy brushed felt with a velvet ribbon, a jet beaded band, and a few discreet feathers tufted on the left side. The front was embellished with a little hint of black veil. Nothing too dramatic, just formal enough to show respect. She packed it away and slid the box up onto the top shelf of the coat closet, hoping she would never have to wear it again.

Mary stopped in front of the hallway mirror to smooth her lipstick with a finger. The house was full of people. Nell and Bridget were supervising things in the kitchen, where most of the women had gathered with their casseroles and wineglasses. The bridge-club ladies were getting a buffet set up in the dining room. David was in the living room, serving beers and Irish whiskey. Moving on down the hallway, Mary saw the den was full of kids of various ages. When she lingered in the doorway and held out her arms, Ben toddled toward her, and she picked him up.

Odd, how happy she felt now that it was finally over. The feeling wasn't denial. It was sheer joy.

She suppressed an involuntary grin, sniffing the magical clean-baby scent of her grandson's neck and feeling the comfort of her friends all around her, an envelope of love that warmed her like a hug.

The service was attended by all the family, innumerable close friends, and the most prominent members of the local business community. Thomas would have been pleased. Wherever he was, he was smiling.

Mary chose to believe that after his death, Thomas had returned to his original rational state. For the past several years, she could only talk to him in her imagination. The body that looked like Thomas hadn't housed his true self for quite some time, so there had been no use talking out loud to it. Mary looked forward to easier communication with his spirit now that the body was out of the way—even easier than when his mind and body were still one and healthy, because after he had met God, she felt sure he had attained a much better understanding of what it was to be human.

Mary carried Ben into the kitchen and put him in his high chair. Nell swept in with a bib and sippy cup, sliding a plastic dish of macaroni and cheese in front of him. The three-year-old's big blue eyes widened, and he gulped from the cup while a neighbor sat down and took up the spoon to feed him.

"You go on and talk to your friends," she said to Mary with a shooing motion.

Suddenly, David was at Mary's elbow with a gin and tonic in his hand. "Mom? Is this good, or would you prefer wine?"

Mary smiled at her young son-in-law. Nell always made such good choices. They were a well-matched couple, smart and attractive. He was in an executive training program with a good company in New York, on a career path headed straight for the top. She was comforted to know her youngest daughter would always be safe and happy.

"Lovely. Thank you, dear." Mary took the drink and kissed David on the cheek. He held her hand for a moment then squeezed it and headed back toward the low rumble of male conversation and the scent of burning tobacco.

Mary sipped her drink and listened to voices filling the rooms where she had lived with Thomas for most of their marriage. Where they'd hosted birthday parties, Christmas dinners, book club meetings, and poker nights. Where the girls had been babies, grown up, become women, and moved on. Where she had loved her husband more than anything in the world when they were young and idealistic and didn't really know each other. Before things had changed.

Thomas Reilly's plane had gone down on a bombing mission when he'd only been in Vietnam a few months. When Mary heard he'd been found and was being flown to an army hospital stateside, she reacted with joy, but by then her life had changed so drastically that at first she didn't know what to do.

Mary had taken the diamond engagement ring out of her jewelry box and worn it to the hospital when she went to visit him after her tour of duty was over. When she saw the smiling Irishman again, she made the decision to keep wearing it. They were married in the Catholic Church a year later and lived with his parents while they looked for a place of their own.

Then they found this house. Four bedrooms upstairs and three full bathrooms. Perfect for a family of five or six. They planned on filling the place up with kids. Bridget was born two years later then Nell three years after that. But the babies stopped coming, and Thomas never got the son he had hoped for. He loved his girls, and they idolized him, but Mary knew he was disappointed. It gnawed at her and filled her mind when she couldn't sleep at night.

Maybe she should have handled things differently. Mary had never felt she could tell Thomas her secret thoughts or longings. She was sure they would all be forbidden. The laughing Irishman became a stern man with a bad temper. Thomas was a pillar of the business community who demanded that his family always present a proper image to the world in general and their hometown in particular. He would never have condoned Mary's behavior had he known everything. It was so much easier just to not talk about it.

Mary looked up as Bridget came over and sat next to her at the kitchen table. The young woman had a glass of wine in her hand and wore a gorgeous black designer dress with a low-cut back.

"Hi, Mom, how are you doing?"

"I'm just dandy, actually. It's good to know your father is at peace." Mary reached for her daughter's hand. "How are you, sweet pea?" She searched her daughter's eyes, so easy to read.

"Me too. We can remember him however we want to now. He can't stop us." Bridget smiled, and Mary laughed.

"He'd try if he could."

"Mom, we were talking. Me and Nell and David."

"About me?"

Bridget nodded. "Have you thought about the house?"

Mary looked around at her home again, feeling the weight of it hanging on her like chains. She thought of her cottage in Vermont, where she'd been spending a lot of weekends. Being able to escape had helped her get through what she had to do in caring for Thomas. She loved her getaway spot and the friends there who had supported her over the past ten years.

"I can't live here anymore, honey," Mary said. "But it must hold such memories for you girls. I hate to take that away if you're not ready."

"It's okay, Mom. We have our own homes now. And we both want you to know that if you're interested in living with one of us…"

Mary interrupted. "No, dear, I do thank you for the thought. I'm nowhere near ready for that yet."

Bridget looked relieved. "Well, what did you have in mind?"

"Actually I was thinking of a little place…" Mary's voice drifted off as she tried to figure out how to open the subject.

"Like the new senior community in South Amherst? Maplewood?" Bridget leaned toward her and nodded. "We were thinking the same thing. It would be perfect, Mom. It's close by, so you'd be near your friends. There are some two – and three-bedroom townhouses with nice little gardens. You'd have as much independence as you want, but if you need help with anything, there's always someone around to call. No mowing the lawn, no worrying about trash pickup or whatever." Bridget had obviously been doing her homework. "You could take your car too. They have garages." She stopped to sip her wine, staring expectantly at her mother.

Mary tried to be a good sport. "That sounds lovely, dear. Maybe we should drive over there tomorrow and take a look. I'll see if I like it. One of your dad's associates is a realtor. He can give us an appraisal on the house. Then we'll see how it looks financially."

Bridget smiled, and it was like sunshine coming out from behind the clouds. Mary was struck, as always, by how beautiful her daughter was both inside and out, though the young woman didn't know it.

Nell came over and stood behind Bridget. "Are you talking about… what we were saying? What do you think, Mom?"

"I think you two are going to take very good care of me." Mary looked at her daughters with loving eyes. "But don't worry too much, please. One of these days I just might surprise you."

But not now. I can't tell them with all these people here. They're both so intent on parenting me. It's wonderful. Best to wait until the right time.

Nell and Bridget exchanged a glance that communicated victory.

"Let's all drink to it, shall we?" Bridget raised her glass.

"To Mom's new home, wherever it may be." Nell touched her glass to her mother's.

They clinked and drank, and the house throbbed with life as everyone who had loved or hated Thomas Reilly celebrated his passing, and his widow planned her next step toward freedom.

CHAPTER 17

Nell ~ 2014

NELL KISSED MOM GOOD NIGHT and went outside as the sun slid down toward the rim of the mountains, making long shadows on the town green.

Stopping by the little market in the center of town on her way home, Nell bought a pound of ground beef, salad greens, and a loaf of fresh-baked bread for dinner, which would happen whenever her sister might appear. Everything else she needed for spaghetti was already in the kitchen cupboards. She picked out a bottle of red wine, and on second thought, made it two.

On the way home, she rolled down the windows of her car and let the sweet air flood the inside. Her mouth watered as the vibrant green scent filled her body. Feeling her eyelids flutter, Nell shook herself back alert.

As she drove along the lakeside road, the bold orange sunset was shining on the water, and its dazzling rays bounced into her face. She pulled down the visor and held one hand over her squinted eyes, slowing down. A small, four-legged form scurried across the road right in front of her, silhouetted against the inferno.

Nell slammed on the brakes, and the tires squealed. She felt a sickening thump.

Her heart pounded as she shoved the gearshift into park, wrenched the car door open, and leaped into the road. Nell staggered around to the front of the car and stared at the wheels.

In front of the car was a large tree limb.

Nell's relief was so enormous that her head spun for a moment. A small snorting noise came from nearby. She raised her eyes, taking a deep, steadying breath.

Standing in the middle of the road, wagging his tail and smiling at her with his white teeth and pink tongue making a happy curve, was Winston.

"Want to play?" his body language said. He ran over and tugged at the tree limb, tail wagging. He tried to drag it off into the grass.

"Winston, what are you doing in the road? No, no, no. Oh, you bad little sweetie. Oh, my good boy," Nell crooned, picking him up to hug him.

"Sorry about that," came a voice from the shore. "I should have kept a closer eye on him. Guess he saw you coming. You've got him charmed, you know." Adam stood silhouetted by the fiery light. He'd been waiting on the dock across the street from Mary's house. Nell noticed that his truck was parked at the curb.

"How's your mother?" He walked up to scratch Winston behind the ear as the dog snuggled in Nell's arms. His hand smelled like furniture polish and lemons.

"Good," she said. "Improved." Nell looked up at his face and felt that sense of déjà vu again. *He must look like someone on TV.*

She admired his square jaw line and high cheekbones, his even white teeth and full lips. His eyes were bright, sky blue. And they were looking at her with a warm expression that comforted her like a badly needed hug.

"I stopped by to see Ellie earlier, while you were out. She does seem better, I think."

She nodded, blinked back tears, and swallowed, unwilling to trust her voice at that moment.

"Need some help?" Adam asked, looking at the grocery bags in her car.

"Sure." She got back into the driver's seat to pull into the driveway. Winston rode the short distance as her copilot, sitting on her lap with his head poking out the window. Nell parked and unlocked the front door, bringing the groceries through into the kitchen.

Helping her empty the bags onto the counter, Adam motioned toward the lake with his head. "You need to see this sunset. It's outrageous."

"I'd love to," she said, pulling out the wine. "Why don't we open one of these? I got it for my sister, but there's plenty."

"Your sister?" Adam pulled open the cooking-tools drawer to get a corkscrew. Nell realized he knew this kitchen much better than she did.

"Bridget is flying up to join me tonight." She watched for his reaction.

His eyes sparkled, and he grinned, one eyebrow raised. "Another beautiful Reilly woman? Can't wait to meet her."

"Yeah, well, she wants to meet you too. You should join us for dinner."

"Bring it on." He popped the cork out of the bottle.

Nell found some plastic cups and held them while he poured. She checked to make sure her mobile phone was in her pocket. The nurses had promised to call if there was any change.

"You want to come watch the sunset too?" she asked Winston. He broke into a grin and wagged his tail. "You have to be good, you know. You cannot run into the street."

His ears flicked down, and he hung his head, peeking up at her from under his eyebrows. She picked up the leash just in case.

She grabbed her sunglasses as they went out the front door to stroll across to the dock. The narrow, sandy road was quiet, not a car in sight. "There's a lot more traffic where I live."

Adam followed her across the street. "New Jersey?"

"You know a lot about my family, don't you?" She turned to see his reaction.

"Ellie used to show me your pictures all the time when I was young. We talked about you." Adam led the way toward two folding chairs perched on the end of the dock.

"I wish we had known about you too," Nell said. "I feel really weird about that. Kind of... mad."

"At your mother?"

She nodded. "For keeping it all such a secret, not sharing this place with us. We would have loved to come here. I just don't get it."

"I didn't realize for a long time that she had kept the house a secret. It did seem funny that you girls were never here, even in the summers, but I didn't think about it much. Kind of got used to it."

The sky had darkened to glowing crimson streaks, reflected in the glassy water below. The pines surrounding the lake looked flat and black, like jagged paper cutouts. Their zigzag shape etched a double-edged horizon that separated the two mirrored worlds.

Adam and Nell looked out at the flaming vista. The air itself was tinted red. Nell took a deep breath and let the magic wash over her. Her mind still flickered with intense images of her mother's pale face, but she could smell the rich, dark soil, the water, and the coming night, cool and soothing. A loud plop in the grasses near the dock reverberated across the ripples. There were no mosquitoes to bother them yet, but fish were rising to feed. The voice of a distant frog sounded, quickly answered by many others.

Sipping her wine, Nell basked in the glow. Adam did the same, and they sat in easy silence for a while. Winston lay at their feet, gazing out over the lake.

"Why do you think she did it?" Nell said.

"Your mom? I never asked."

"Me, neither. Yet. But I will, soon as she can talk. And what's the deal with your dad and my mother?"

"What do you mean?" he said, turning to look at her. "He's known her a long time. Always been dazzled by her, I guess. So was my mom. So was I. When Ellie was around, we were always celebrating holidays, birthdays, at my folks' house or down at the town beach, with all the neighbors and a big gang of kids. Everybody loves her."

They sipped and lounged a while longer. The air grew cooler as the sun went down, and Nell rubbed her arms but was reluctant to leave the view.

"What was your father like?" Adam said.

"Dad? Sweet, wonderful, super smart, kind of melodramatic sometimes."

"Family man, eh?"

"Exactly. There at every basketball game and school play, cheering us on." Nell remembered how her father used to whistle and hoot when the team scored, leading cheers from the parents in the stands. He had gone even crazier if the basket was hers, and she always knew he was proud. It was worth the long hours of practice and training just for that.

"Chasing away the boyfriends, Nell?" Adam teased.

"Yes, mostly Bridget's, though. Mine were pretty mild mannered."

Adam laughed and raised one eyebrow. "No bad boys on your dance card?"

"No, only honor students with glasses and sweaty palms." Nell smiled.

"Those are the most dangerous guys," he said. "All that pent-up sexual tension."

They both grinned.

"Dad was great," Nell continued, "if a little on the strict side. He was kind of a big shot in town, and I was proud of him. I worked hard to do as well in school as he wanted. His confidence in my ability spurred me along. I got into a great college on a scholarship. I won a summer internship with the *New York Times*. Then he started to get sick. After that, things got really bad, and it was hard to go home."

"How old were you?"

"About eighteen at the beginning. A freshman at Vassar."

"So you weren't living at home?" he asked.

"Only on vacations and holidays. I noticed it first that summer."

"What happened?"

"There was a thunderstorm coming." Nell stared out across the water, remembering it so clearly that a sudden pang of loss twisted her stomach. "He kept nagging me to put the convertible into the garage before it rained…" Her voice faltered. "He wouldn't stop asking me, over and over, so finally I went out to do it. But the car was already in the garage." She looked at Adam.

"You mean he'd done it himself?"

She took off her sunglasses to look at him more directly. "There was nobody else home."

"So he'd just spaced out?"

Her throat tightened and she wanted to cry, even though so much time had passed since that day. Her voice came out with an emotional crackle in it. "Adam, it's more than just spacing out when you completely forget something physical you've done just minutes before. It's a blackout."

"My father has had those, too, but he always did it on purpose." He punched her gently on the arm then slid his hand around to pat her on the back. "That must have been rough, Nell."

"He had Alzheimer's. It got much worse. That day was the beginning of the end. He was never the same." Nell closed her eyes. There was a blazing red world of light behind her eyelids.

"Maybe that was why she did it." His voice came out of the flames.

"Because it was so awful?"

"Yeah. To get away."

"From Daddy?" Nell demanded, her eyes flying open. A spark of anger toward her mother smoldered again. "She could have done that and not lied to all the rest of us. And anyhow, the worst of Daddy's illness was much later. She had been coming up here for a while by then. There are earlier dates stamped on some of those photographs."

Adam sat back in his chair and sipped wine. "Maybe she saw the signs before you did. Maybe she wanted to get away from the fact that it was happening."

"I still don't get it," Nell snapped. Obviously, her concerns about her mother's secrecy weren't important to him. "What's your point?"

"What I mean is…" He seemed to choose his words carefully. "Up here where nobody knew about it, she could pretend it wasn't true."

Nell's anger deflated in the face of that statement. He could be right. Every time her mother had looked into Nell's or Bridget's eyes, she'd have seen their pain and her own. There was no escaping it when they were all together. And everyone in their hometown had known about the situation after a while. Mary couldn't even go to the grocery store without facing her neighbors' kind expressions of sympathy.

With Nell off at college and Bridget interning at a design firm in Connecticut, Mary had been at home alone with Daddy to bear the brunt of his care and the horror of the disease. There were kind people who helped, of course, personal-care assistants. Occasionally, when Nell called home back in those days, one of them would answer. When Mom went on jaunts with her girlfriends or alone to a spa, everyone thought it was healthy for her to have a little fun.

"I wonder…" Nell mused. "Mom used to go on little trips with her friends. Every few months or so." She and Adam exchanged looks.

"You think she came up here instead?"

Nell nodded, sure of it. "It's all starting to add up. Somebody must have covered for her, probably our neighbor Charlotte Morris. She was Mom's friend and another army nurse. They served in Vietnam together. But she died a few years ago, so I can't ask her for the juicy details."

"I'll bet if anyone knew the whole story, my mother did," Adam said. "They were so close. It was like Ellie was part of the family."

At least Mom had not been alone in her time of fear and despair. She had found a safe place to indulge her grief privately without the whole town watching. A haven of solace, where her friend Ginnie helped her mime normalcy and where Mom, by acting as if everything was okay, made it so. At least for a little while.

Had Jake been the stalwart and dashing protector of the two women? Perhaps he'd been jealous and resented sharing his wife with Mom, who needed so much attention.

But why did Mom come up here in the first place, before things got so bad at home? Part of the mystery had been explained but not everything. And something that Adam said had rung a bell in her mind... what was that? She couldn't remember anymore.

The sun had gone all the way down behind the trees, and the air was cold. Their cups were empty. Winston had run off to bark at some creature in the shadows along the shore.

"What time is Bridget coming?" Adam asked.

"Her plane lands at around eight thirty if it's on time. She'll let me know."

"Does she need a ride here?"

"No, she's renting a car."

"Independent, like you?"

"You'll be amazed." Nell laughed. "I am a total pussycat next to my daring sister."

Adam looked at her and raised one eyebrow. "Can't wait to meet her."

"You said that already."

"But now I mean it," he said, grinning. "Before, I was just being polite."

They both laughed, and she squeezed his arm. "Come on, then." Nell got up out of her chair and reached out her hand to him. "You'd better come inside and help me cook dinner. Besides, we need more wine."

He stood up and tightened his grasp on her, pulling her in for a quick hug.

"Sorry this is all so hard for you, kid," he said in a gruff voice. She felt it rumble in his chest.

"Better quit being so nice, or I'll cry again."

He kissed the top of her head. An alarm went off in the back of her mind, and she stiffened. The image of David's face flashed in her mind, and guilt confronted her. Nothing had really happened, but the circumstances were definitely borderline suspicious. No more hugging, she vowed.

She pulled away and took a few steps down the dock, whistling for Winston and trying to look casual. He came bounding out of the bushes and looked up at her expectantly, tail alert.

"Time for puppy supper?" she said.

His eyes shone, and he trotted along by her side as they crossed the road and went inside. Adam followed and closed the door behind them, flipping on the lights.

"Want some music?" he said, walking over to the CD player on the sideboard in the living room. "Your mom has some great jazz. She used to play it at parties."

"Sure, I didn't even know she liked it." Nell frowned. "But then, apparently there are lots of things I don't know about my mother." She was starting to get used to that concept though it still made a swell of anxiety pulse in her chest.

Nell went into the kitchen, where the light from the old-fashioned fixture was golden and warm. She scooped some kibble into Winston's bowl. Kicking off her sandals, she wrapped a big white dishtowel around her waist. Opening cupboards, she found Mary's largest pot and put it under the faucet in the sink to fill with cold water for the pasta.

"Italian?" His voice came from the doorway as the mellow notes of a female jazz singer's husky voice floated into the room.

"Did the row of canned tomatoes on the counter give it away?"

"Want me to chop anything? I'm a great prep chef. Worked my way through college in a restaurant."

"Sure, by all means," she said. "Cooking is definitely a team sport."

He moved to the sink and redirected the water for a minute then washed his hands. She went over to wash hers too, and they bumped hips. Grinning at each other, they did it again, jostling for the best position at the sink like little kids. He seemed to bring out the brat in her. The music played something about "love, love, love." The fun and the wine rushed to her cheeks. After being so stressed about Mom, she needed to let go for a minute.

"I guess in a way you actually *are* my cousin. Like you told Maplewood," Nell said, rinsing onions and peppers in the sink. She gave them to Adam, who stood at the cutting board, sharpening a knife.

"How do you figure that?" He began to slice and chop.

Nell cleared away the peels and seeds as he pushed them to the side. "We shared family. Our moms were like sisters. We just didn't know it at the time."

"I used to sit in there and watch TV," he said, pointing down the hall with the knife. He stared at her, remembering. "I looked at your pictures on the wall when we came over for dinner. I daydreamed about you and Bridget."

"What did you think of us?"

"That you were the two most beautiful girls I'd ever seen, and I was in love with you both. Kind of how you get a crush on a movie star." His voice was serious though his lips were smiling.

Nell put the pasta pot on the stove to boil and drizzled olive oil into a sauté pan, while he continued chopping and the jazz singer crooned, "lover, come back..." She poured more wine in stout little jelly jars.

"Don't trust me?" he asked when she handed him the short glass.

"It's me I don't trust."

"Oh?"

"I always knock wineglasses over. Cheers." She clinked her glass against his.

"*Santé*," he answered. They stood together in the little pool of light by the stove. The ambiance was like gathering around a cozy campfire. Nell felt her face glow.

"French?" she asked.

"French Canadian on my mother's side. My grandparents live near Montreal."

"And what about Jake? Where did he come from?"

"Maine. His people came from England, settled in Portland. Shipbuilders."

"Ah. Hence his fascination with all things nautical."

"You said it." Adam slid all the chopped vegetables into the sauté pan. He turned the burner on, picked up a wooden spoon, and devoted his attention to stirring as the pan started to smoke and sizzle.

Nell mashed some butter and chopped garlic together in a little bowl then sliced the bread and spread it with the mixture. They moved back and forth together in the workspace as though it were a dance, slipping past each other gracefully, coordinated by intuition.

"So what's your story?" she said playfully as she wrapped the bread in tinfoil.

"Grew up happy and married my college sweetheart." He avoided her eyes and stirred the vegetables intently. "We tried to have kids but couldn't. She left me for someone else, they got married and had twins."

There was a moment of silence in the room as the music paused between songs, and he stopped stirring to turn his head and look at her. His bleak expression said much more, and she caught a glimpse of disappointment.

Everything she thought she'd known about him changed in that moment. She saw a different person. The atmosphere in the room went from lighthearted to tense. He turned back to cooking, his jaw clenched.

Nell touched his arm. "I'm so sorry."

"It's okay." He spoke in a matter-of-fact voice. "It was eight years ago. I'm surprised someone didn't tell you. Sarah took off about ten months after my mom… passed. She left most of her things behind and just walked away. They moved to Colorado."

Nell felt sick to her stomach. He had lost his mother and his marriage, both within a year. What a total disaster. He was not the happy-go-lucky guy she had imagined. He seemed so confident and self-possessed. But he must have been a deeply wounded soul underneath it all.

"That's awful, Adam."

"The worst year of my life so far." He still wouldn't meet her eyes.

"You must have been devastated."

"But Ellie, she helped a lot. She was there when it happened."

"When your wife left?" Nell felt confused.

"No, when my mother went overboard. When she drowned. Your mom was on the boat. The three of them were out on the lake together when a storm blew up."

Nell shook her head, trying to register these new facts. "So Jake wasn't alone with your mother? There was a witness? Mom?"

Adam looked surprised and nodded. "That was why they let him off. Your mother testified for him. I told you, she helped a lot." Adam turned the burner on the stove down. "They had him in jail for suspicion of murder, you know."

"Yes, I heard."

"But he didn't do it."

"Yes, I heard that too."

That was exactly what Mom had told her that first day in the hospital. JAKE DIDN'T DO IT. Now it seemed she might have meant, *He didn't kill his wife…* at least, not with deliberate intent. But what about through criminal negligence? He could have made some stupid move that resulted in Ginnie's death.

Nell turned her attention back to Adam. He poured in the canned tomatoes, she sprinkled some dried basil and oregano on top, and he stirred again. The aromas rising out of the pan made her mouth water despite everything. They both leaned together over the steam, sniffing the scents. She imagined taking him in her arms, as she would her son, to comfort him. Adam turned the burner all the way down to simmer, and they left the pan bubbling softly on the back of the stove.

He pulled out a chair at the kitchen table and collapsed into it, raking his hands through his hair. "I know people around here still talk about it." He had a brooding expression. "But some things are better off left in the past."

"So people can move on?" She sat down in the other chair. They looked at one another across the table.

He nodded. "So *life* can move on."

When eight o'clock came and Nell still hadn't heard from Bridget, she finally thought to look at her cell phone. It showed no bars. Walking around the house, she discovered there was reception only on the second floor. She sat at the top of the stairs and retrieved messages from David and Bridget.

"We'd better go ahead and eat," she called down to Adam, receiver to her ear. "Her flight has been delayed." Nell listened to the next message and heard the impatience in David's voice, but she turned the screen off and went back downstairs. She'd call him back later when she was alone.

They ate at the kitchen table, savoring the sauce, the music, and the company. Nell's feelings toward Adam had deepened with the revelation of his tragic experiences. Now she saw he needed to be taken care of, he was vulnerable. Jake was his only living relative nearby, and that wasn't saying much. The son took care of the father, from what she could see.

With the table safely between them, they both reached for bread at the same moment.

Nell tried to think of David, but her focus slipped away, and instead, she stared into Adam's intense eyes. Her mind reached out for his, and she felt their spirits brush up against one another. He was such a sweet man. Bright, strong, responsible, and asking nothing though he obviously needed a lot. Sitting with him, she felt free and light.

After dinner, they brought mugs of chamomile tea out into the backyard, sitting on the old-fashioned green-canopied glider next to the rose arbor. The air was cool and moist, filled with the whispers of small creatures. The moon shone down from behind the trees, casting shadows like dark tentacles that snaked across the lawn. The woods seemed to creep into the yard, sneaking up on civilization. Fireflies twinkled in the bushes, and the black sky was full of stars, many more than Nell ever saw at home. Mom's sweet little garden had become a place where the wild had power, and Nell felt herself responding to its call.

They swung gently, and her shoulder bumped against his. Something dark fluttered across the yard, flying low. An owl hooted.

No matter how drawn to him she felt, it just wasn't that simple. She was happily married, for the most part. Her life with David needed work, but she wasn't giving up yet.

As though he knew what she'd been thinking, Adam put down his empty mug and stood up. Turning, he reached out to touch her cheek. "Night. Thanks for dinner."

She looked up at him. "Thank yourself, chef. You did all the cooking."

Taking her hand in his, he tightened his grip firmly and pulled her up to standing. He stepped forward as she rose, bringing her into his arms. Wrapping his warmth around her, he held her. Without thinking and despite her previous vow, Nell leaned into the hug. It felt natural, comfortable, like hugging an old friend. A lump rose to her throat, and tears welled in her eyes.

"Relax, I'm not going to complicate your life." His pulse beat against her cheek. "I love your mom, and I'm here for you too."

"But..." She breathed, closing her eyes, shutting him out, while at the same time she held him tighter with her arms.

"Hey, look at me, Nell." He gave her a little shake, and she opened her eyes again. "I mean it."

She nodded.

"You and Bridget are my perfect, up-on-a-pedestal imaginary girlfriends. Don't want to screw up something like that." He bent to kiss her on the cheek. They both smiled.

As she caught her breath, her wits began to return.

"Now, you can say good night… if you still want to, that is." He released her from the hug but still held onto her hand.

She nodded mutely and bit her lip.

He took one step backward and shoved his hands into his pockets. "Okay," he said in a gruff tone, then his voice softened. "Sleep well."

She nodded. "Okay. You too."

"See you tomorrow." He took one step away.

"Yes. See you then."

Adam took one more step. "Night…" He bowed his head in farewell, turned, and walked around the side of the house toward where his truck was parked out front. She heard the door creak and slam, then a long silence. Finally, the engine started up, but it idled for a time before he finally pulled away from the curb.

It's much better this way. Really, it is. We'll be friends. Solid, loyal, supportive friends. It's fine.

Nell listened to the night for a few minutes, then she went inside and locked the doors. She climbed up the stairs to her little room, where Winston was already waiting, curled up on the pillow. She got into bed and talked to her husband on the phone in the dark.

Nell was on the phone with David for over an hour. He poured out long descriptions of everything that had been happening in their family life, while she lay there and propped the phone up with pillows after her hand cramped and she couldn't hold it any longer. She said, "Uh-huh," encouragingly over and over again in all the right places. She laughed when he told her about funny things the kids had done and said.

Stroking Winston with her spare hand, Nell made sympathetic noises and said, "Oh, no" when David told her there was trouble at work. "I'm sure you'll straighten it out, honey. You always know just what to do."

They talked about Mary, and Bridget's imminent arrival. For some reason, Nell couldn't bring herself to open the subject of Mom's big secret. The thought of explaining it all, everything she had discovered, seemed too long and involved. Her sleepy eyes were closing already.

So she didn't mention it. Any of it. Keeping this strange story all to herself was her little secret act of rebellion. She didn't speak of the cottage or of Jake Bascomb and Ginnie. She didn't even mention Winston, who lay there on his back with his pink belly turned up while she scratched his chest. And certainly, she did not mention her dinner guest.

Instead, she yawned and asked her husband what the kids had eaten that night then reminded him that their daughter needed to bring her leotard and ballet slippers to school the next day. She promised to call after the kids got home the following afternoon, and she sent her love.

David talked his heart out and seemed reassured, as though somehow Nell was still controlling everything from afar. After they hung up, a tsunami of guilt hit her.

There she was, angry with Mom for keeping part of her life a secret for so many years, and yet when the chance came for Nell to come clean with David and fill him in on the whole story, she had backed away. What a hypocrite she was.

She was a secret keeper too.

That night, she had wished for a little while that she was single again because she wanted to feel that sensation of lightness, of unlimited choices. Nobody depending on her, nobody to disappoint, no examples to set, and no repercussions. For a few hours, at dinner with a stranger, she had felt like that. It had been exhilarating, almost enough to make her lose her famous self-control.

Was that what had happened to Mom?

Nell tossed and turned as the dream floated into her consciousness. Her eyelids twitched while images flashed through her mind.

Women laughing. A white sail against a gray sky, red rays of the sun shooting into her eyes as she squinted. A face staring, angry. Hands clutching at her as someone shouted. A splash of blood shining on a white surface.

There was something under the dark water. Something horrible. The woman's hair streamed out from her head like snakes.

Nell moaned and flopped over onto her stomach.

Music was playing, the sounds of a party. He danced with Ginnie, with Mom, with both. Nell watched, almost a part of it, hovering near her mother's shoulder. The three of them with their arms around each other, laughing as they swayed. She watched them hug and kiss, the women turning to kiss him, one for each cheek. His arms around their waists, he was warm between them, happy and safe. His girls. The music played, and they danced on.

Then Nell's viewpoint changed, and she sank down beneath the green water, her forehead blooming red and opening horribly, falling apart, disintegrating. White bone, jagged on the edges. An expression of mild surprise. Someone was crying.

When she woke up just before dawn, her pillow was wet with tears.

CHAPTER 18

Bridget ~ 2014

BRIDGET ENDED UP SPENDING THE whole night at the airport, waiting for a plane to arrive that could take her to Burlington. High winds and heavy rain had hit Georgia and the Carolinas, and it affected flights all along the East Coast. Reagan National Airport was full of people, everyone waiting. They walked around, looked at the kiosks, drank coffee, napped in the uncomfortable waiting-area chairs, and watched movies on their laptops. Parents with small children put them to bed on the floor.

The airport was predicting flights would resume the next day, so it didn't seem worthwhile to get the car out of the garage, find a hotel, and not be able to hear the latest announcements. She needed to get up to Vermont as soon as a flight was available. So Bridget stayed. She roamed the hallways and lounges, trapped in a metaphor. She had left her old life behind, but she couldn't move forward. She worried about her mother, but she couldn't do anything to help. She was in nowhere land, the in-between. She tried to call Nell around ten but got her voicemail. Bridget left a message and promised to appear just as fast as she could. At least she had moved out of *Eric's house*, as she already thought of it, and that was settled. The transition had begun. She'd feel a lot better when she got out of town, though.

Bridget settled into a corner where she could look out the window and had a good view of the gate entrance. Using her big purse as a pillow, she tucked Lulu into the front of her jacket, and they napped. Half-asleep, she let her mind wander to the memory of her daughter, born that spring day in Stockbridge, Massachusetts. Then she thought back even further to the summer before, when she'd been a seventeen-year-old waitress at a family resort in the Berkshires.

There was a dormitory over the garage where all the summer girls lived, and they slept in a long room filled with bunk beds. A similar facility for males was located in the barn. Some of the girls were from other countries, wanting to learn English and get a green card so they could immigrate permanently. These were the housekeeping maids, who didn't need to speak to the guests. Other girls were college students traveling the US, looking for a place to sleep for a few months. And some, like Bridget, were high-school kids who had lied about their age to get the job and spend the summer away from the watchful eyes of their parents, who didn't know the whole story. They worked as maids, in the kitchen, and as waitresses, depending on their skills and how presentable they were. Bridget, with her blond good looks and educated speech, was employed in the dining room, where she waited on the most prestigious families at the resort.

Her eyes half-lidded as she relaxed and hugged Lulu close, Bridget remembered the first night she waited on the Longworth family and met their eighteen-year-old son.

Cole was tall, aristocratic, and clean-cut, headed to Yale in the fall. He absolutely reeked of old money and entitlement. That boy looked at Bridget as though she were an ice cream cone on a sweltering day in the desert. He just couldn't peel his eyes off her. Naturally, she went right back to her bunk and changed from ponytail-with-tendrils, artsy, Danskin to loose-and-straight, preppy, J. Crew. She knew a good thing when she saw it, and he was the most beautiful sight she had seen all summer.

She remembered sneaking off after clearing tables to go skinny-dipping. Cole's smooth, nearly hairless body was lean and toned from rowing on the crew team at his exclusive prep school. All these years later, Bridget could barely picture his somewhat generic face, but she still remembered those sculpted arms. His skin was the color of honey, and his hair was licked with blond from the sun.

She took him to the reservoir down the road, and they snuck under the fence. A big white moon was shining on the water, and it helped them find their way down the hidden path to the beach. Swimming was forbidden there, but the summer kids did it all the time.

Cole stripped off his T-shirt and shorts to stand there nude, daring her to follow. He watched while she slowly unbuttoned her blouse and unhooked her bra, but before he could grab her, she wriggled out of her pants and jumped into the water. She knew there was a pretty deep drop-off where kids liked to cannonball into the water. Bridget flipped up her feet and dove like a seal, disappearing.

She heard him jump in and swim to where he'd last seen her. Bubbles rose as she floated back to the surface, gliding up along his slippery body. She could still remember feeling his erection bump against her as she slid past and pressed her breasts against his chest. He held her there while they floated in the dark water, wrestling, and he filled her mouth with his eager tongue. Her lips were bruised and swollen when she looked in the bathroom mirror before going to bed. She lay in her bunk that night and stared at the knotty pine ceiling, a maddening throb between her legs and her nipples tingling, and decided he would be the first. She wanted him. It was that simple.

That summer, Cole taught Bridget things about sex she had always wanted to know. Indoors, outdoors, in cars, in the barn, in the pool house, on the golf course, anyplace where they could sneak out of sight for ten minutes. They made love on the garage roof in the dark and lay there afterward, naked and sweating in the hot breeze, watching the stars. They talked about life, about sex, about protecting themselves from AIDS. He showed her how to carefully roll a condom onto his erect penis, and she loved the way he swelled even larger at the touch of her hand.

"Doesn't it make the feeling less intense?" she asked, stroking him.

He nodded, watching her hands. "It's worth it though, don't you think? You should go on the pill too. All the girls are on it now. It's safer."

"In what way?"

"Condoms break sometimes. You should still use one unless your partner has been tested for diseases, but only birth-control pills are a hundred percent effective against getting pregnant."

Bridget was coming into her power as a woman. She saw how it affected him when she licked him or squeezed or straddled him and bounced. In those moments, he was her slave. He would have done anything she asked just to be allowed to touch her breasts. Now she understood what it meant when other men looked at her that way, and she realized it could be used to her advantage. Sex could be a gift, a tool, or a potent weapon.

The affair went on for the whole of July and part of August. He had to go home, and so did she. They planned to get together when Cole was at Yale, which was only a couple of hours from Amherst, where Bridget's family lived. At the end of the month, she missed her period. Weeks later, still nothing. She told Nell, who told their mother. Mom helped her write to Cole and wrote to his mother. But that was the end of Bridget and Cole's relationship. When the letters arrived, his parents took over. They refused to be involved with her pregnancy, and Cole never communicated with her again. Bridget's father talked her into doing what he thought was best, to have the baby and give her up for adoption. She had always felt that it was probably the same story for Cole. She didn't blame him. Neither one of them ever really had a choice.

Bridget sighed, stroking Lulu to comfort herself.

She napped, on and off, until the sun came up over the landing strip and she smelled bacon and coffee. She took Lulu to the ladies' room, where the poodle relieved herself on a doggie training pad and drank from a paper cup.

If only they hadn't been so young when they met. Cole might have been the one. After all, they'd made a beautiful little girl together. Wherever she was, she had a mother who loved her and always would.

Too bad she'd never know.

CHAPTER 19

Mary ~ 2003

MARY SHADED HER EYES WITH her hand as she drove along Lakeshore Road. In the second weekend of October, the trees were at peak fall foliage, and the red maples and orange oaks glowed with rosy light. The wooded mountains along the highway coming north from her apartment in South Amherst had been utterly spectacular, but at the lake, it was all reflected in the water for a double vista—even more beautiful to Mary's eyes. The crisp air wafted in through the open driver's window.

"Hey. Here I am at last." She waved to her friends, who sat gathered on the dock across the street for the sunset view, then she pulled into her driveway and stopped in front of the garage. Jake ran over and pulled the sliding door up, holding a squirming Winston while she drove inside. Mary stepped on the parking brake and turned the engine off, glad to be at home in Vermont again. She stepped out of the car and popped open the trunk to unload her things.

"Howdy, neighbor." Jake doffed an imaginary cap. He put Winston down and watched him race to Mary's side. "I knew you'd make it in time for the sun."

She laughed as she reached down to pat Winston, who was leaping for attention. "I'm in time for the cocktails, not the sunset."

"But it's always time for cocktails…"

"Ha. Not after I brush my teeth, Jake. I do have some scruples."

"So unless you brushed them in the car on the way up here, you're right on time?" He winked at her and stroked his shaggy salt-and-pepper moustache, grinning.

"Exactly." She closed her eyes for a second, turning her face toward the warm rays shooting across the water.

Jake's voice came from close by. "Okay, then let me take your bags inside while you go join the party."

She opened her eyes. He was standing with one arm propped against the car next to her shoulder. He leaned down and kissed her lightly on the cheek, and she ducked to open the car door and put it between them. She frowned a warning at him, but he just grinned again.

"There's a chair and a gin and tonic waiting for you. Just watch this little rascal on the road. He's feisty tonight."

Mary grabbed her bag of snacks and tucked Winston under her arm. "Thanks," she said, backing away. Then she turned and strolled across the street to walk down the dock and say hi to the group of neighbors who were clustered there with coolers and trays of appetizers. She chose a seat next to Ginnie.

"Hello, my dear." Mary greeted her friend with a hug around the neck. She found the drink Jake had mixed for her and took a long sip.

Ginnie's hands were busy with her plate and cup, so she didn't return the hug, but she smiled and welcomed Mary to the gathering. "Ready to help out for the big day tomorrow? We're all exhausted, but everything is ready. We're celebrating."

When Mary had come through town, she'd seen the town green was set up for the annual Fall Festival. One of the events was a charity auction that Jake and Ginnie had been running for years. Jake donated some of the used furniture he and Adam had been unable to sell at the antiques barn, and others in town did the same. The money raised was donated to the Hartland Public Library.

"I saw the stage and chairs set up and waiting," Mary said. "It all looks wonderful. I like the new striped awnings over the food booths."

The conversation moved along and around them as Mary and Ginnie put their heads together.

"You look a little tired. Is driving back and forth to Massachusetts taking its toll?"

"No, no… it's fine. I just stay in the slow lane and let everyone pass me. I wish I could see better in the dark. My new glasses don't work very well. I can't read the signs at all. Luckily, I know the way."

"I hate wearing glasses, don't you?"

"Yes. It's bad enough still getting hot flashes at night. At my age, that's supposed to be over and done with. Now I need reading glasses to look at a menu and distance glasses to drive my car. It's ridiculous."

"I know." Ginnie fanned herself with an empty paper plate. "For me, it's hot flashes all day long too. I feel so damn grouchy. It's like bugs are running around under my skin. Know what I mean?"

Mary looked at her. "Not really," she said, one eyebrow raised. "Bugs?"

"Oh, you know." Ginnie's eyes flashed with impatience. "That itchy, crawly feeling. Right before the heat explodes and you start sweating. I can't stand it. And Jake... he's so cool and collected I'd like to kill him."

"Well, you are a few years behind me," Mary said. "It does get better as time goes by."

"Still, it's just not fair that Jake gets to look more and more handsome every year while I have sagging skin and the joys of menopause. Memory loss, weight gain, a new allergy to my laundry detergent... sometimes I think I'm losing my mind."

Jake rejoined the group, pulling up a lawn chair next to the two women. "So," he said, pulling his cap down to meet his sunglasses. "What are we talking about, girls?"

"You really don't want to know." Mary laughed.

"If you say so, I believe you. Anybody need a refill?"

"Yeah. Here you go." Several of the men tossed their empty cans at him. Jake fielded the empties deftly, opened a cooler, and tossed beers toward his buddies, who caught them with smooth expertise. The sound of tops popping echoed across the water as they all watched the sun settle down onto a bed of pines across the lake.

"There she goes," Jake said, and everyone nodded. The sun moved faster then, slipping down behind the jagged silhouettes. It was whole, then half, then quickly it sank to just a thin sliver of gold that coated the rim of the horizon with dazzle. And then it was gone.

Mary's neighbors applauded, and from the docks down near the town beach came whistling and cheers.

Everyone began to stand up and fold their chairs, gathering their things to head for home.

"Good night, all," Mary said, waving as some of her friends went off down the street. She turned to Ginnie, who was still sitting in her chair. "Need a hand with your things?"

"I've got it," said Jake, hoisting their cooler up onto his shoulder. "Come on, Virginia. Time to go."

"You go," Ginnie said with a nasty gleam in her eye. "I'll stay with her for a change. It's my turn."

Mary glanced at Jake uneasily. He shrugged and turned to go. As he passed his wife, he reached down and took her hand, tugging on it.

"Come on, Virginia. Time to make dinner. Be a good girl, and I'll treat you to my world-famous cabbage steaks tonight."

The dark mood seemed to pass, and Ginnie laughed. "Oh, no, anything but that."

"Cabbage steak?" Mary said, doubting her ears.

Ginnie glanced at her as they walked across the street. "He must have cooked it for you one of these nights. When the two of you..." She turned her head, and her voice trailed off.

Jake frowned and shook his head silently at Mary, who had taken a breath to protest. "Virginia, don't get yourself carried away with imaginary trouble."

"Oh, I won't, Jake. I don't have much of an imagination. You ought to know that."

Mary quickly went up her driveway into the garage, where Jake had left the light on by the kitchen door.

"Come, Winston. Bye. See you tomorrow." She waved and reached up to slide the garage door closed. She saw them walk down the sidewalk to turn the corner onto their street.

What on earth had that been about? There was nothing going on between her and Jake anymore and no reason for Ginnie to behave that way. No reason at all. All these years, they had been nothing but friends, the three of them. Despite substantial temptation. Mary had been lonely, and Jake was always very... attentive. Ever since they'd met, there had been such a strong attraction between them. It had not been easy to resist, but Mary didn't want that kind of trouble. There was too much at stake for everyone.

She hoped it was just the menopause starting that had upset Ginnie. They did say some women had a hard time with depression when their hormones were changing.

Feeling a little spooked, Mary went inside and carefully locked the kitchen door.

CHAPTER 20

Nell ~ 2014

WHEN NELL WENT BACK TO the hospital early the next morning, she immediately noticed a difference in the manner of the nurses standing at the desk in Intensive Care. They greeted her with cautious eyes.

"What's the matter?" she said, immediately fearful. "What's happening?"

She peered into Mom's cubicle, where the lights were dimmed and the TV was turned off. It was strangely quiet inside. Nell realized that the breathing tube had been removed from her mother's mouth and the constant sucking noise of the machine had been silenced.

"Fantastic. The doctor took away that awful machine, thank God."

The women looked back at her without comment.

"It is good news, right? She's better, isn't she?" Nell could see Mom's chest moving up and down, proof that she was breathing on her own. She wasn't coughing or wheezing. She still looked frail and shrunken in the bed, though, as if the infection had taken its toll on her strength.

"The doctor wants to talk to you, Mrs. Williams," one of the nurses said. "We really don't know anything except that her condition is still serious. I'm sorry."

"Oh. All right. Is he here now, at the hospital?"

The nurse suggested that she sit with Mom while they paged the doctor. It was good to see her mother's face again after days of seeing the ugly breathing tube taped into her mouth. Mom slept on, stirring every once in a while. Her eyes would flutter open for a moment then close, and she would drift back off. Once, she muttered something incomprehensible in protesting tones and tried to sit up, looking around wildly without focusing then falling onto the pillow again, asleep.

Nell asked the nurses to check on her. They said it was probably a reaction to the drugs, and not to worry. But it didn't seem right to Nell. She felt something was on Mom's mind—something had changed. The day before, she hadn't been upset. In fact, the opposite. They had spent the day together happily, and her mother had seemed peaceful, even serene.

Nell went out to the nurses' station. "Was anyone here to see her earlier today? Before I came?"

"No, nobody's been by today," the nurse said. "Not since I went on duty at nine o'clock anyhow."

Nell paced back into Mom's cubicle.

She sat in the bedside chair and stared at her mother. Then she noticed something on the little table that hadn't been there yesterday, a book about gardening. She picked it up and looked inside the front cover.

"*Virginia Bascomb*," the spidery handwriting said, inscribed in blue ink across the title page.

Nell's jaw tensed, and her eyes hardened.

A knock came from the doorway, and she turned to see Dr. Hicks standing there. His expression was solemn, and when he smiled, it didn't reach his eyes. He beckoned, and she went out into the hallway to hear the news.

"What's happening? How is she?"

"We removed the breathing tube late last night," he said. "Keeping Mary on the respirator any longer would have made it hard to wean her off it. The infection has improved, and her lungs will probably continue to clear. Of course, there's always a chance of reinfection."

Nell knew that secondary infections were common in hospitals, where super-bacteria that resisted antibiotics lurked. "So we're not out of the woods yet?"

"No. But if all goes well, she could move to a rehab facility in a week or two. Her insurance won't let us keep her here if she's stabilized."

"How long would she be there?"

"It's hard to say. Maybe a month, maybe two, maybe... six. She might recover well and go home again. Or she might go from there into a nursing home, where they can care for her permanently. To be frank, she's very weak, and at her age, the odds are not great."

"I see." Nell swallowed hard.

"You do know, I hope, that when your mother was admitted, she signed a DNR order? Is this something you have talked about?"

"A what?"

"A do-not-resuscitate order. It means that if she arrests, we are not to try to revive her. She doesn't want to be kept alive by machines."

Nell stared at him. Obviously, he thought there was a real possibility that this might happen. Her heart sank, and she swayed, a bit nauseous.

The doctor's cell phone rang, and he turned away to answer it.

Nell folded her arms close to her body and walked outside to sit on the bench near the hospital entrance. Sunlight beat down on the top of her head as the day warmed up. She leaned back against the brick wall, her emotions spinning. She had been fooling herself. Mom would probably never get better, not really. This was the beginning of the end. Things would never be the same again.

She pulled her cell phone out of her jeans pocket and dialed Bridget. The phone rang and rang, then it went to voicemail. Was she still stuck in the DC airport?

"Hey, sister. It's me. I... I have some not so great news about Mom. I really, really hope you can get up here soon. I think... I really can't handle this by myself anymore. I need you, Bridget. Call me?"

Nell flipped her phone shut and closed her eyes, feeling the sun on her face. Well, at least she could try to make Mom feel happy with whatever time was left. To "maximize the quality of her life." That was the phrase people used, right?

She thought of her mother's restless sleeping and the muttering, then she remembered Ginnie's gardening book on the bedside table. Jake must have been there earlier. And whatever he had said, it upset Mom. Not surprising. That man was a mess, and trouble seemed to follow him like a shadow. Nell scowled.

Well, that was not going to happen again. Not even if she had to take her complaints all the way to the top.

She stood up and strode back inside, ready to make as much trouble as was necessary to keep Jake Bascomb away from Mom. She consulted the floor plan mounted on the lobby wall and headed down the corridor toward the administrative offices.

Later, while Mom was sleeping, Nell drove back to the cottage by the lake. It was a beautiful blue-sky day in the sixties, and after the major meltdown she'd just had at the hospital, she needed some exercise. Used to jogging every day, she was way too edgy. She had to get her emotions under control. Her heart was still pounding, and she felt a little foolish.

Winston watched her change into a sports bra, shorts, and a T-shirt, pull on tennis socks, and tie her running shoes. His head cocked first to one side then to the other, his eyes imploring. She tucked her phone into her fanny pack and fastened it around her waist.

"You want to come too?" She laughed, and his tail burst into frantic wagging.

He raced down the stairs ahead of her and waited to see which direction she would choose, his ears perked and every muscle alert.

Nell snapped a long leash onto his collar and went out the front door. As usual, there was no traffic on the shore road. She led Winston across the street and decided to explore farther along the coastline.

She started out walking while Winston trotted obediently alongside. In a few minutes, she picked it up to an easy jog, and the dog matched her pace. The two ran along under the trees, the sunlight bouncing off the water alongside. It dappled the street with bright flashes that dazzled as she ran through them, spurred along by the sound of her feet hitting the ground. Lulled by the rhythm, her mind wandered. It replayed the nasty scene she had made at the hospital that morning. She ran faster, trying to shake it off.

Oh, crap. Shouldn't have gotten carried away like that.

It was Jake's fault, anyway. Why couldn't he mind his own business? Every time he was there, Mom got upset.

Stay away. Stay away. Stay away.

Why was he so important, anyhow? He was bad for her. Dangerous. Trouble. Not even part of the family.

Get out. Get out. Get out.

The hospital president, Mr. Levine, agreed that it wasn't good for Mom to be so agitated. Nell had barged into his office after the nurses in ICU told her they were powerless to do anything.

Leave her alone. Leave her alone. The words pounded in her head as she ran.

Mr. Levine had said there was nothing the hospital could do to keep Jake out as long as Mom was conscious and wanted to see him. Jake hadn't broken any rules, the little bald man said. Nell went off on him then, raising her voice and jumping out of her chair to pace the office. She called him uncaring and irresponsible and threatened to sue. She glared at him. The executive had cringed, sinking back in his big black desk chair to get away from her.

Damn, she shouldn't have done that. Now he'd think she was a nut. He'd know it, actually. She was just so worried about her mother. He must understand.

Nell's face reddened with embarrassment as well as exertion as she ran down the road. After she passed a long row of cottages, a side street came in from the left. At the intersection, a dirt pull-off on the right led to a small parking area by the lake, filled with vehicles. Several busy docks stretched out into the water, and wooden stairs led down to a stretch of sandy beach. The sign said it was reserved for town residents.

Slowing down to take a look, Nell felt Winston tugging at the leash and followed him into the parking lot. Thinking he might need a drink of water, she walked toward the stairs. People were sunbathing and playing in the lake, the kids screaming with laughter and splashing around on inflatable toys. The docks were loaded with little dinghies, motorboats, and a few larger yachts. A boat towing someone on water skis zoomed past the entrance to the cove, a white plume of spray flying up into the air behind it.

Winston pulled on the leash, leading her away from the beach and onto one of the docks. Nell followed mindlessly, dazed by the blinding sunlight and the sound of splashing water.

A beautiful sailboat was tied up at the end of the pier. She squinted at it. A couple of red coolers were sitting on the dock nearby, and someone was bent over in the stern, tossing empty beer cans into a trash bag. Golden script across the back end of the boat spelled the name *Belle*.

With a jolt, Nell recognized it as the boat in the photographs at Mom's cottage. Then she took a closer look at the man in the stern, who stood up to stare at her with a scowl on his face. It was Jake. Her rage came flooding back with a force that left her breathless.

"You," she cried, pointing at him. "You'd better stay away from my mother!"

He looked at her with surprise, the scowl replaced by raised eyebrows. Winston pulled the leash out of her hand and jumped down into the boat, putting his front paws up on Jake's leg to beg for a petting, his tail wagging in excited little circles.

"You know what I'm talking about." Nell glared at the big man. "Don't pretend with me."

"Are you out of your mind, woman?" Completely unfazed, Jake looked her over with a bored expression.

"Don't underestimate me, either, you old… grouchy… crybaby. I have legal rights, and I can stop you from seeing her at all if I want to."

Jake scowled again, brushing Winston off his leg and taking a step up onto the dock next to Nell. All of the sudden, he was looming over her, the huge mass of him, and she flinched. He seemed to know he was scaring her and leaned a little closer, an amused look in his eyes.

She got even more furious and stood right up in his face with her finger pointing, and she yelled at him. "I'll take her away from here if I have to. I'll fly her down to the hospital where I live. I can do it if I want to. You stay away, do you hear me?"

"What the hell are you ranting about?" he yelled back, and his breath stank of alcohol.

"Stay away from my mother," she repeated, with a little more control.

"Why should I?" He batted her hand away and stepped toward her.

She shrank back but blurted out, "Because you've already hurt her enough. It's your fault she's sick. And now you're killing her, Jake."

"And how the bloody hell do you figure that?"

"Every time you come to see her, she gets so upset she loses ground. I've seen you in there, dumping all your troubles on her, making her comfort you. Don't bother to deny it."

His eyes changed. He looked guilty for a second then turned stubborn and defensive. "None of your concern, little girl."

"My mother, my concern." Nell gritted her teeth and shot a beam of hostility from her eyes. "You stay away from her. Or else."

"I'll do what I want. You mind your business."

"I'll take her away, I swear."

He took a step back. Crossing his big arms in front of his chest, Jake spoke in a gruff voice. "What exactly do you want from me, Nell? You want me to never see her again?"

"Not right now. She shouldn't be upset."

He raised his hands in the air helplessly, swaying on his feet. "Okay." He seemed to give up. "Whatever you say."

Nell nodded, triumphant.

"But you'd better understand something, little girl," he growled. "Ellie and I, we've known each other real well for a long time. There's a lot of water gone by, a lot of water. That's not going to stop just because you say so."

"Just give her a chance to get well, Jake."

"Hey, I want that just as much as you do. You only just found out about... all this, but Ellie is part of our family too. We care about her."

Nell realized that what he said was true. Her anger deflated, the wind sucked out of her sails. "I know that." She felt calmer. "And I don't want to blame you just because I feel so left out and disappointed."

"Disappointed? Don't be. Ellie may not be perfect, but she's a lot closer to it than most people I know."

"I suppose so."

They nodded in agreement. Winston jumped back up onto the dock next to them, and she reached down to pick up the leash.

"So." She cleared her throat. "You'll stop visiting Mom every day for a while until I say?"

His face was deadpan, his eyes unreadable. He didn't answer.

"Good," she said firmly as though he had agreed. She turned her back on him, leading Winston back down the pier.

Nell didn't look back as they went out through the parking lot and resumed their run around the lake. She didn't want to risk feeling sorry for him.

CHAPTER 21

Nell ~ 2014

NELL GAVE WINSTON A BOWL of fresh water and went upstairs to shower and dress. She saw the little green envelope flashing on her cell phone and picked up another voicemail from Bridget. Playing telephone tag was driving Nell nuts, but it seemed to be the normal way of things up in the mountains.

A hurricane off the Atlantic coast had screwed up all the flights, but her sister was finally on her way. Relieved to hear that Bridget would be in Hartland in a few hours, Nell drove back to the hospital to see how Mom was doing.

It would be so good to have someone to share this with. Her mother's second life wouldn't be a secret anymore.

Not totally, anyhow. She still hadn't said anything to David. In fact, she hadn't even tried to reach him since their phone call the night before. For some reason, she just didn't feel like talking to him. Or listening to him talk to her. Nell's feelings about her marriage were starting to push up toward the surface and make themselves known like weeds sprouting. Something needed to change, she realized. It wasn't working for her anymore. The appeal of Mom's secret house was a signal, telling her to pay attention. Maybe when she had more time, she'd give it some serious thought. For the moment, she tried to concentrate on her mother.

Nell could tell as soon as she arrived at the ICU that Mom was worse again. The nurses looked worried, and the TV was turned off in her mother's cubicle, the lights dimmed.

Mom lay with her eyes shut, her chest rattling as she struggled to breathe.

Nell sat down and took her hand. Mom opened her eyes and looked at Nell, unfocused for a moment then tuned-in and sharp. She smiled.

"Hi, Mom. How are you feeling?"

Her mother frowned and shook her head slightly. Pointing at her chest she whispered, "Bad."

"I'm so sorry, Mom. I love you. I wish you were better."

"Me too," Mom mouthed. Her eyes were solemn.

"Bridget is coming, Mom. She'll be here soon."

Mom's face lightened, and she smiled broadly. She squeezed Nell's hand. "Good," she whispered then closed her eyes again, exhausted.

"I'll be right back." Nell wasn't sure whether her mother was still awake. Mom didn't react, so she quietly left the room. Out in the hallway, the women at the nurses' station were waiting.

"We called the doctor." Jennifer spoke in a quiet voice. "She's not responding well to the antibiotics anymore. He may want to change the medication."

Nell nodded. She looked at her watch. Only a little while until Bridget arrived.

She went back to her mother's bedside and picked up the library book she'd been reading aloud. Mom's eyes fluttered open when she heard Nell's voice, and she gazed at her daughter's face, watching with loving eyes, laboring for each breath. The doctor came, dressed in his golf clothes again. He examined Mom and wrote something on the chart, smiling at Nell before he moved on to the next cubicle. She read on and on through it all, her voice even and steady, soothing.

Mom kept her eyes on Nell, focused only on her words, enthralled in a trance of love and calm. The doctor went out, and soon Jennifer came in with a syringe filled with medicine that she put into the IV line. Nell read on smoothly, never stopping or hesitating, one hand holding her mother's on the bed while the other turned the pages. Time passed, Mom's breathing evened out a bit, and finally, she fell asleep again.

Outside the hallway window, the bright afternoon had ripened into that buttery yellow light that came late in the day. Slanting rays made long shadows that striped the grass on the town green when Nell walked across to the market.

She stood in line at the butcher counter, her face blank and her mind numb. Her heart was breaking, but the tears did not come. Instead, she was empty and dazed, a zombie. She held herself back at a distance from reality like someone sitting in the stands at a tennis match, watching the ball bounce back and forth.

This was really happening. The world would never be the same again. Everyone else would move on, and Mom would not. She would just... stop. Her part in the story of their lives would end. They would be alone now, Nell and Bridget, with both parents gone. Forever. Moved up to the head of the line, the next ones in the family to grow old.

The next ones to die. Would it be Nell first or her sister? It was all so hard to grasp. The changes were happening so fast.

It seemed like yesterday that they were little girls in pigtails with red ribbons, sitting on Santa's lap while Daddy took their picture with the home-movie camera. Now they were adults, rushing toward death on the downward slope.

When it was her turn in front of the butcher, Nell asked for chicken and watched the plump, red-cheeked man wrap the meat in white paper. After picking up a couple of other things, she got in line at the cash register. The room throbbed around her as she stood there spacing out. She heard the little bell ring on the front door as someone entered, and then there was a warm hand on her elbow as Adam said, "Nell? Are you okay? Do you need to sit down?"

Nell swayed on her feet, clutching the shopping basket.

"Come here a second. Have a seat." He led her over to a table.

He went away for a minute and came back with two cups of tea, stirred sugar into one of them, and put it in her hand. "Sweet tea. My mother always said it's the best thing for a shock. You look like you need it."

Nell sipped it, feeling the warm sweetness begin to bring her back. She looked over at him. "Mom is getting worse, not better. I think she's dying." Her voice creaked as her throat tightened.

Adam put his hand over hers, and it covered her like a warm blanket. "I hope not. But if so, at least she'll know she was loved, Nell. Because you had a chance to tell her."

Nell nodded, but the background noises pounded in her head, and she searched her pockets for a tissue to wipe her watery eyes.

"When it comes by surprise with no time to get ready, that's the worst," Adam said. "Never knowing how much people loved you."

She realized he was talking about his mother.

"Everyone always says they want to die in bed, to just not wake up one day. But that's the same as dying in an accident… you never get to say good-bye." His voice was breaking up too.

"It's much harder on the family when it happens that way, isn't it?" Nell whispered, understanding.

"Yeah. It's like, the movie is just getting really good, and then the power suddenly goes off and you never get to see the rest. You always wonder what was going to happen."

"Your mother might have been here with us now." Nell pictured Ginnie alive and helping them all through this.

"Dad was incredibly torn up back then. And there was a lot going on. The police were all over him. It took a long time to go away. But eventually, they let him go. Thanks to your mother."

Nell stared at him. "What do you mean by that, exactly?"

"Ellie said they were all drinking, and she and Mom got into a big fight. A wrestling, punching kind of fight."

"No way." Nell's mother in a fistfight with her best friend, or anyone else for that matter? Impossible.

Adam nodded. "True. She said they were shouting at each other when the boat came about, and the boom knocked my mother over the side."

"She never shouts at anyone, ever. I don't believe it."

"Neither did the police. That's why they didn't want to let Dad go."

"So why did they release him?"

Adam looked her straight in the eyes. "Because your mother testified, over and over, that if anyone was at fault, she was."

Nell stared at him, aghast.

"Nobody ever believed her, but the judge finally ruled it was an accidental death."

They sat at the little table in a private bubble of emotion, while all around them customers busily filled their shopping baskets and chatted with their friends.

What an amazing puzzle it is—what love will make us do. There was no doubt in her mind that Mom saved Jake out of love. She also believed that Mom had ultimately suffered for it. She'd lost Ginnie, and she would lose Jake too. What else could she do but help him? A woman of much conscience, Mom would have struggled with telling less than the truth, the whole truth, and nothing but the truth. But Nell still didn't believe that Jake was totally innocent, no matter what Adam might think or Mom had testified. The accident had conveniently rid him of a jealous, unwanted wife and cleared the way for a deeper relationship with Nell's mother.

What we do for love... to ourselves and for each other.

CHAPTER 22

Mary ~ 2004

MARY LIFTED THE PICNIC BASKET over the side of the boat. Jake dragged the cooler down the dock and hoisted it onto the deck, where Ginnie pulled flotation seat cushions out of the storage compartments. The sun was still bright and warm, but rain was predicted, and Mary eyed the clouds on the horizon with a measuring glance. They had planned to get going in time for one big lap around the lake before the weather changed.

Jake reached out a hand to help her climb on board, looking up at her with a warm smile.

"Do you have to do that?" Ginnie's voice had a nasty tone.

He turned around, the smile still on his face. "Do what?"

Ginnie stood, pouting. She pointed as he steadied Mary by holding her elbow. "What do you think I mean, Jake? Do you have to touch her all the time?"

Mary stepped onto the deck and went to Ginnie, putting an arm around her friend. "Now, Virginia, you know Jake was just being polite. An old lady like me needs a hand now and then." She spoke sweetly and broke the tension.

Lately, Ginnie had been nervous, behaving oddly. Jake flirted with Mary a little more than usual, pulling the tiger's tail, but they'd decided years ago that it would never go further. At sixty-five, and a widow, the last thing Mary wanted was to shake up the comfortable arrangement she had with her neighbors in Vermont. Jake didn't take the situation seriously enough and insisted on making mischief, but Virginia's emotional outbursts concerned Mary, who recognized some potentially dangerous symptoms. Her friend seemed deeply depressed.

Ginnie had always been high-strung, but her moods now swung back and forth for no apparent reason. Younger than Mary, she complained about the typical woes of the onset of menopause, but that didn't seem like enough to explain her paranoid behavior. As an army nurse and married to Thomas for so long, Mary knew a lot about post-traumatic stress disorder. Ginnie's symptoms were much the same. It seemed as though something had happened in the Bascomb home while Mary had been busy taking care of Thomas. Ginnie and Jake's relationship had deteriorated.

Their house echoed with remembered laughter and footsteps since Adam had moved out, a hard transition for every aging couple. Mary knew Jake drank a lot, probably too much. She wondered if the couple had fought about it. He went off into the woods to do it and thought nobody would notice. She came across the empty gin bottles when out walking Winston.

Somehow, Ginnie fixated on the idea that after all this time, Mary had suddenly decided to steal her husband. When the night sweats woke her up and he wasn't in bed, she decided he'd gone to see Mary.

Jake unhooked the moorings and pushed off from the dock, motoring slowly out beyond the harbor area before he raised the sails. Focusing on Ginnie, Mary diverted the conversation to chat about the new library addition. Ginnie seemed to relax, and for the moment, her mood passed. The two women sat together and chatted, enjoying the margaritas, corn chips, and guacamole. Jake piloted them halfway around the lake to the remote area where very few houses hugged the shore and the boat traffic dwindled to next to nothing. He lowered the sails and dropped anchor.

Laughing, drinking, and acting goofy, they were the three *amigos* again. Jake wore Mary's straw hat, with its long red ribbon, and stood at the tiller like a gondolier, singing in Italian. Mary wore his Red Sox cap and took a swing at an apple with one of the oars, knocking it over the port side. They watched it sink, then rise back to the surface and bob. The thermos of cocktails went down fast and easy, so Jake and Ginnie started on the jug of white wine he kept in the cabin below. Mary felt drowsy and lay down on one of the bench seats in the sun and rocked, her eyes drifting shut. When she woke up a while later, the sun was gone, the air was chilly, and Ginnie was at it again.

Pulleys squealed as Jake started to raise the sails, preparing to head for home.

"I know everything, and you don't think so," Ginnie teased in a singsong voice, following him around as he readied the boat for sailing and took his seat at the tiller.

Jake sent her a venomous look. Mary guessed he'd had enough of Ginnie's irrational nagging. And it looked as if the two of them had polished off the whole jug of wine while Mary napped. Ginnie staggered and tried to plant her feet more firmly on the deck of the rocking boat.

"Shut up, Virginia. You don't know shit," Jake shouted with a snap of temper.

"Don't you swear at me, Jake Bascomb." Ginnie's voice slurred as she watched him with squinted eyes, her curly hair whipping madly in the wind.

The sails flapped noisily as they rose. Mary sat up and reached for her jacket, noticing the storm blowing in from the west. Big, dark thunderclouds huddled on the horizon, spreading toward the lake.

"I'll say whatever I want," Jake taunted, moving clumsily to get the boat in motion. "You're a crazy old biddy, that's what you are. Now shut up and sit down."

Ginnie screamed with rage and leaped on Jake, using her fingernails and knocking him away from the ropes he was trying to secure. His forehead was bleeding. Mary shook her sleepy head in shock, slow to respond. The boat was rocking back and forth as they scuffled.

"You trying to get us all killed?" Jake yelled, shoving Ginnie down on the other bench seat, across from Mary. She sat sulking. He struggled to get the boat under control as the breeze picked up, caught the sails, and sent the vessel gliding out into the middle of the lake where the water was dark and deep. Gusts of wind pushed them on a bumpy course, and whitecaps foamed on top of the ragged chop.

Mary could see that at the other end of the lake, everyone had either tied up or gone home to their private docks. The sky was nearly dark now, and the wind moaned. The thought occurred to her that they might be in serious trouble. She looked around for the life jackets. Nobody ever wore them, but Jake kept them on the deck when they were sailing.

Mary's eyes refocused, and she saw Ginnie standing in front of her, fists clenched.

"Stay away from my husband," the woman growled. "Stay away from my family. You've had your chance. You think now that your husband is finally dead, you can take mine."

"That's not true, Ginnie." Mary reached toward her, pleading, but the boat lurched, and they both lost their balance. Mary sat down again hard, and Ginnie fell to the deck onto her hands and knees. "I'd never do anything to hurt you," Mary shouted. "Please believe me."

"Virginia," Jake yelled. "Don't be an idiot. Sit down and stay there." His face was furious, and the look he gave her was lethal. "Weather's going to catch us, Ellie. Go in the cabin and get the rain gear. You girls will freeze. Hold on and be careful."

He fought with the sails and the tiller as the bow rose up and crashed down again, splashing them with frigid water. He headed across the lake diagonally, pushed by the wind coming from the west and using its power to help the boat cut through the rough waves.

Mary half crawled to the cabin door and got it open, dropping down into the quieter dry space below. She spied the yellow slickers and quickly put one on, bringing two more back out to the slippery deck. She slid the jackets over to Jake and to Ginnie, who put hers on but left it open, flapping in the wind and doing little good. Jake got his snapped seconds before the storm struck.

The wind howled, and with a loud rushing, seething sound, the rain came. It fell hard enough to sting where it lashed Mary's bare skin. The gray surface of the lake was textured with craters and spouts. The water churned and foamed like a boiling stew.

Jake seemed to be trying for one long tack across the widest part of the lake, and he gestured for the women to stay seated and hang on. The boat tipped and moved along fast, nearly on its side, as they all leaned against the tilt to keep from capsizing. Jake took his eyes off the sails for a moment to check his passengers, and Mary returned his smile of encouragement. Ginnie saw them exchange glances and stood up to scream at them again.

"You're still doing it. You won't stop. You'll never stop." Ginnie's wet hair streamed out behind her like snakes as she crouched on the deck, sobbing, and flung her hands in the air. "You and your secrets. I can't take it anymore. I hate you both."

"Ginnie, watch out! It's not safe." Mary reached for her hand.

"Virginia, sit on the bench. We don't have time for this bullshit. I need to come about now. Get ready, stay down."

Jake fought the wind and the thrashing waves, hanging onto the tiller with both hands.

Mary stood up and lurched to Ginnie's side, slipping on the wet deck. She threw all her weight on top of the woman, pushing her down on the bench seat. From the corner of her eye, she saw Jake nod at her and turn the tiller. The boom began to swing across the deck when the sails caught the wind.

"Don't touch me," Ginnie screamed, squirming on the bench until she wriggled free of Mary's hold. Grabbing for her again, Mary's hands slid off slick, wet skin. Ginnie got up and stalked toward Jake to leap on him again, hands like claws.

"Ginnie, don't," Mary shouted, but the wind picked up her voice and carried it away.

The boom moved faster as the sails wheeled about and the boat turned. Mary saw the look of surprise on Ginnie's face as she noticed the heavy wooden spar coming straight for her. Jake lunged for his wife to push her down, but it was too late.

The boom hit Ginnie squarely on the side of the head with a sickening smack. It lifted the small woman up off her feet and flung her over the side to disappear into the water with a little splash. Mary watched in a state of shock, unable to believe her eyes. Jake, a desperate look on his face, dropped the sails and dove into the water.

Then the hissing noise of rain on water was the only sound. Mary sat alone on the lake, the only living thing in a steel-gray landscape of misty, foaming water. She couldn't see the docks anymore or the shoreline. The air had filled with clouds of condensation and darkness.

In a second, they will both come up to the surface, and we'll bring her home. She'll be cold, and we'll have to watch out for shock and concussion. Mary started going over first-aid procedures in her mind, thinking about clearing Ginnie's airway, doing CPR. Then she saw Jake's head bob up near the spot where Ginnie had disappeared. He gasped for air and dove again, then again. Mary got up to toss out a few life preservers, but they immediately floated away. There was no sign of Ginnie. No sign at all.

The boat was drifting, so Mary lowered the anchor. She yanked open the cabin doors and ran downstairs to call for help on the radio then came outside with a handful of emergency flares and started firing them off.

Still, Jake dove and dove again. When the flares were all gone, Mary leaned over the side and shone a big flashlight into the water, but it was even darker in the deep. Finally, the rescue boats came with underwater lights and divers in scuba gear. The professionals took over and made Jake get out of the water to rest. They had dry blankets for him and Mary and hot coffee.

The divers searched for hours, the rain finally stopped, and eventually, they found Ginnie's body on the bottom of the lake, hooked under a fallen tree.

When they pulled up at the town dock, towing Jake's sailboat behind, police cars waited with their lights flashing silently. A policewoman took Mary home, convinced her to take a hot shower, then had her write and sign a statement. She got to lie down in her own bed that night, crying herself to sleep, filled with dreams of horror and guilt.

But they took Jake directly to jail. Mary was afraid it would be a long time before he slept in his own bed again.

CHAPTER 23

Nell ~ 2014

NELL KISSED HER MOTHER GOOD night, careful not to wake her. She reminded the night nurses of her cell phone number and drove back to the cottage slowly, trying to shake the spacey feeling that had hung on her for most of the day. She felt as if she hadn't slept in days, though it wasn't true. The constant stress was getting to her, and she desperately wanted her sister to arrive.

Mom was never much of a drinker, maybe one or two glasses of wine with dinner, tops. She said too much alcohol gave her a headache. Nell doubted that she would suddenly change her lifelong habits. And Mom was one of the most even-tempered people that she knew. Even when Nell and Bridget were little and exploded in screaming fights, as sisters did, their mother always remained calm and patient. She said her training as an army nurse taught her to keep her head in the whirlwind. The story Mom had told the police made no sense to Nell. It seemed obvious that her mother had lied to get Jake off the hook.

What really happened? From what Nell knew, only one person on the sailboat that day was a belligerent heavy drinker. According to all accounts, he was at the tiller when his wife went overboard.

Was Ginnie's death a tragic accident, or is Jake really guilty of murder? In a sailboat, the person at the helm controlled the boom, and someone standing in the way could be hit with it quite easily if they weren't paying attention.

But the story just didn't add up. There was something Jake was hiding, Nell felt sure. And for reasons of her own, Mom was helping him hide it.

Nell carried the groceries inside and was greeted by an exuberant Winston, who leapt up and yipped with excitement as he followed her into the kitchen. She opened the back door and let him into the garden, bringing his dish of kibble out to the porch. It was nearly dark, and fireflies were coming out. She got herself a glass of white wine and sat on the back steps to watch the sparkles.

The moon looked full that night. Fat and yellow, it swelled behind the ragged navy-blue and purple clouds, rising so fast she could almost see it move. A dramatic sky soared overhead, filled with mystery—the kind of night when shadows seemed to walk and wolves howled in the woods.

A shape stirred in the trees beyond the rose arbor. Winston pricked up his ears. He ran up the steps to sit beside her, pressing his body against hers as he peered into the shadows.

"Something out there?" Nell said to him. His ears went up, then down, then up again. A little whine sounded in his throat, and he trembled.

Frowning, Nell tried to see into the woods, but it was too dark. Then she heard the noise again… a stick breaking, a rustling.

Winston barked once. The sharp sound made Nell jump.

"Let's go inside, shall we?" She got up to hold the door open. When they were inside, she quickly locked the door.

"Probably just a raccoon," she said to Winston, who looked up at her trustingly.

She put the chicken in the oven and went into the den to snuggle with the dog on the couch in front of the TV. While dozing, she heard a knock at the front door, and Winston went crazy with barking.

Nell flipped on the outside lights and swung the door open. Bridget stood on the front porch with Lulu under her arm, a puzzled expression on her face that quickly turned to a smile when she saw Nell.

"Hey, there she is. Hooray!" Nell threw her arms around her sister. "You can't imagine how glad I am to see you."

Bridget hugged her back, nearly squishing the little poodle between them, then set the dog down in the yard, where she scampered around and sniffed the plantings, her tail wagging.

"Me too." Bridget had tears in her eyes. "Glad to be here, baby sister."

"Let's get your luggage inside." Nell headed for the driveway, where a red Jeep Cherokee was parked behind her rental car. They hauled Bridget's bags inside the cottage, and she called Lulu to follow.

"Who's this?" Bridget asked as Winston greeted the newcomers with a flourish of his feathery white tail. The two dogs raced around in happy circles.

"Mom's dog. His name is Winston," Nell answered with a sly grin.

"Mom has a dog?"

"Yep."

"They let her have him at Maplewood?"

"Nope. Guess again."

"Mom snuck him into Maplewood?"

"Nope. One more guess."

Bridget paused and looked around at the living room of the cottage. She sent her sister an impatient glance. "Mom got him up here? On vacation?"

"Nope. Last guess. You lose. Though he does live here—you were right about that."

"Eleanor Reilly, you tell me what is going on right now. No more fooling around." Bridget stood with her hands on her hips.

"Okay, calm down." Nell couldn't resist teasing and raised her hand with a welcoming gesture. "Welcome to Mom's very own secret hideaway, our new, old country cottage."

Bridget walked slowly through the living room and into the kitchen, where the delicious aromas of dinner cooking rose out of the oven. There was a suspicious look on her face, and she frowned at her sister.

"In here," Nell said, leading her into the den and turning her around to face the wall of photos.

Bridget's mouth fell open, and she stumbled. Nell guided her until they were both sitting on the couch.

"Surprise." Nell watched as Bridget scanned their family history.

"This really is Mom's house? She... *owns* it?"

"Yep."

"For how long?"

"I don't know exactly. About thirty years, I think. That's how far back the photos of her in here go." Nell indicated the photo album she had left out for her sister to see.

Bridget gasped. "Why? Why would she do this? How did she get away with it?"

"You tell me, sister. I've been trying to figure that out all week."

"Is there a man involved?" Bridget raised one eyebrow knowingly.

"Unfortunately, I guess so, sort of. His name is Jake Bascomb. But his wife was one of Mom's best friends until she died. I don't think they ever met until Mom moved in here. I'm just guessing."

"So that wasn't the reason?"

"No, I don't think it could have been."

"But then, why?" Bridget looked at Nell with disbelief in her eyes. "Why wouldn't she tell us? Didn't she trust us?"

Nell put her hand over Bridget's and squeezed it. "I know. I felt that same way. I think it might have to do with needing some time to herself."

Bridget looked back up at the photos so lovingly arranged on the wall.

"She wanted a place of her own? We were too much trouble?" A tremor wobbled in Bridget's voice.

"Maybe at first, anyhow. And probably it was Daddy more than us." Relieved to discuss her theories, Nell was eager to explain. "But then, I think, it got complicated."

Bridget kicked off her shoes and settled back against the pillows. "Okay. Start talking. I've got all night."

"Well," Nell began, picking up the photo album and turning to the first page. "Apparently, she met Jake and Ginnie at a neighborhood picnic…"

The two sisters talked until late at night, moving into the kitchen at one point to eat dinner then back into the den again to sit with their wineglasses and try to decipher the mysteries of their mother's past, the night her best friend had died, and why Mom had lied to defend the man who was probably responsible.

<hr />

Nell finally went to bed after helping Bridget and Lulu get settled in Mom's room, and she was exhausted. She thought about calling David, but it was nearly the middle of the night by then. When she looked at her cell phone, the green envelope was flashing. She pushed it and put the phone to her ear, expecting a message from her husband.

"Nell. It's me." It was Adam's voice. "Just wanted to say, it felt really wonderful to… share my feelings… the way we did today. Very unusual for me nowadays. That's it. Anyhow, thanks." He sounded like he needed to clear his throat.

Nell sat down on the edge of her bed and stared into space while the final beep sounded and a recording automatically told her there were no more messages. Surprised and touched by his call, she forgot to breathe for a minute.

How sweet of him to thank her when he was the one who had come to her rescue in the market that day. Nell sat with a goofy smile on her face, daydreaming, until Winston jumped up next to her and jiggled the mattress.

They snuggled down into the bed together. Nell lay with her head on the pillow, looking out the window at the full moon, which sailed high above the lake, white and bright as a faraway spotlight. It silvered the night and her dreams. Black-and-white images flickered behind her eyelids like scenes from an old movie.

She saw Ginnie and Mary lying on beach towels in their bathing suits, laughing. She saw Jake, like a young Clark Gable with his moustache and dashing good looks. They all sailed off into the lake, the two women sitting arm in arm in the bow as Jake steered.

A huge black cloud loomed over them, and lightning forked down into the dark water.

The boat tilted and shook as wind whipped the sails. Rain came in sheets of water, turning the air opaque and gray. A woman fell from the boat, her body floating toward Nell, the watcher. *It must be Ginnie.* Nell whimpered in her sleep, aware that she was dreaming but still straining to help in some way. The woman floated closer. She was lying on her back with her hands crossed over her chest and waterweeds in her white hair. She looked asleep or dead, with closed eyes in a pale, ghostly face.

But it wasn't Ginnie, she realized when the body came closer.

The woman was Mom.

CHAPTER 24

Bridget ~ 2014

B RIDGET LAY IN HER MOTHER's bed under clean sheets and a warm
quilt from the hallway closet, surrounded by darkness and the scent
of lavender.

She couldn't sleep. Her mind spun with a series of jumbled thoughts.
The drama of her own life faded to a bland memory compared with the
story Nell had told her that night. She couldn't stop thinking about it, and
she couldn't wait to see her mother at the hospital the next morning for
more reasons than one.

It all seemed so fabulously amazing. *You think you really know someone,
know them intimately, and then… you don't.*

Bridget always thought of her mother as a conservative, dutiful woman
who would never dare to challenge the rules of authority to do something
wild and crazy. Among the three women in the family, Bridget thought of
herself as the one who refused to accept what life doled out in carefully
measured portions. Nell didn't fill that role, and certainly not Mom. Her
mother had always seemed so patient with life. She advised them to judge
slowly, to wait and discover the silver lining in every cloud. The thought of
Mom doing something so rash as to run off to Vermont and buy a private
haven for herself was staggering.

Giggling to herself, Bridget shook her head in wonder, filled with
admiration. *You go, girl.*

Somehow, she knew that when they learned the whole story, a man
would be at the heart of it. She agreed with Nell that at first, Mom had
probably been looking for a place to get away alone, and then she eventually
needed a respite from the horror of watching Daddy deteriorate. But it

sounded as if over the years, Mary's relationship with her neighbors had become personal and deeply involved.

An open-minded ménage á trois? Possibly. A man in love with two women? Conventional yet titillating. Or a woman in love with a man and her best friend? Very twenty-first-century liberated.

How exciting. No wonder Mom found a way to drag herself up to Vermont even during the past few years when she didn't have transportation and lived among a circle of well-meaning eyewitnesses.

Bridget wished there was something in her own life so compelling. At the moment, all she had was a big, sleazy rat who she hoped would never speak to her again except through her lawyer.

The day before, while she was waiting in the airport, Bridget had called the answering machine at home and left a message for Eric. She'd told him she'd been called away due to Mary's failing health and said that Heather was spending the next few days with her friends. Neglecting to mention where she would be staying or even the name of the town, Bridget doubted he'd care enough to be curious. He had her cell number, and that would be enough to satisfy him for the time being.

Her lawyer was working on a plan to get back as much of her money as possible. He thought there was probably some equity left in the house. Bridget's private detective was looking into it as well. By tracing the company that had installed their safe at home, he found out that Eric had a second safe at the office. They planned to get a court order to open it and see what kind of goodies he'd stashed there.

Bridget was hoping for gold, bonds, or foreign currency. *Either way, I win and you lose. Satisfying, but not like snuggling up to a lover on a cold night.*

She tossed in bed. Lulu, who liked to sleep on the pillow curled up next to Bridget's head, got up and put her paws on the windowsill. She looked out the open window into the night, sniffing. Bridget leaned up on one elbow to look out at the nearly pitch-dark backyard as the moon shadow cast by the house inked it a dark gray. The woods beyond were whitened by moonlight on the front side of the trees and outlined by black shadows behind them.

Something was moving. The form of a tall man detached itself from the vertical tree shapes as he walked along the edge of the perennial bed and stepped through the arch into Mary's dark garden.

Sitting up straighter, Bridget peered into the gloom, trying to see where he had gone. A subtle movement drew her eye to the swinging glider, and she heard a creaking sound.

Lulu gave an airy woof, a timid doggy whisper.

"Shhh." Bridget tapped her muzzle lightly with one finger. The little dog was silent though her ears remained perked.

The swing creaked again. Bridget could see it moving as her eyes had adjusted to the shadows. A man was sitting there, his face turned toward the house. She saw the clean angle of a strong jawline.

He was watching. A hint of gleam revealed his eyes.

She wondered if he could see her with all the lights out in the house and the sky bright with moonlight behind the black outline of the building. Probably not.

What was he looking at, then, so intently? And who was he?

She had a feeling it was that man, Jake Bascomb. Nell had said he lived beyond the woods and took care of Winston whenever she was away. Maybe he missed Mom. Perhaps he couldn't sleep, either, because he was lonely like Bridget.

She propped her chin on the windowsill and watched as he slowly rocked in the glider, a rhythmic creaking the only sound that broke the stillness of the night.

CHAPTER 25

Mary ~ 2006

MARY PARKED NEXT TO THE town green and looked up at the handsome brick eighteenth-century building across from the market. Adam and Sarah had built a beautiful apartment upstairs over the law offices that leased space from them. The couple had bought the historic building, which used to be an inn, back when they were first married. They spent the next four years renovating it, staying as true to the original design and materials as possible.

The renovation came out perfect, like everything Adam did. He had always been driven, competing with himself to do better and better. He was the opposite of his father, the king of resignation. Adam was ambitious. He and Sarah were going to buy old properties, fix them up, and rent them or sell them at a profit. She would do the research and design while he supervised the construction work.

That's what they had planned to do, Mary corrected herself. Now it was just Adam. He'd been hiding away at home alone for a month since his wife moved out.

Mary had left him to his mourning long enough. It was time for Adam to rejoin the world, to get on with his life. Jake didn't want to intrude on him. He said the boy would call if he needed anything. But Mary couldn't stand to watch Adam hibernate in his den of sorrow any longer. The sun was shining, and the sky was blue. It was time for the bear to come out of his cave and sniff the air.

She followed the cobblestone sidewalk to the steps that led up to the second floor, holding onto the black wrought-iron handrail as she climbed up to the landing. Before she could knock, the door opened.

"I saw you coming." Adam leaned over and gave her a hug and kiss.

"Isn't it a lovely day today? I think Heaven has floated down to give us a little preview." Mary let him help her out of her coat and scarf, and he took them away. She stood in the little kitchen with its cute antique furniture from Jake's endless inventory. Getting busy, she filled the electric kettle and washed her hands. When he came back, she was putting teabags into two mugs.

"Are you really ready for this project?" The kettle boiled, and Mary filled their mugs.

He hesitated, dunking his teabag a few times. "I suppose so. It's got to be done sometime."

"If it's easier for you, I can come in while you're at work and take care of it. Just say the word."

He smiled gratefully. "Thank you. I appreciate so much that you're here. You've always been another mother to me, Ellie, and now that Mom is gone... well, it's just really good to have you with me, that's all."

A flash of joy shot through her. "I love you so, my beautiful boy. You must always know that."

"I do know. And the feeling is mutual." He kissed her hand and gave a quick smile. "Okay, let's get started." Adam's expression turned grim, but he seemed determined.

"Shall we pack her clothes first?" Mary hooked her arm through his and led him toward the bedroom. "I'll take them to the Salvation Army donation box on the way home. Someone in need will benefit."

"I've already boxed up her books and artwork. I'm going to mail them to her. She doesn't want anything else."

They went into the bedroom, and Adam opened the closet door to turn on the light. Sarah's rumpled jackets, wrinkled blouses, and dusty rack of shoes had a lost, abandoned look. Her dresses drooped on their hangers.

Mary took a large trash bag out of the box and shook it until it opened. The snapping noise echoed through the silent rooms.

"Come on, then." She stepped forward. "Let's get to it."

He nodded.

"You take them off the hangers and hand them to me, and I'll fold." Mary demonstrated, pulling down a pink dress and folding it then putting it in the bottom of the trash bag.

Adam saw her waiting for the next one and slowly pulled it off the hanger. His hand trembled, and he kept his back turned to her, but he passed Mary the dress and moved on to the next one.

They worked that way for several hours until Sarah's half of the closet was finished and her dresser drawers had been emptied and vacuumed. Mary threw away all the lotions and potions from the bathroom, Sarah's makeup, and her hair things. By the end of the afternoon, none of Sarah's things remained in the house, and the backseat of Mary's car was full of bags.

Adam stood on the sidewalk and hugged her. "Thanks, Ellie. Couldn't have done it without you… again. I feel better already."

Mary hugged him back, patting his shoulder. "I love you, sweet pea."

"Love you too."

"Adam, you need to believe that this wasn't about something you did or didn't do. She told you that, right? Do you understand it?"

"Yes, I guess so. She never got over her old feelings for him. I never really had a chance with her. Pretty pathetic."

"I think she did love you, honey, in her way. Just not enough to stick with it."

"Wish she hadn't married me if that was how she felt."

"People do stupid things. Even the best of us." *Even me*, thought Mary. *Even your father and me and Ginnie. She would be here right now instead, telling you the same thing, if it weren't for our stupid mistakes.*

As she pulled away, Mary looked back and saw him heading up the stairs to his lonely apartment and remembered how it had felt when everyone finally left her alone in the house after Thomas died. *A bit different.* A lot different, actually. She had been happy, excited to be alone.

Adam was crushed. It was such a sad disappointment for him. But he wasn't alone, not really. He still had her and Jake.

And Adam's life had a long way to go. Wonderful things could be ahead. Especially if Mary had anything to say about it.

CHAPTER 26

Nell ~ 2014

NELL AND BRIDGET GOT UP at dawn, made coffee, and drank it while they walked the dogs by the lake. The sky was pink and birds were chirping. Everything smelled clean and fresh. The green forest was glowing its usual brilliant neon hue. It was just another fairy-tale morning in Vermont, Nell assured her sister, except for Mom's illness.

Bridget said, "I see what you mean. Do you hear that? It's so quiet."

Lulu and Winston trotted alongside the walkers, alternating between sniffing things and roughhousing. Winston was tolerant, a good thing considering that Lulu was half his size. But tiny Lulu threw herself into trying her utmost to wrestle him into a submissive position.

The dogs' antics kept Nell and Bridget occupied while they walked down to the town beach. Nell pointed out Jake's boat, tied up at the docks. Nobody was around yet, so they walked the dogs on the beach and let them run off leash and play in the gentle waves that lapped on the shore. The wind was calm, and the smooth dark-blue water mirrored the trees along the shoreline with crystal precision.

"It's a beautiful place." Bridget gazed out across the water while Nell threw a stick for Winston.

"Can you taste the flavor of the air?" Nell said. "It's like maple sugar." Both women stopped to breathe in through their mouths. They looked at each other and nodded.

"The sweet taste of freedom," Bridget said. "For Mom and maybe for us too."

"I love it here." Nell watched Winston race down the beach and pounce on the stick.

"Mom's secret."

Nell turned to get her sister's attention. "Ours too, if we want."

Bridget raised her eyebrows. "Our secret?"

"I haven't told anyone. Have you?"

Bridget shook her head, smiling. "You didn't tell David? Why not?"

"Guess I didn't feel like it."

"Why, you little devil." Bridget looked at her admiringly. "Are you thinking we should take up the family tradition?"

"Could be." The idea sent an excited rush through Nell, though she knew it was only a remote possibility.

"Everything okay with you and David, honey?"

"I guess so," Nell said in an unconvincing, flat tone. "Nothing has changed, anyhow."

"Do I hear a little dissatisfaction in that voice? Are you getting bored?"

"Maybe."

Bridget examined her sister's face. "Nell, are you involved with another man?"

"No. Maybe."

"My dear lord—I never thought I'd live to see the day."

"We haven't done anything. Except hug. I'm married, and we're just friends."

"My dear lord, Nell hugged another man." Bridget threw her hands up in the air, appealing to the sky and laughing. "And how was it?" she whispered and sidled up to Nell.

"Great," Nell said, grinning and staring into space.

"Really. And who is the man? Some local lumberjack?"

"Adam Bascomb, the guy who's been driving Mom back and forth to Maplewood."

"Is he nice looking?"

Nell grinned. "What do you think?"

"Are you leaving your husband for him?" Bridget sounded hopeful.

"Don't get carried away."

"Of course not, Nell. You know I never get carried away."

"No, really, it's just a kindred-spirit thing, that's all. So we hugged. No big deal."

"Is he married?"

"No. But I am," Nell said firmly, whistling for Winston and walking away.

She changed the subject to Bridget and Eric, and Bridget soon poured her heart out about recent events. She went on to deliver a humorous description of her last meeting with him, which kept them in giggles all the way home from the beach.

The two women showered and dressed and headed for the hospital in the red Jeep. They arrived at Mary's cubicle just as the doctor was coming out. Bridget's eyes were wide and solemn. Nell knew her sister must be shocked to see their mother's tiny, translucent form lying in the tangle of tubes and wires.

The doctor looked concerned. "Mrs. Williams," he said, shaking her hand. She introduced him to Bridget. "Let's go sit down together for a minute." He led them down the hallway.

―――――

"Ladies, Mary has contracted a secondary infection, and she hasn't yet responded to the new antibiotics. We cultured her to identify the bug, and I changed the medication early this morning. She's being fed and hydrated now through IV. Our options are limited at this point."

Nell and Bridget held hands, squeezing tightly.

"We can intubate her again and put her back on the respirator," he said, "or we can hope she continues to fight and the new meds work."

"What are her chances?" Bridget asked, her eyes brimming with tears.

"Reasonably good. We can keep her comfortable, and when the antibiotics kick in, she may rally. Your mother strikes me as a strong woman. I vote we wait and see if she improves, but it's up to you ladies. Nell, in particular, as health-care proxy."

"I want to see her." Bridget stood up. There was an emotional edge to her voice.

Nell realized that her sister would have to decide for herself, and she exchanged glances with the doctor. "We'll discuss it." Nell smiled her thanks.

The doctor nodded. "Page me when you're ready. I'll be here all morning."

Bridget went in and sat down next to her mother's bedside while Nell watched from the doorway. Mom labored for each rattling breath. Bridget carefully took her limp hand and held it.

"Mom, Mom. It's me, I'm here."

Mom's eyes remained shut as she struggled for air. A little frown creased her forehead. Nell came into the cubicle and stood behind Bridget while Jennifer took Mom's vital signs and wrote them on the chart. Bridget's shoulders shook under Nell's comforting hands. She was crying.

"She looks so… old." Bridget's voice trembled.

Nell agreed. "At first she was getting better, but yesterday, she took a turn for the worse."

"She's pretty heavily sedated right now," Jennifer said. "When she had trouble breathing a little while ago, she got panicky. The doctor had us give her something to calm her down." Jennifer brushed Mary's hair back from her forehead.

"They had her hooked up to a breathing machine when I first got up here," Nell said to her sister. "It was horrible." She and Bridget looked at each other.

"I remember the conversation we had about this," Bridget said. "When we three went on that yoga retreat."

"Yes. It's what she wants. No machines."

"Okay," Bridget whispered, reaching out for Nell. They hugged.

"She should be more alert in a few hours," Jennifer said. "You might have a chance to talk with her a little bit then."

Bridget squared her shoulders and wiped her eyes with her hand. "Good." She settled into the bedside chair. "I need to say a few things to her."

Nell stood at the foot of the bed and watched as her sister stroked Mom's hand. After a minute, she left the room to roam the hallways, leaving the two of them alone. It was Bridget's turn.

Nell went to the little market and picked up what she needed for hamburgers and salad, plus a bag of charcoal for the grill on the back porch. Bridget wanted a few things that hadn't been in the kitchen, so Nell browsed to see what she could find. People in the aisles smiled at her, and she recognized a few of their faces.

The man behind the meat counter asked about her mother. Someone had obviously told him who she was since her visit the previous day. It had been only a short time, but she was already starting to feel at home here. People were friendly. They seemed to care about each other. It was very different from her other home.

Not only was her New Jersey town jam-packed with human beings, but most of them came and went in a flash. She could count on one hand the number of houses in her neighborhood where the owners had been in residence as long as she and David—nearly seven years at that point.

People were always moving because of their careers or because they traded up to bigger, better houses. The town was constantly growing as more people came to work at new technology and research companies that had sprung up in the area. Despite all that togetherness, people somehow still managed to be cold and impersonal, uninterested in each other unless they had gathered for a business party or an organized social event. There were so many newcomers that someone coming into town for a few days was unremarkable. Nell had only been in Vermont for less than a week, but already, she had friends there. *Perhaps enemies too*, she thought, remembering her encounters with Jake.

She came out of the market and put her grocery bags in the back of her car, which was parked in one of the diagonal spaces along the edge of the town green. Beyond the sidewalk that edged the wide lawn was a row of ancient maple trees, enormous in diameter, probably hundreds of years old. Huge gnarled roots rippled across the sandy dirt, and the lower tree limbs were thick as an elephant's leg.

Nell had noticed the townspeople gathering on park benches in the shade of the maples to gossip and read the paper. Small boys played with their toy trucks among the twisting roots. Adventurous teens climbed up into the broad green canopies and carved their initials into the bark. The trees on the green were the center of a vibrant social network, the beating heart of Hartland.

She bought a newspaper and sat down on a bench to flip through it. As her mind went numb, her imagination dissolved the view into a dream of living quietly in Hartland alone as Mary had done. *Running by the lake in the sunshine, breathing in the lovely air, watching the clear colors of nature throb with life. No responsibilities.*

But Mom didn't have a husband like David, who was always trying to help in that anxious, managerial way of his. When Nell came home, he'd want to read her journal and discuss each epiphany. Then he'd show her the towers of neatly folded, spanking-clean laundry he'd produced during her absence and say how easy it had been thanks to his new high-efficiency system. *Just helping out, baby. I emailed you the flow chart.*

Nell wondered whether her father had known about the cottage. Had Mom been planning to leave him? Back then, Nell had been distracted by finishing high school and choosing a university, but she did remember thinking Mom seemed mad at Thomas for quite a while after Bridget caved in and put her baby up for adoption. Mom had been even more upset than Bridget. She seemed to take it personally for some reason.

Did the diagnosis of his illness stop her from leaving him? The timing seemed right.

Is that what kept her tied to him? She'd been unable to abandon Thomas in his time of need even while she yearned to escape to her new home, the house she kept in her back pocket like the photo of a secret lover, pulling it out to sneak a look when she needed cheering up.

Nell knew that she'd probably have to tell David about the cottage before long, and he'd want to come up and bring the kids, and it would turn into a family vacation spot. The kids would swim at the town beach, and David would get a little sailboat. He'd go fishing with Ben at dawn every day, and they would bond. The kids would buy popsicles from the ice cream truck that stopped at the beach parking lot on summer afternoons, and Lauren would make friends with a gaggle of little girls. Nell would still get to go running by the lake, but she'd spend most of her vacation cooking and cleaning and taking care of everyone as usual. The house would be full of laughter and the sound of running feet. At night in Mom's old room, her husband would kiss her, and they'd make love in the soft light of the moon shadow that glowed darkly in the garden window.

But not yet. At the moment, it was still Mom's place and Nell's and Bridget's. Their private retreat. Perhaps if the sisters both really wanted to, they could arrange their lives so that every once in a while, they could sneak off together or alone and enjoy the stillness, the solitude.

After all, men had their hunting cabins, their fishing camps. Their wives knew about them, but they certainly didn't want to tag along and interfere. It was Man Land.

She might be able to tell David she just needed some time to herself.

She might say, "Don't call. I'll be back in a week or two. I'm going to write some poetry."

Nell imagined the look that would come over his face if she ever said that.

"I still love you," she'd say. "It's not about you."

And his eyes would fill with panic. A wife who vacationed alone for weeks at a time was not part of his picture of the ideal marriage. No, David would not find this idea easy to handle.

But for the moment, Nell sat on the park bench and basked in the feeling of independence.

Driving through town to bring the groceries home and let the dogs out, Nell experimented with a few logical shortcuts and found herself in familiar territory. She saw the antiques barn coming up on her right. Adam was in the driveway, unloading furniture from his pickup truck. His back was turned to the street, and she saw his broad shoulders ripple under the blue work shirt as he lifted a table up in the air. She beeped the horn, and he looked up, breaking into a smile.

"Hey there." Nell pulled into the parking area, rolled down the window, and slowed to a stop.

Adam came over to the side of her car. "Hey yourself."

She smelled the lemony scent of his furniture polish. "How are you?" Relieved for a moment, her anxiety level plummeted. He seemed to have that effect on her.

"Sad." He leaned on the car near the open window. "Stopped by and saw your mom again early this morning. She wasn't doing so well."

Nell forgot to pay attention, and her foot slipped off the brake. The car rolled an inch or two before she stopped it, and they both laughed, a tight nervous sound.

"Well, yes," she said. "She's asleep again now, and they're trying a new medicine. My sister is here."

"Aha, the elusive Bridget finally appears. Can't wait to meet her." He grinned and nodded.

"She can't wait to meet you, and your father too," Nell said. "Not that I'm eager to socialize with Jake. He's been annoying the hell out of me."

"Hey, don't get your Reilly up." Adam stepped back and raised his hands defensively. "I'm not responsible for the offensive things my dad does."

"I know," she said, mellowing. "He acts like a jerk sometimes without your coaching."

"Nobody likes it when he gets obnoxious, you know. Least of all me."

"Okay, sorry. Just letting off steam." Nell unclenched her fists and took a deep breath.

They looked at one another in silence.

"Gotta go put some stuff in the fridge," she said.

"Bye." He stepped back. "Take care, Nell."

She lifted one hand and waved, backing up to pull out into the road and continue on her way. Before she could change her mind, she stepped on the brake and leaned out the window.

"Adam."

"Yeah?"

"Why don't you come for dinner? Meet Bridget?"

He grinned and bounced a little like an eager puppy. "Are you sure?"

"Yes, definitely. Mom would want us to all be together. I feel it."

"Okay." Adam stood with hands on hips. "I'll bring the wine if you promise not to get me drunk again."

"No promises. Bring plenty. Seven thirty unless you hear otherwise." Waving again, she drove off down the street.

CHAPTER 27

Bridget ~ 2014

BRIDGET SAT NEXT TO THE hospital bed all morning and watched her mother fight to pull air into her congested lungs until finally, in the early afternoon, Mom's eyes fluttered open, and she looked at her oldest daughter. A smile spread from her eyes to her lips. Lifting her arms a scant inch off the mattress, she reached out, and Bridget bent over the bed to thread her arms between the tubes and wires and fold her mother's tiny body into an embrace. It was like hugging a bird.

"My girl," Mom whispered, then she burst into a spasm of coughing, and Bridget drew back, grabbing for a tissue from the bedside table to offer it to her mother.

Jennifer came hurrying into the room and reached behind Mom's back to lean her forward as she coughed in great rattling shudders. Pulling a sturdier tissue from a packet on the table, the nurse said, "Spit!" and Mom did, filling the tissue in Jennifer's hand with dark-gray mucus. "Good girl." Jennifer rubbed Mom's back. "That was a good one."

Mom smiled up at her weakly, beads of sweat on her forehead. She lay back against the pillows and took a shuddering breath.

Jennifer held a glass of water to her lips, and she sipped from a bent straw. "Better?" the nurse said.

Mom nodded, and her breathing settled into a quieter pattern.

"She can't talk much," Jennifer told Bridget. "It makes her cough. But she can listen just fine."

Bridget took her mother's hand, and this time she felt a squeeze in return.

"We'll be okay," Bridget said. "Thank you."

Jennifer pointed to where the call button was clipped to the sheets near the pillow. She went back to the nurses' station, saying she'd be in and out but to pay her no mind.

Bridget sat with her mother for the next few hours and talked about whatever came into her mind—memories of childhood, family trips, and mental snapshots from their years together. She'd been a wild teenager, and they had fought more than once over her bids for independence. At the moment, it all seemed humorous rather than dire. Bridget told her mother about similar incidents she'd gone through recently with Heather, saying that now she understood Mom's point of view. She didn't tell Mom about her decision to get divorced again. Her mother didn't need more to worry about.

"I've been meaning to tell you," Bridget said. "There's something that's been hard for me to say all these years."

Her mother looked at her curiously, raising one eyebrow.

"You were right, Mom. I should have kept her."

Mom's eyes saddened, and she gave Bridget's hand a weak squeeze. "I understand," she mouthed.

Bridget laid her head down on the edge of the mattress, unable to meet her mother's eyes for the rest of what she wanted to say. "I was so young and stupid. I never realized I wouldn't have another chance. And I thought it would just be too hard to raise her by myself." She was crying quietly, letting the tears roll off and soak into the sheets. "A few years ago, I started looking for her. I went to Catholic Charities, but they said the records had been lost. So I hired a detective and then another. Nothing. They couldn't find her. I was too late."

Bridget felt her mother's hand on her hair, stroking it. She raised her head. "I should have listened to you, Mom. I wish I had."

Her mother nodded. "Keep trying," she whispered urgently.

"I will, I promise."

The hours passed all too quickly as they leaned toward each other, arms intertwined on the edge of the bed, heads nearly touching. Bridget spoke in a quiet voice, and her mother whispered a reply now and then. Love surrounded them like a bright glow, filling the cubicle with an atmosphere of peace. The knot in Bridget's stomach relaxed.

Her mind wandered off into a vision of her father the day he'd given her a driving lesson and she'd hit the gas instead of the brake, propelling the car off the road. She laughed out loud at the memory of his astonished, angry expression. Turning back to Mary, she found her mother's eyes had closed, and Bridget realized the hand in hers had relaxed.

Jennifer came in to say that Mary would probably sleep for a few hours. She suggested that Bridget take a break and come back later. It was early afternoon, and Bridget hadn't eaten since breakfast. She stood up and stretched, looking around for Nell. She asked at the nurses' station, but none of them had seen her in several hours.

Bridget went outside and saw the red Jeep still parked where they'd left it that morning. Shading her eyes with her hand, she peered across the town green. Down at the far end, in front of the library, stood a swing set and some other playground equipment. She spotted Nell sitting on one of the swings, swaying back and forth.

She remembered their contests as little girls, seeing who could swing the highest and try to hook the moon, inspired by the poem their mother read to them at bedtime. Bridget walked onto the lawn and slipped out of her expensive clogs, enjoying the feel of the cool grass between her toes. She headed toward the girl who was now a woman but was still her baby sister and always would be. It was a comforting thought.

Everything was changing in Bridget's life at a breakneck pace. Thinking about it made her head spin and her stomach churn. But this was how it always happened: things would go along day after day in the same pattern of events and relationships, and then boom, it would all tumble apart, and like a row of falling dominoes, one thing after another would change until everything had been transformed and a whole new status quo emerged from the rubble.

Nothing ever stayed the same for long for Bridget. Her marriages, her addresses, her client list, and even her hairstyles changed completely every few years.

But through it all, there was Nell, stable and sensible, looking up to her trustingly, ever admiring and supportive. Rebuilding Bridget's self-image when it had crumbled into dust and reminding her who she really was. Smiling and beckoning to her from the playground. Inviting her to swing and swing and keep on swinging, side by side, until they could stretch out their feet and hook the moon.

Bridget and her sister went to get lunch at the café and sat at a table outside, enjoying the balmy weather while they ate. Afterward, they walked back to the hospital.

As they drew nearer, Nell's face puckered up in a suspicious squint. She stared at the beat-up old blue truck parked haphazardly across two spaces in the parking lot. "Oh no you don't," she cried, running toward the building.

"What's the matter?" Bridget hurried to keep up.

Nell flew through the double doors, rushing past the receptionist and racing along the familiar path to the ICU. Bridget drafted along in her wake, sending apologetic looks to the hospital personnel, who watched their speedy progress with disapproval.

Coming to a halt outside her mother's cubicle, Nell panted with rage. A man sat in the chair next to Mom's bed, her hand held in both of his. A vase of fresh flowers had appeared on the bedside table. Mom's eyes were closed, and she seemed to be sleeping.

"God dammit," Nell muttered, her fists balled. "Goddam drunken jerk."

Bridget looked through the glass, impressed by the visitor's rugged good looks. "Who is that man, Nell? Is that... him? Jake Bascomb?"

"Yes, it is, and he promised not to come back. He's a bloody liar."

Jake seemed to hear them talking and turned his head. He sneered when he saw Nell then looked curious when he spotted Bridget. Leaning over to kiss Mom's hand, he stood up and walked out into the hallway.

Nell fumed. "You... you... you shouldn't be here."

"Take it easy." He seemed perfectly calm and sober, in contrast with Nell. "She's not even awake."

Nell peered into the cubicle and seemed to relax slightly. "But you promised not to come back until I said it was okay."

Jake finally turned his eyes to Bridget, who was treating him to her most practiced Southern belle smile. A responsive glimmer flashed in his eyes.

"No." He spoke to Nell while he smiled back at Bridget. "You demanded, but I didn't promise." He reached out for Bridget's hand. "And this must be the other Reilly sister, right?"

Wearing rumpled clothes and needing a shave, Jake still looked like he would clean up quite well—not at all what Nell had described. He reminded Bridget of a distinguished silverback gorilla: impressive, strong, and commanding.

"Mr. Bascomb, senior, I presume?" Bridget almost fluttered her eyelashes but managed to suppress the reflex.

"Cut the crap, Bridget." Nell's tone was impatient. "Every time Mom sees this guy, she goes into a tailspin, and we can't afford that right now, can we?"

Jake and Bridget looked like two kids caught passing notes in class.

"Of course not." Bridget gently withdrew her hand. "She's right. We really do have to keep Mom calm and quiet."

Jake glanced through the glass at the sleeping woman, and a troubled look flickered across his face. "Sure, no problem." His voice was gruff, and he turned to face Nell. "Don't be so uptight, little girl. I just wanted to check on her."

Nell scowled at the term *little girl*, which was obviously meant to annoy her. "Okay, so you checked. Now, go."

His eyes smoldered briefly, and he glared at her. Without another word, he nodded to Bridget and strode down the hall, covering the yards swiftly with his long legs. Then he was gone.

"My lord." Bridget fanned herself and stared as he walked away. "You didn't tell me we had anyone like that up here in the woods."

"I did too. And wait until you meet Mr. Bascomb, junior."

"Oh no, honey, I'll leave him to you. I've been waiting a lot of years to see you meet the man who could stir you up. No offense to your husband, of course. He's very cute too, if you like the conservative, obedient type."

"I do. I like that type very much."

"Yes, yes… so you said. But let's not forget the famous hug, shall we?" Bridget needled her with a mischievous grin.

"No chance of that." Nell sighed.

"Poor baby." Bridget patted her on the shoulder but couldn't resist teasing. "And did you talk to your husband yet today?"

"Yes."

"Is he coming up to join us?"

"Not yet. He's taking care of the kids. Sends love."

"Hmmm," Bridget said, pretending to examine her fingernails.

"Shut up."

"Whatever you say. Shall we sit with Mom a while longer, then?" Bridget headed toward Mom's cubicle.

"I'll get another chair." Nell turned to ask the nurse for help.

Mom slept for the rest of the day, her breathing growing easier. It looked as though the antibiotic was working. When she awakened, she seemed much better and sat up to talk a little, her voice nearly normal. Ben's "Get Well Soon – Or Else…" card had arrived, with a picture of a skunk on it, and they all had a good laugh. As evening approached, the nurse settled her down for the night.

Mom kissed Bridget and Nell good night, whispered, "I love you," and smiled then shooed them away with her hands. She seemed to have turned a corner, and there was a little sparkle in her eyes. The ICU nurses promised to call if there was any change.

Bridget left the hospital feeling relieved and optimistic.

CHAPTER 28

Mary ~ July 10, 1967

MARY STOOD OUTSIDE AT THE 3rd Field Hospital in the city of Saigon, Vietnam, waiting for the next ambulance to appear. There were already eight of them parked in front of the long, two-story building. Some contained up to six soldiers lying on stretchers stacked on racks like bunk beds. The dark-green trucks emblazoned with Red Cross signs had delivered casualties flown in to Tan Son Nhut Air Base by medevac planes, from two ongoing battles in the Central Highlands. It had been going on all day, and the beautiful mosaic tile floor of the covered porch was slippery with blood.

Her lower back ached from being on her feet since dawn. Mary stretched out the kinks and took this brief chance to straighten her white cap and duty uniform. There wasn't anything to be done about the bloodstains or the sweat. It was monsoon season, and working outside on triage duty in the humid heat was like torture. Not to mention the stress of having to choose which patients would be patched together first and which would have to wait.

She silently cursed General Westmoreland, who was the reason she couldn't wear lightweight fatigues instead of the heavy whites. He insisted that seeing women nurses in white uniforms and stockings was good for the soldiers' morale, and he had ordered it for Mary's hospital. He was headquartered in Saigon and liked to bring important visitors and reporters to tour the hospital. Everybody said he wanted the nurses to look good to give the impression that everything was under control. *Nothing like a lot of relentless white sheets and walls and uniforms to banish the image of blood from your mind's eye.* Mary had noticed that the tours only came on slow days.

In a busy section of the city, the compound of relatively modern buildings had a stateside type of atmosphere, with air conditioning in some of the rooms. Most of the best surgeons in Vietnam had been attracted to the staff. Mary felt lucky to be stationed there, especially considering how bad the situation was in lots of other field hospitals.

Mary knew she would be the first American woman most of these boys had seen in many months. They saw her as a true angel, and she didn't want to let them down.

An ambulance pulled into the driveway and reversed to back up to the porch. Mary calmed herself and put a welcoming smile on her face. When the engine shut off, two medics jumped out of the cab and ran to open the rear doors.

All the racks were occupied. A boy in one of the top bunks turned his head to peer out at the light. His left eye was covered by a field dressing that was wrapped around his head. When he saw Mary, he began to sob. She had gotten used to the sound, but it never failed to move her.

"Hey there, soldier." Mary stepped forward and reached for his hand while the corpsmen slid the stretcher off the rack. "It's great to see you. We're going to take real good care of you, so don't you worry about a thing. Let me just take a quick look..." She rambled on in a soothing tone, understanding the positive impact of a woman's voice that sounded like home.

The boys still inside the truck heard her too, and they began to stir and moan, calling to their girlfriends, their sisters, their mothers. Mary knew that at the moment, she was all of these. She answered, calling the soldiers "honey" and "my boy." With her heart firmly under control, she put sunshine and picnics and apple pie into her voice, and it brought them comfort.

The men lowered the stretcher to the ground, where she quickly examined the wounded soldier and made some notes on her clipboard. She told them where to deliver him and turned to the next casualty. More men came to help unload the truck as Mary sorted those who could wait for care from those who needed immediate attention. When the ambulance was empty, the driver and his partner jumped back inside and tore off toward the air base for a refill. The whole exercise had taken approximately ten minutes.

Later, the quiet in the air told everyone that helicopters had stopped coming in from the north and the rush was over for the time being. Mary's shift was finally finished, and she had stopped outside for a moment to look up at the night sky. It had cooled off a bit, and the stars were out. A medical corpsman was rinsing blood-soaked stretchers with a garden hose and stacking them upright against a wall to dry. He turned off the water and looked over at her.

"Good work today, Lieutenant Sullivan."

She squinted across the shadowy porch. "Thanks, Sergeant. You were driving, weren't you?"

"Yep. Cigarette, ma'am?" He walked over, a pack of Marlboros outstretched.

She took one and leaned close to the flame as he lit a match. When he bent to light his own, she saw his face in the light. Brown hair and blue eyes, quite a bit younger than she was but not a kid like so many of the soldiers in Vietnam.

"You look familiar... Bascomb?" She read the name printed above his right breast pocket as he had apparently read the tag pinned above hers. "But you're new, aren't you?"

"Aw, sweet thing, I'm crushed. You don't remember me?"

Then it dawned on her. "Honey's. In Honolulu. You're the guy who saved me from unthinkable embarrassment, right?" She laughed, remembering how she had almost hit the floor that night.

He nodded, smiling. "It's Jake. What's yours?"

"Mary Ellen Sullivan. Haven't seen you here before. You just get transferred to Saigon?" He looked different now, with long sideburns and a moustache. Kind of like the Beatles on their new album cover. Mary thought he looked exotic. Very attractive, especially after a day of examining unspeakably mangled limbs and oozing head wounds.

"Yeah, I got here last week." He looked at her left hand, where the diamond ring still sparkled. "So Mary Ellen, how's the boyfriend?"

"Fine, last I heard. He flies a Skyhawk for the navy."

"God bless him."

"Yes, exactly."

"You headed back to your hooch now?" He used the nickname that nurses in the field had adopted for their improvised quarters.

Her living situation was relatively good, in the former school complex that had been converted for US Army hospital use. It was fenced and patrolled by MPs who made sure nobody entered without permission. The female nurses had their own building, where Mary shared a room with five other women. They had decorated it with posters, pretty bedspreads on their bunks, and colorful curtains, but it was definitely still a *hooch*.

She nodded. "Time for laundry and sleep. I'm beat."

"I'll walk you if it's okay?"

"Sure. Thanks, Jake."

They ground out their cigarette butts in the driveway and strolled down the road that led into the group of buildings. Jake offered her a swig from his pocket flask, exactly the kind of "fraternization" that was questionable between an enlisted soldier and an officer.

She shot him a mischievous grin. "Since we're old friends, how can I say no?" Mary sipped and tasted whiskey. It went down like smooth, sweet fire.

Somebody had the radio on, and it was playing Aretha Franklin's new hit record, "Respect." The song echoed through the hospital complex. Mary giggled and sang along. She needed to forget about the horrors she had seen all day. Grabbing her hand, he swung her around, rocking, as they danced down the middle of the road. The buildings they passed were shuttered and shaded with little slashes of light where windows had been left open to let in the breeze. Laughter and soft voices leaked out into the night. The rain clouds had cleared off, and a tiny sliver of crescent moon was in the sky. When she looked up and ignored everything else, Mary could almost imagine she was back home.

Jake admired her footwork. "You're pretty agile when you're not drunk, sweet thing."

"Better give me some more in that case." She took the flask from his hand again.

"Long as you're not on your ass when the next security sweep comes around." Jake grinned at her as she swallowed twice, choked, and gave him back the whiskey.

"Those guys are my buddies anyhow. No problem." She unpinned her cap and took it off, letting the breeze cool her head. She caught the spicy scent of warm male skin that wafted her way when he swayed close, and she studied him. "What's your story, Jake? Where are you from, and how did you end up here?"

He took a long pull on the flask and handed it back to her. "Born in Maine, grew up in Vermont. Dropped out of college after one semester and got drafted. Ended up in the medical corps because I had CPR certification and a clean driving record. Six months in the field, then hello Saigon. End of story."

"Well, I hope not."

"Yeah, guess you're right," he said, laughing quietly. "We'll go home someday, and life will go on."

"We've lost a lot of wonderful guys, Jake." Mary took an extra swig and handed him back the flask, almost empty by then.

"President Johnson says the fighting is almost over. I heard on the radio last week."

"You really think so? That would be fab-a-lush. I mean, fabulous." Mary burst into laughter, stifling the sound with her hands over her mouth.

"Enough for you, sister. You're cut off." Jake stopped walking to grin at her.

Mary glanced up with an embarrassed smirk. "Sorry," she mimed, and they resumed walking. When they reached the nurses' quarters, she flopped down to sit on the front steps, and he sat beside her, pulling out his cigarettes. He lit one for her and another for himself.

"I'm from New England too," she said. "Boston area."

"No kidding? Howdy, neighbor." He solemnly held out his hand, and they shook on it.

"Funny how far apart that seemed when we were home. But now…"

"It seems like right next door." Jake finished her thought.

"Yes. Even California seems close to home, from here."

Jake looked at her through a cloud of smoke, his eyes dreamy. "I wouldn't mind living right next door to you, Mary Ellen Sullivan. Not one bit." His eyes wandered down her body, along the line of her legs stretched out on the steps.

She squirmed and tucked her legs under her. "Be careful what you wish for, Jake Bascomb. Don't you have a girl waiting for you at home? Or maybe several?"

"Her name is Virginia. We might get married some day, unless you change your mind about that pilot. Be sure and let me know. I'll give her the brush-off and marry you." His eyes were dark blue with a spark of something in them that she didn't want to see.

Jake seemed a little dangerous, and a twinge of nerves made her shiver. Anything could happen if she wasn't careful. In Vietnam, everything was so unreal—part nightmare, part wild and exciting. The fear of death gave people permission to misbehave. Lots of her coworkers were having affairs, even those who were married. It was a way to pass the time when work was slow and to feel intimacy while surrounded by strangers. Mary had been out on a couple of dates since her arrival but nothing serious. She was trying to be loyal to Thomas.

"I'd better go inside." She stubbed out her cigarette and stood up to brush off the seat of her skirt. "Good to see you again, Jake."

He stood up and backed away, one eyebrow raised. "A little nervous about me, are you? We can't have that, sweet thing. Just teasing... sort of."

"I know, it's okay. Good night, then. See you tomorrow, probably."

Jake tipped his imaginary cap and turned to walk away down the road.

Mary went inside and climbed the stairs to the crowded little room where she lived. It was empty at the moment, and she could hear her roommates chattering down the hall where the other women had gathered. She threw her cap on her bunk and shrugged out of her short-sleeved shirt, pausing to unbutton the waist of her skirt.

Then she noticed the brown envelope propped up against her pillow. It was a telegram. She immediately thought of her parents and her sister and tore into it to read the news:

SORRY TO INFORM YOU LT CDR THOMAS REILLY MISSING IN ACTION -(STOP) – REPORTED ENGINE TROUBLE ON MISSION THAI BINH PROVINCE – (STOP) – FOLLOWING RELEASE OF ORDNANCE HIS SKYHAWK DOWN OVER GULF OF TONKIN – (STOP) – PARACHUTE NOT SIGHTED – (STOP)-

Mary stopped breathing and stared at the page in her hand. She read it again, not trusting her eyes. Then she gasped, and a moan slipped out of her trembling lips. She sat down on her bunk and read the telegram a third time. "Parachute not sighted." That meant he had still been inside the plane when it crashed. He was classified as "missing in action" instead of "killed in action" because they hadn't found the remains.

Thomas was likely dead.

The telegram fell from her hand, and she felt the scream building inside her. When it burst from her throat, the other nurses came running.

CHAPTER 29

Bridget ~ 2014

WHILE NELL WENT FOR A jog around the lake, Bridget lay down on the sofa and tried to nap, but her eyes kept popping open. She was tired but too wound up to sleep. Visions of her mother struggling for air haunted her.

Wandering from room to room, she inspected the cottage. She looked in the drawers and closets. In the living room cupboard, she came across a treasure trove of family memorabilia, things she had never seen before or not for many years. Pulling out boxes and cartons, she sat down on the braided rug to inspect them.

A large, flat white box tied with blue satin ribbon drew her eye first. It looked like the kind of box a sweater or a suit might come in from a nice department store. Inside was an old navy uniform, carefully folded. Lying on top of it was a framed photograph and a single dried red rose, shriveled and crumbling.

Bridget knew that Daddy had flown a plane in the Vietnam War in the 1960s and Mom had been an army nurse in Saigon. The photo was in black-and-white, a close-up shot of Thomas and Mary on a dance floor. They were both wearing military uniforms though Mom had taken off her jacket. Looking closer, Bridget saw that her mother held a dark rose in her hand.

Mom had gone to a lot of trouble to keep this iconic moment forever. It spoke of a deep and magical love. She wanted to remember him the way he was then, bright and sharp as a tack, and their relationship the way it was then as well—passionate and consuming. Staring into the white box was like looking through a window into the past.

Then Bridget saw the engagement ring on Mom's left hand and understood: that was the night they decided to get married.

Bridget looked at the photo and touched the dried rose, thinking how trivial all her relationships had been compared to the spark and intensity of her mother's. That beautiful love was what had sustained Mom through the sad years when Thomas disappeared and a stranger inhabited his body, looking out at her fearfully through his eyes.

Bridget carefully closed the white box and set it aside then pulled a box of odds and ends toward her. First, she found a well-worn stuffed lamb, familiar to her fingers, and a little pink-satin jewelry box with a dancing ballerina on top. The music that played when she opened it summoned a vision of her and Nell getting dressed for church, wearing necklaces of tiny pearls with their matching pink dresses.

Bridget looked deeper into the carton. In the bottom was a mirrored tray scattered with costume jewelry, matchbooks, and tiny keepsakes. She remembered it from many years ago, when it used to sit on Mom's dresser. Mementos of her mother's travels when she was young, the rings, bracelets, and brooches sparkled with the rich colors of Africa and Asia.

Buried beneath a large Italian cameo, a button peeked out. Its green-and-gold hexagonal pattern caught her eye. Simple dull plastic, homely compared to the flashy rhinestones and semiprecious gems surrounding it, the button called out for attention. It had a story to tell.

She picked it up and examined the six-sided barred design. Two holes in the center still held a frayed olive-green thread where it had been attached to some article of clothing. A full two inches across, it must have helped to fasten a coat, jacket, or sweater—something big and heavy.

Bridget looked at it again, and a thought came to her. A framed portrait of Mary and Thomas in the early days of their marriage hung on the wall in the den. She went in there and lifted it off the nail for a closer view, looking carefully at the suit her mother wore in the photo. Sure enough, holding a tweed jacket closed under Mom's breasts was the button. Just the one. It did the whole job on its own.

They looked happy in the photo, young and hopeful. The world was theirs to explore together. Little did they know that Thomas would be taken away long before his time, leaving his wife to care for him, bury him, and hold the family together on her own, all alone.

Bridget was going to hold things together alone too. For the first time ever, she'd left one man when she didn't have another waiting in the wings. *Time to make it on my own.*

She tucked the green button away in her pants pocket. Maybe it would bring her luck.

Bridget put Lulu and Winston on leashes and took them out for a quick walk around the block. She turned left at the town beach. The sidewalk led her past a row of gingerbread cottages painted pastel colors and a large white Colonial farmhouse with the porch decayed and falling off. A rusty old blue truck was parked in the driveway.

Winston suddenly yanked on the leash, pulling it out of her hand. He darted off toward the farmhouse and ran down the driveway and around the side, past the woodshed.

"Great," Bridget muttered to herself. "Winston!" She picked Lulu up to hurry after him.

She came around the end of the house just in time to see the little white dog disappear inside the back door. She ran up the porch steps, dodging a crate filled with empty beer cans, and looked up breathlessly into the eyes of Jake Bascomb, who stood in the doorway with Winston in his arms.

Jake scratched Winston's chest and looked at her and then at Lulu, tucked under her arm.

"Walking your... cat?" There was a glimmer in his eyes.

"Toy poodle." She smiled, and her cheeks tingled.

He raised one raggedy eyebrow. "Beats me." He shook his head. "You want to come in? I just made coffee." He held the screen door open.

"Why, thank you, kind sir. Very neighborly of you," Bridget sang out in her faux Southern accent, a flirtatious reflex. She batted her eyes a little bit as she passed him and went inside.

Jake put Winston down, and the dog ran for the water dish, lapped at it greedily, and then smiled with his pink mouth open, panting and dripping on the floor. Lulu wiggled, so Bridget put her down.

Jake watched the black fluff ball with a bemused expression and laughed when she turned around and leapt onto Winston's head for one of their wrestling matches. "Well, it doesn't look much like a dog, but I see it has some spunk… like you girls." He waved her toward the table, which was clean and shining. In fact, the whole kitchen looked as though it had recently been tidied and scrubbed. Bridget wondered again why Nell was so set against this man. Maybe he was depressed and did have a drinking problem, but at least he was trying. He poured them each a cup of coffee and sat across from her.

"Yes, our mother trained us well. I'm sorry, though, about Nell. She seems to be feeling extremely defensive about Mom. I hope you'll forgive her rudeness."

"Wasn't exactly the soul of good grace myself. I call a spade a spade."

"Frankness is an admirable quality," she said cautiously.

"She just doesn't get it. Me and Ellie, that is." Intense emotion flickered in his eyes. He was clearly upset and trying to hide it.

"And what exactly is there to get, if you don't mind my asking?"

"I adore Ellie. Always have, always will. The best friend I ever had. I'd do anything for her." Jake shook his head sorrowfully, and his face began to crumple. A tear splashed onto the table. "Seeing her in that hospital bed is a nightmare. I can't hardly stand it."

"Me too." Bridget covered his hand with hers, and her emotions flooded out. "I can't even sleep. I just keep seeing her gasping for air. It's horrible." She tightened her jaw as her throat contracted, and she tried not to cry too.

Jake nodded. "I know your sister thinks I did something to hurt Ellie, but it's not true. We were out on the lake in my boat, and the wind came up. It got rough, and I turned back. Ellie was fighting to bring down the sails. There was a big wave, and we rocked. She went over the side." Jake looked stricken and shivered at the memory. "I got her right out again, but it was freezing cold in that wind. I made her take a hot bath, tucked her into bed, and went home, but…" He hesitated, his eyes begging for her approval. "I should have stayed and watched her. Why didn't she call me? I would have been there in seconds."

"It's okay," Bridget said, patting his hand. "You did what you could to help her. It was an accident."

"Tell that to your sister."

"I will. It's just I think Nell's worried about another boating accident. Something about Mom and your wife. We don't know much about what actually happened."

His eyes darkened, and he lowered his face, looking at her from under his brows. "You mean the night Ginnie died, the worst night of my life?"

"Yes." Bridget watched his face.

Jake took a long swallow of his coffee and stared out the window into the yard. They sat in silence for a few moments while he seemed to make up his mind. His voice shook when he finally spoke. "I told them I killed her, you know. I said, 'I'm guilty. Lock me up.'"

Bridget looked into his eyes, seeing only sadness and defeat. He was a man who had given up, not a man who was hiding the truth. Still, his statement made her nervous.

Jake leaned toward her, his eyes wide. "You don't know what I mean, do you?"

"You killed your wife?" Bridget tensed and sat up straight.

"No, I did not."

Bridget relaxed again. He looked as if he might feel a little better too. The stress and exhaustion of holding the secret close for all those years was on his face. His hand shook when he lifted the coffee cup for another sip. He put it back down on the table and watched her, waiting.

"Tell me." No stranger to desperate confessions, Bridget was drawn to the man. Having been so close to rock bottom herself several times before, she recognized the signs.

Jake seemed to teeter on the edge of the decision then decided to take a plunge. His big hands wrapped around the coffee cup and engulfed it as he looked her straight in the eye. "When they pulled my wife's body out of the lake, and I saw her lying there like a dead fish in the rain, it was like my head exploded and my mind just... went away somewhere."

"I can't even imagine."

"Your mother was there, and the police, and the EMTs, and a bunch of people. There were lights flashing and people shouting. And Ginnie was... lying on a tarp on the ground, and they wrapped it up around her a little and kind of dragged her along toward the ambulance, and her head... bounced..." His voice broke, and his face folded into a grimace. He wiped his eyes quickly with the back of his hand.

She was holding his other hand now too. "Jake," she said, shaking her head. "Don't... you don't have to tell me. It's too awful."

"No, I want to. You still don't understand. I never talked to anyone about this before except Ellie. She's the only one who knows what really happened."

"Yes, Nell told me."

He looked disgusted. "Nell doesn't know shit, if you'll excuse my French."

"Well, that's true sometimes. You tell me, then."

"I thought about this a lot while I was in jail. Adam lost enough that night. His mother was dead. No need for him to lose all of us by knowing everything. There was no good way to explain it to him, why it really happened. That's why I never told him. Adam came back pretty well from that night." Jake's voice took on a note of pride. "He took over the family business and threw himself into it."

"And you?" she asked.

"I do okay," Jake answered in a gruff voice, but his face said otherwise.

She saw the chaotic house, the empty liquor bottles on top of the refrigerator and the unfinished projects scattered around the yard. He had cleaned up recently, but she could still spot the signs of a soul in pain. Self-loathing radiated from the man sitting across from her, and he had told his story haltingly, glancing up at her between phrases for reassurance.

Bridget's generous heart went out to him, and she understood why Mary had been so involved with his family all these years. She'd been a physical caretaker at home with Thomas and a spiritual caretaker in Hartland. Between the two, Thomas and Jake had satisfied her instinct for healing. Mom hadn't become a nurse by accident—it was her true calling. She had been needed, appreciated, and loved. *Hard for any woman to turn away from that.* Bridget had never fully experienced being needed that way, and she could see the attraction.

The trust that suddenly blossomed between Bridget and Jake was a gift that did them both good. Jake bared his soul, and Bridget accepted the honor of his confidence, thinking that in all the years of their marriage, Eric had never been this honest with her, not once. He'd given her diamonds, clothes, and a big fancy house, but he'd never given her the truth. She'd never really known him.

But this vulnerable man was sharing his most private secret with her, and they had only just met that day. Fancy that. Bridget heard him in silence and consoled him with her eyes, their fingers entwined on the table between them.

CHAPTER 30

Nell ~ 2014

NELL WENT BACK TO THE cottage and started dinner. She turned on the music she and Adam had listened to and daydreamed while she worked. At first she thought Bridget must still be napping upstairs, then she realized the dogs were gone. *Probably at the town beach or walking by the lake.* She made a mug of tea and went into the garden to wait, sitting on the glider. She checked her phone and answered a text from David, automatically adding the heart graphic she always used as a sort of signature in their family messages.

The sky had become overcast, and a cold breeze was pushing gray clouds in from the north. Nell wished she'd worn a sweater. But the warm drink in her hands helped, and she felt lazy, so she sat and sipped while she rocked.

Emotions swirled inside her. Mom seemed better again, but that had happened before and had given her false hope. The stress of uncertainty was wearing Nell down. Half of her wanted to rush back and watch over Mom all night, while the other half wanted to believe things were improving and simply escape for a while. She needed David's support but didn't call because she couldn't offer hers in return. Her attention to her own needs seemed selfish, but yet, there it was. The conflict buzzed in her head.

We must all feel this way from time to time, Nell rationalized. *It's part of normal life to want to run away from it once in a while. That's why God invented the vacation.*

Then she thought of Adam, who was probably on his way over. Adam made her feel as if he really cared what she thought and wasn't just waiting for her to finish talking so it would be his turn. With her family, Nell was the confessor but had to keep her worries to herself. It was in her job description.

With Adam, she felt as comfortable and easy as with her most trusted women friends. His presence nourished her spirit. It used to be that way with David, but they had fallen into a pattern of routine and habit that kept them partitioned off in separate areas of responsibility. They intersected at one or two daily meals, at the kids' most important life events, and when asleep. She realized that as time had flowed onward, their relationship had faded and been pushed to the back of a dusty closet. There was no time to be friends—it wasn't on the agenda.

Wind tossed the trees, and leaves flipped up to show their silvery undersides. The forecast said that night they were going to get rain from the remnants of the hurricane, which had blown itself out halfway up the coast. It was getting dark fast. She heard voices, a man's and a woman's, coming from the woods behind her. A moment later, Winston came running up to jump into her lap, and Jake Bascomb walked into the yard, followed by Bridget with Lulubelle tucked under her arm.

Bridget looked flushed, and Jake had put on a clean shirt. His thick white hair was neatly combed, and he had shaved.

Nell narrowed her eyes suspiciously.

Bridget spoke in her most charming tones. "I've invited one more for dinner, darlin'. I hope that's convenient." She looked at Nell, flashing her a quick mental message that demanded a positive response.

Nell opened her eyes wide and nodded obediently. "Sure, that's fine. Plenty of food," she stammered. Far be it for Nell to question a psychic order from her big sister.

She looked at Jake, standing behind Bridget as though she were his bodyguard. He met Nell's eyes without the usual sullen expression. In fact, he looked... friendly, that was it. Sort of hopeful and relieved. Nell decided to experiment by smiling at him.

He smiled back.

Very interesting. Bridget had apparently inspired Jake to clean up his act and behave, but Nell still didn't trust him.

The women went into the kitchen to pour wine, and they served crackers and cheese while Jake started a fire in the grill. He came inside, and they all sat down at the kitchen table.

Bridget nudged Jake. "Tell her. Go on."

"Tell me what?" Nell said.

"It's about the night his wife died, Nell," Bridget said. "That's what you've been trying to figure out, isn't it?"

"Don't tell me you already know something I don't. And you only just got here. Typical Bridget. You're such an overachiever." Nell turned to Jake. "How come you told her and you wouldn't tell me? All you ever do is growl at me."

"All you ever do is tell me what to do." Jake met her eyes, and the tension began to rise.

"If you weren't so grouchy all the time, I might trust you more."

"If you didn't tell me what to do, I wouldn't be so grouchy."

Bridget burst out laughing, but the other two didn't join in. They glowered at each other across the table.

Jake leaned toward Nell. She shifted and sat back in her chair, moving away from him.

"The fact is I adored your mother the first time I saw her. So did Ginnie. We thought she was the most sophisticated, beautiful person we ever met."

Nell and Bridget exchanged questioning glances, and Jake answered their look.

"Ellie was traveled, and educated, and she's older by almost ten years, you know. She always looked so damn good for her age, you'd barely guess it, but it showed in how she acted." Jake leaned on his crossed arms. "We all followed her lead, that's for sure."

Nell nodded, remembering how Mom always liked to be in charge of things.

"Ellie didn't want to hurt Virginia. Neither did I. So that was how we kept it. Nothing happened, and everything was fine." Jake paused as his voice faltered. "Until that night out on the lake," he said, tension in his face. He looked down at his hands.

Nell waited, skeptical about what would come next.

"My wife was what my mother called 'high strung.' Everyone around got sucked into the drama, whatever Virginia had stirred up on any particular day. That was the fun of high school —living dangerously, making a statement. Back before I found out what real fear was and took crazy off my Christmas list." He rolled his eyes, sat back, and put one hand on his hip, shifting in his chair. "I came home from 'Nam and should have known right then. But Ginnie said she'd changed, too, was ready to settle down now, wanted a family. We got married, and Adam showed up. Then we went to couples therapy. Then separate therapy for each of us. Then family therapy when Adam was a little kid. Ginnie was diagnosed as manic-depressive, bipolar II, which explains a lot. But it's damn hard to live with. Your mother helped a lot. She was so patient and generous."

Jake looked at Nell and Bridget. "She's a born healer, you know. She has magic in her hands—I've seen it. And heard it in her voice." He smiled, love in his eyes.

Nell's prejudices began to crumble. She had a flash of sympathy for the man and lowered her guard.

"At the time of the accident, Ginnie was delusional, on and off. She had a history of hormone troubles, only had one ovary left after uterine-cancer surgery, but it sure did kick up a lot of fuss. Keeping the one ovary was supposed to be good for her, but it was the opposite." He scratched his chin then laced his fingers together and put his hands on the table.

"We all had a few drinks that night. Ginnie had a few too many. She called your mother terrible names, accused her of trying to break us up. I guess that's why I was so distracted. And the tequila... it was my fault." There was a solemn look on his face. "I was the captain."

Nell felt a lump in her throat as she imagined how her mother must have reacted. Knowing she was partially responsible for Ginnie being upset in the first place. No wonder she was so quick to defend Jake to the police. "So Mom didn't lie. Ginnie's death was an accident. You tried to save her."

"I sure am sick of how everybody in this town still acts like something different happened." Jake sent Nell a sullen look.

Then there came a knock at the front door, and the dogs ran barking into the living room. Nell let Adam in and introduced Bridget, who gazed up at his tall form with approval. Father and son did not seem surprised to see each other. They pounded each other on the back, the macho hug. Nell knew the air had been cleared between her and Jake, though she guessed there was still more to discover.

The men grilled the meat and the women made the salad, tasks divided as they'd always been since cookouts were invented. A light rain had started to fall, but father and son stood under the overhang on the back porch and drank beer while they talked about politics and flipped the burgers. Bridget and Nell giggled at the sink while they washed lettuce and chopped carrots, and their mother's music filled the air with a woman's husky voice and a smooth saxophone. Nell kept expecting to look up and see Mom standing nearby, watching them.

Nell and Jake didn't fight, and Bridget didn't flirt with Adam enough to upset her sister. Adam watched Nell like a cat at a mouse hole. Jake looked at Bridget like a kid who had just opened his Christmas package and found the most wonderful, magical present in the world. At around nine o'clock, the phone rang. Nell answered it while they all listened.

"Mrs. Williams? It's the ICU at Hartland General calling. I'm so sorry..."

Mary Ellen Reilly had ended her struggle for life. Her spirit had moved on.

"Is there anything we should do?" Nell asked the nurse, her voice calm and rational while her heart pounded loud in her ears and tears began to roll down her cheeks. "Should we come over there? Are there papers to sign or something?"

"Why don't you give us a call in the morning? We're all so sorry. She was a lovely person." Then the woman said good-bye.

Nell turned to the others. They were all staring at her.

"It's awful." Her voice started to shake as she was flooded with guilt, and her throat contracted painfully. "While we were all here in her house having a good time, Mom died alone. We should have been there."

"No." Bridget stood up and went to her. "Because we gave her some privacy, she thought it was all right to stop hanging on for our sake. It was a good thing. She pushed us away, remember?"

Jake escaped into the garden and stood alone in the rain. Adam took the dishes over to the sink and began to wash them while Nell grabbed a clean towel and dried, tears rolling down her face. Bridget sat down at the kitchen table again, her face in her hands.

The jazz album ended, and the cottage was silent.

Lightning flickered, and a little while later, thunder rumbled with a rolling crash.

Adam and Nell worked smoothly, their movements efficient. They seemed to fit together like parts of a machine. Nell realized she was still crying. Mom's image was before her eyes, and her familiar scent seemed to fill the room. Adam cupped Nell's face in his hand and wiped her tears with the dishtowel. His eyes were solemn.

"Go for a walk?"

She nodded.

They grabbed slickers and took a big umbrella from the stand near the front door. He took Nell's hand and led her out into the night. It was dark under the clouds and the trees, and there were no streetlights along the lake road. Rain was coming down steadily now.

Lightning flickered again, closer this time, and the boom of thunder followed soon afterwards. Nell saw the lake illuminated briefly, its dull surface textured by lashings of raindrops. Blasts of wind tossed rain under the umbrella, immediately soaking Nell's hair. The water ran down her neck inside the jacket, but she didn't care. They walked along briskly, her arm tucked into his.

She'd been waiting for this to happen, expecting it. But now it seemed unreal.

Mom was dead.

She had no one to run to anymore when things fell apart. No one to call on the phone when something really great, or really awful, happened. No one to remember the things she had forgotten, like Grandma's middle name or how old she was when they first went to Disneyland. The matriarchy was Nell's responsibility now.

Time raced along so quickly. Nell's whole life had passed in a flash. Already, it was nearly over, especially with Mom and Daddy both gone.

I miss you. I miss you guys.

The sound of her pain caught in her throat. A wave of bleak desolation swept over her, and she wept. Striding along on the uneven ground, stumbling over rocks and through deep puddles, Nell clung to Adam's arm and sobbed as he pulled her along. Rain came down in thick, wet sheets, slapping her in the face to mingle with the tears, but they kept on going. The wind gusted and turned the umbrella inside out then ripped it out of their hands. They had reached the town beach. Adam led her down to the docks, where the big yacht was moored.

"Come in here," he yelled over the sound of the storm, jumping aboard and holding out a hand to help her onto the tossing deck. He opened the doors to the cabin, and they climbed down the stairs. He slammed the doors shut, and they were standing in a small, dark space. It was like a secret clubhouse. She could hear the sound of water dripping on the floor while the storm raged outside. Her heart was pounding, and blood pulsed in her cold cheeks and fingertips. She tried to slow down her ragged breath.

A match scraped, and Adam lit a candle lantern that hung from the ceiling. The little cabin was revealed, neat as a pin and fitted with wooden cabinets and two berths, a built-in table with two bench seats, and a tiny galley kitchen. He opened a cabinet and took out a towel.

"Get out of that wet jacket." Water streamed from his hair, chin, and eyebrows, but he offered her the towel first. Nell's heart melted, and she reached out to him. He folded her in his arms and sat her down, rocking.

They talked about Nell's mother for hours, lying together in a single berth with their arms entangled. They remembered things she'd said and done, and the warmth of her eyes filled with love. They remembered how she had called them both "sweet pea" and how she'd kissed them on the back of the neck after tucking in their shirts.

"But wait," Nell said drowsily, her eyes still leaking tears but calmer at that point. "How old were you then?"

"Oh, ten or twelve, I guess. All gangly arms and legs—no butt. My pants were always falling down."

"You must have been in your early twenties when Mom bought the cottage. The oldest photos in the album I found in the den were dated 1991."

"Oh, I knew Ellie way before then. She came to visit when I was a kid, maybe even still a baby. I don't remember exactly. Seems like she was always part of my life."

Nell frowned in confusion, but her head ached, and her heart was sore, so she let it go.

When they got back to Mary's cottage later, the rain had stopped, and the moon was coming out from behind the clouds. It shone down on the raindrops sprinkled like millions of fallen stars in the wet grass under their feet.

Nell kissed Adam on the cheek and watched him drive away. Then she wept again for Mary, and for Thomas, and for Ginnie too. But mostly, Nell cried for herself.

CHAPTER 31

Mary ~ January 31, 1968

MARY'S WARD WAS QUIET THAT night. The GI who had lost both his legs to mortar fire had stopped crying in his sleep. The three infantrymen who'd come in together the previous week after walking into a trip wire attached to a grenade were still playing cards, but they were keeping their voices down. She didn't mind night shift when it was nice and slow like this. Her stomach had been bothering her that day, so it was good they weren't swamped with new patients. The pace wasn't likely to pick up since the next day was Tet, the Vietnamese New Year, and there was an informal ceasefire agreement in effect. Saigon would be in full celebration mode with decorations and costumes and fireworks in the street.

"Nurse?" A sweet kid from Iowa called to her. He said he was eighteen but looked about twelve.

She walked over and stood next to his bed. "Private? Some water?" He nodded. She held the cup to his mouth. Both his hands were covered with gauze where the skin had been burned off by Napalm when he'd rescued a little girl caught in the crossfire.

"Thanks, Lieutenant." He smiled up at her. "How long before I can have more meds?"

She checked his chart. "You were due when you were sleeping, so I'll get them now if you like."

"I like, ma'am."

Mary smiled. "Be right back, then."

She walked down the row of beds toward the nurses' station, near where the card game was in progress. Using her key to open the drug cabinet, she spoke to the players.

"After midnight, boys. The casino is closing. Time to cash in your chips."

"Casinos never close, Lieutenant. I should know. I'm from Vegas."

"No kidding? Did you ever play one of those machines where you pull the handle and money comes out?" Mary counted out two pain pills into a paper cup, helped herself to an antacid, signed them out, and locked the cabinet again.

"You mean the one-armed bandit?" One of the white-gowned soldiers glanced at his buddy, whose arm had been amputated from the elbow down. Mary cringed, but all three of them burst out laughing, and the amputee chuckled loudest. He was heading home and would be discharged with a bronze star while the other two would be sent back into the war when their wounds had healed. After all she had seen and heard, Mary wasn't sure which was worse.

She delivered the pain meds and helped her patient swallow them with another sip of water then straightened his clean white sheets and stroked his forehead with a cool hand.

"Back to sleep, baby," she said softly. "It's the best medicine."

He gazed at her with a trusting expression and closed his eyes. His rosy cheeks and golden curls looked angelic. He didn't even have much of a beard yet. Earlier, she had helped read his mail from home since he couldn't hold it himself. There was a letter from his mother about getting a heifer he had raised ready to enter a competition at the state fair. Mary had wiped his tears for him when she finished reading it aloud.

That's what I'm here for.

The look on that boy's face had been her reward. It was hard not to get too close. After they left her care, many of these soldiers would go back to the war and be killed or injured again. She couldn't think about that and still be able to do her job. She needed to stay focused on the here and now.

Mary helped the card-playing GIs back into their beds, turning off the lights clamped to their headboards. Everyone had settled down. Sitting at the desk, she turned on the electric kettle to make a cup of tea and flipped through *Glamour* magazine. At two in the morning, she got up to monitor vital signs, taking her blood-pressure cuff out of the desk drawer. Glancing out the window as she bent over the first soldier, she saw some strange flashes of light in the eastern sky.

"Looks like the celebration is starting early. Fireworks." Mary smiled at the soldier, who was quietly watching her pump the cuff. She looked at the dial, then the air slowly hissed out and the cuff relaxed.

More flashes caught her eye, and she turned her head to watch. She noticed glowing red-and-green lines in the sky. The distant sound of an explosion broke the quiet, then another.

"What's that?" Mary wondered aloud, and the soldier sat up to see what she was watching.

He clutched her arm with excitement. "That's mortar fire, Lieutenant. Something's going on. Those are tracers, not fireworks."

"It's the air base." Mary guessed what might be happening. "Could they be under attack?"

More explosions sounded, a thudding sound in the sleepy silence, and the water in the glass on the bedside table rippled. The eastern sky was full of tracers.

"Shit." The card player from Las Vegas shuffled over to the window to look outside. "That's Tan Son Nhut, where Westmoreland is headquartered. This is no ceasefire… it's a trick. How the hell did they sneak into Saigon?"

The other soldiers were all awake at that point, and those who could walk gathered at the windows. Mary went to the telephone and dialed the hospital headquarters. The line was busy. She ran out into the corridor, where people were rushing around with supplies and clean linens, getting ready for incoming wounded. Mary spotted the shift supervisor, Captain Clark, a stout, black-haired woman who had served in Korea too and always seemed calm.

"Sullivan," the captain snapped, her eyes wide with alarm. "Get those men away from the windows. It's not safe."

"Yes, ma'am." Mary hadn't thought of it, but of course if there were Viet Cong or North Vietnamese Army troops in the city, fighting could break out anywhere. Her heart raced and stomach clenched, just as they did whenever she heard ambulances driving into the compound. For the first time in her life, Mary felt the cold fear of real danger.

She ran back into her ward and urged the men to return to their beds, but only a few cooperated. Then they all heard an enormous boom and saw a flash in the southeast part of the city, much closer to them. The entire building shook, and everyone went silent for a moment.

"What's over there?" A soldier with his head wrapped in bandages pointed.

"Government buildings, I think," another said.

"Any of them ours?" the soldier from Las Vegas wanted to know.

"The US Embassy. It's in that direction." Mary put her hand on his shoulder as they both stared out the window. They could hear gunfire from the direction of the explosion, and a steady hammering of mortar rounds.

"Holy shit. They're blowing up the fucking embassy."

"What should we do?"

"Nurse, what's the emergency protocol?"

"Where's the weapons and ammo, Lieutenant?"

The voices all sounded at once, a garbled chorus. The men were looking at her expectantly. Mary was the only officer in the room, and she had no idea what to do. There hadn't been an enemy attack inside the city since she'd arrived—or ever, as far as she knew. There was no hospital protocol for this situation.

An army colonel carrying an M16 rifle rushed in from the corridor.

"Any walking wounded in here who can help with security?"

"Yes, sir." The soldier from Las Vegas spoke up along with two others. They saluted, their white hospital gowns riding up when they raised their arms.

He looked them over and shrugged. "Let's get down to the basement. Find you some real clothes and some weapons. We don't have much ammo, but it's better than nothing. They're making Molotov cocktails down in the surgery area—we'll have those too."

The rocket fire at the air base had swelled, and they could hear planes taking off. Mary ran to the window to look up and saw them pass directly overhead, going north. She could hear rifle fire in the distance, and the ground shook constantly. Those B-52s were taking off under fire, which had to be terribly dangerous. She wondered where they were going. There had to be fighting somewhere else as well. That meant casualties would be coming soon from upcountry too. How would they get them in here without the planes being shot down?

Mary wiped her sweaty palms on her skirt. Her stomach growled and burned. "Colonel, what was that big explosion a minute ago?"

"They fired a rocket through the perimeter wall of the US Embassy." His eyes flashed with anger. "VC sappers are shooting into the building through the windows. Radio chatter says the MPs and marines inside are returning fire. We need to get ready for anything. Follow me, men."

He strode out of the room, his volunteers limping behind him.

"Ma'am, don't you have a security force here at the hospital?" The boy from Iowa sounded scared.

"Not really." Mary's voice was high and shaky. "There are two MPs who guard the gate and patrol the grounds, but we've never had this kind of trouble before. It's always been safe here in Saigon."

"Not anymore," the boy said, his eyes solemn.

Later that morning, Mary heard the news that US forces at the embassy had killed nineteen members of the elite Viet Cong C-10 Sapper Battalion. Five Americans were also dead, but the embassy had been saved. The battle at the air base raged on. Apparently, many other strategic sites in South Vietnam were also under attack by a huge, well-organized army. Wounded soldiers started to arrive at the hospital soon after the fighting began. Thousands more were expected, and the hospital was preparing for their arrival.

At first light, Captain Clark sent Mary down to the courtyard to set up an additional triage area. Ambulances were coming in from the air base, where brave medevac pilots were flying in and out under heavy fire while US troops defended them. Since the hospital complex was in the city and didn't have the space for helicopters to land, there was no other way for wounded to get there by air. As Mary and the other nurses hustled to prepare for more wounded, she thought again of the men she loved, and she prayed for their safety.

Six months had passed since the telegram about Thomas arrived, and Mary was still wearing her engagement ring but didn't feel there was any real hope he was still alive. His remains were probably at the bottom of the ocean. It all seemed like a nightmare.

But Jake helped to push the horror out of her mind. They had been seeing each other secretly for a while after he found out about a room down the street from the hospital where one of the Vietnamese orderlies lived.

When Tuan was working, he was only too glad to rent the place to US soldiers who wanted some privacy.

With Jake's strong arms holding her, the images of multiple amputees and massive trauma cases dissolved. When they lay together on the narrow pallet, life seemed almost normal, and home didn't feel so far away.

"Tell me more about your town," Mary had said just the day before the Tet attacks. Her fingers were threaded through the curly hairs on his chest while her head rested on his broad shoulder.

Jake's chest vibrated when he spoke, a deep rumble. "It's a little place called Hartland, deep in the Green Mountains. The kind of place where people don't lock their doors, everybody knows your name, and neighbors pitch in to help without being asked. Sunset on the lake is a sight to behold, the most beautiful colors I've ever seen. You'd love it there, sweet thing."

Mary dozed, wrapped in his warmth and the peace of that moment. "Tell more about the trees on the town green," she murmured sleepily. "Did you climb them when you were a boy?"

"Every kid in town climbed those maples, with or without their parents' permission. All the way to the top. It's a rite of passage." Jake ran his finger along the curve of her shoulder, sending shivers through her body. "I used to sneak out at night to meet my buddies there and show off for the girls."

"Didn't the girls climb trees too?" She raised her head to look at his face and saw him watching her with softness in his eyes.

"A few of them did." He grinned. "The ones who didn't mind the guys looking up their skirts."

"I would have worn jeans," Mary said, laying her head back down. "You don't get your legs all scratched up."

"You probably would have beat me to the top, sweet thing. You are one determined woman."

Mary sniffed. "You better believe it. When I was a kid, my sister and I used to climb all the way to the tippety-top of the old pine tree in our yard. Pine bark cuts like crazy, and we'd get covered with sticky black sap, but we could see the whole town from up there. When the wind blew, the tree swayed. I loved it."

He leaned over and kissed her gently on the mouth, pulling her close. The spark between them flared again, and he turned to cover her with his lean, muscular body, deepening the kiss. She took his tongue into her mouth and tasted his intoxicating flavor, breathing in the warm, spicy aroma that radiated from his skin. He groaned. She felt him harden and press against her thigh. Her legs slipped open, and she took him inside, welcoming the total focus on the here and now that sex with Jake brought her. Eyes locked together, energy flowing on the deepest level of communication. She felt their minds connect. They rocked together in the hot little room, sunlight slanting in through a shuttered window to fall in bright stripes through the air, bodies slick with sweat as they slid against one another and she arched toward him, absorbed by him, until a brilliant flash and a deep shudder flew her away to another world where nobody was bleeding and the only color surrounding them was the marbled green of a cool Vermont forest.

"Tell me," she whispered in his ear when they lay next to each other again. "Tell me about the lake."

They didn't speak of love, but she felt it surrounding them. For the time being, this wonderful intimacy was enough. The seven-year difference in their ages didn't seem important anymore. They were equal when working side by side to save a wounded soldier's life. The losses were huge, appalling. One man died out of every three they tried to save, and it would be easy to feel their mission was hopeless. For Mary, the affair had become a way to assert that she was still alive while so many around her were dying.

Jake was off duty, catching up on sleep, when the Tet attack began and the call went out. Mary knew he'd end up driving one of the ambulances back and forth from the air base, which would put him in grave danger.

She set up the clipboards and waited by the back door. Several other nurses were supposed to join her. The medics had been told to bypass the front of the hospital and drive around back to unload the wounded. One very large truck pulled up, a two-and-a-half-ton vehicle. The driver who got out wasn't a medic but an MP officer. Two others jumped out to help him.

Mary walked over to talk to them. "Lieutenant? How many wounded on board? Do you need help?" Nurses and medical corpsmen were coming out of the back door, ready to deal with the wounded about to arrive.

The officer turned toward her. His expression was grim, his face was pale and dirty, and there were rips in his flak jacket. He had obviously been in the fighting.

"Thanks, but we can handle it, Lieutenant Sullivan. I doubt your people would want to waste their time with this lot, anyhow."

Mary frowned, wondering why he would speak that way.

His men opened the back of the truck, and Mary recoiled at the sight, nearly overcome with nausea. All the bodies from the morning's massacre at the embassy were piled inside. The MPs began to carry the dead into the grassy courtyard and lay them out in rows. While they were working, the first ambulance rounded the corner and parked on the edge of the grass, then the next, and a third.

Jake was driving the third. He looked over and flashed Mary the brightest smile she had seen all day. She smiled back, caught on his eyes like a fish on a hook. He winked, and suddenly she felt fine and strong again.

They worked into the night, and still, the wounded kept coming. There were patients in every available space, lying on cots that lined the hallways and outside on the covered porches. The nurses worked twenty-four-hour shifts. It was a nightmare, but nobody had time to be terrified.

Mary glimpsed Jake every hour or so when he pulled up and unloaded. By sundown, most of the grass in the little courtyard had been churned to mud, and everyone was covered with it. Around sundown, he finally parked at her station, and they had a chance to talk for a minute. The corpsmen and male nurses had carried all the loaded stretchers inside, and Jake was about to jump inside his truck for another trip to the air base.

"What's it like over there, Sergeant?" Mary approached, careful to keep her voice impersonal. She knew her heart showed in her eyes and he'd see how she felt.

He smiled at her, and she saw his feelings written on his face as well. "Like shootin' fish in a barrel… except I'm the fish. Our guys are doing a great job. They're pulling the flak off us pretty good when we stop to load up."

"Glad to hear it." She wanted to kiss him or at least to touch him. "You take care, soldier." She smiled and reached out and patted his shoulder, a neutral supportive gesture. The warmth of his arm through the fabric made her chest ache with emotion.

He seemed to know what she meant and saluted, then tipped his combat helmet with a twinkle in his eye. "You take care too, ma'am. Be seeing you soon."

Mary watched him drive away as she blinked away tears, but then the next truck pulled up in front of her, and there wasn't time to worry.

Later in the evening, Mary realized she hadn't seen Jake in a while or the corpsman who had worked by his side that day. "Is everyone getting through the line okay?" she asked the next driver who pulled into her station.

"There's one truck down, flipped over by a mortar round. No wounded were inside yet, thank God."

"Everyone okay? Your guys?"

"They both got beat up pretty bad, I heard. Somebody brought them in here a while ago. The driver got his leg broke and caught a bullet. Bascomb, I think his name is."

Her stomach twisted, and black spots swam in front of her as all the blood seemed to drain out of her body. Mary's knees buckled, and she sank toward the ground.

"You okay, ma'am?" The ambulance driver pulled her up by the elbow, and she steadied on her feet.

She took a deep breath and straightened. "I'm fine. Thank you, Sergeant. It's been… a hell of a day." She wiped the sweat off her forehead with the back of her hand. Silently, she started to pray.

"Hell of a day, ma'am." He nodded and turned back to his work.

Mary robotically straightened her white cap to greet the next wounded soldier. It took every ounce of discipline she possessed not to turn and run inside to find Jake.

She got off duty at around nine o'clock that night after working since the day before with only a few breaks to eat, hydrate, and go to the bathroom. The rush of wounded showed no sign of abating. Soon, they would have to move some of the stabilized patients out, perhaps send them away from the war zone to recover. Her white uniform was dappled with layers of bloodstains, and she desperately needed a shower.

When Mary went to find Jake, she discovered he was in surgery. He had a compound fracture of the right leg and a gunshot wound in his left arm. They had set his leg and were working on the arm. It looked as if he would probably stay alive unless an infection set in, and Mary sent up a prayer of thanks.

She went back to her quarters to shower and change into fatigues. The nurses had abandoned their whites, which were impractical under the best circumstances and impossible during a catastrophe like this. They had been commanded to wear their helmets when outdoors, something never considered necessary before that moment in Saigon.

Mary tried to think of what to bring Jake. A magazine? Flowers? She grabbed a paperback copy of the latest James Bond book off the table in the lounge, slapped her helmet on her head, and trotted down the dark road toward the building where the surgeons had been operating on Jake.

While she jogged, Mary thought about what might happen next. Most likely, Jake would be sent home, with two serious injuries and a bad break in his leg that could stop him from driving a vehicle for a long time.

What will I do here without him? It was a selfish thought. She tried to wipe it from her mind.

At least her tour of duty would be over in a few months. Mary had been playing with the idea of re-enlisting, but after the past day's events, it didn't seem like the right step. She wasn't cut out to be an army nurse. Working in the emergency room in Boston would be like a luxury vacation compared to triage in the mud.

She wondered where Jake would go after he recovered in an army hospital stateside. He had spoken so fondly of the little town in Vermont where he grew up. It sounded beautiful. A lovely place to raise kids, grow old, and die.

Mary reached the hospital and went inside to find the man she was picturing by her side as they lived happily ever after in a place called Hartland. A week later, just after she and Jake had kissed good-bye and she'd watched medics carry him onto a plane to start the long journey home, Mary received word that Thomas Reilly was alive.

CHAPTER 32

Nell ~ 2014

NELL AND BRIDGET'S MOTHER WAS buried next to their dad in the family's hometown of Amherst, Massachusetts. When they all walked out of the cool stone church after the service, the brightness outside was dazzling. Nell heard people say that the heavenly gates had opened to let Mom in, and a flash of God's light was shining through.

Many of the Reillys' old friends attended the funeral, families who had been there when Nell and Bridget were growing up. In the graveyard, an army honor guard shot off a three-gun rifle salute, folded the American flag that had covered Mom's coffin, and presented it to Nell and Bridget while the bugler played taps. Nell cried all the way through it, holding tightly onto her sister's hand.

The sisters stood by their mother's grave, wearing the black linen A-line dresses that Mom had made for them when Grandma died. Nell wore her dress plain with a simple strand of pearls while Bridget had jazzed hers up with a Hermes silk scarf, fastened at the shoulder with a gold pin. Wearing clothes that Mom had sewed for them so lovingly was their salute to her. Ben had pointed out that his grandmother's DNA was probably embedded in every fiber. Nell felt the dress embracing her like a ghostly hug, and Mom seemed present among the family as they gathered to say good-bye.

Nell had finally told David about her mother's cottage, which she and Bridget had inherited. As she'd expected, he was excited to come up and see the place. The kids wanted to swim in the lake and go fishing.

Bridget was planning to stay on in Vermont until her divorce was settled, maybe even longer. The peace and quiet were addictive, she said.

Nell promised to let her enjoy the solitude for as long as possible, so for the moment, the cottage was still the sisters' private space.

David looked handsome and dignified, greeting their old friends and neighbors with a firm handshake as they filed by to express their condolences. Ben stood next to him, and when she saw them side by side, Nell realized he was nearly as tall as his father. She still had to help make sure his tie went with his shirt and his socks matched, but despite Ben's color blindness, he was growing up fast and finding ways to compensate on his own. She glanced at his feet and noticed that he had chosen one navy and one brown sock. With his dark-blue suit, he was half-right. *Close enough.* She knew he would be off on his own soon. He would learn to get along without her just as she would somehow learn to survive without her mother.

This chain of connections and separations is how our lives pass. It was a continuum, with rich memories in the past, a tiny blip to indicate the fleeting present, and vast misty expectations in the future. Nell wanted to learn to be more in the present—to stop and smell the maple trees, to feel love for her mother without the intrusion of selfish grief, and to celebrate Mom's life as the amazing thing of beauty it was.

"What a wonderful friend she was, my dear. What a sweet and gracious lady," said one of her mother's friends, in her eighties and on the arm of a grandson when she stepped up to shake Nell's hand. Nell nodded and smiled, but an empty place echoed in her heart. Her eyes blurred, and when she blinked, Jake and Adam were standing next in line.

Father and son both wore dark suits and perfectly shined black dress shoes with white shirts and black ties. Jake had hidden his eyes behind sunglasses and carried a bouquet of purple lupines that looked like the ones that grew in the garden of Mom's cottage. He dropped it gently onto the mound of flowers at the gravesite and then turned to shake David's hand.

"Jake Bascomb. A friend from Vermont." He looked stiff and solemn. Nell wondered if he had been drinking yet. At least she couldn't smell it, and Adam was probably driving. Hopefully, there wouldn't be a scene at the gathering after the funeral. The less their friends and neighbors knew about Mom's connections in Vermont, the better.

"Thank you for coming, Jake. It's good to meet you." David passed him on to Ben, who gave his hand a manly shake.

Adam stepped up and stood in front of David. Nell watched the two men meet eyes as they shook hands.

"Sorry for your loss. We'll miss her too." Adam's expression was guarded. He glanced at Nell, who was staring, fascinated.

It shocked her to see them standing there together, both tall, even featured, and clean shaven. In a way, they might be brothers. Except for the color of their eyes and David's slightly darker hair, they looked quite similar. Cut from the same piece of cloth, Mom would have said. But such different personalities. Not really alike at all.

"David Williams," Nell's husband said, looking at the other man curiously. "And you are…?"

"Adam Bascomb. One of the Vermont neighbors." Adam's eyes squinted as they slowly shook hands, a man-to-man gesture like two bucks sizing each other up.

David nodded, satisfied. "Glad you could come. We appreciate it."

Then the next mourner stepped up, and the line moved along. Nell could practically feel Adam's eyes staring at her as he moved down the reception line. He stepped in front of Ben and shook his hand with a polite nod. Both of them started to talk at the same time, then they laughed and introduced themselves. Next, Adam stood in front of Nell. He looked at her face, which was covered in tears, and frowned, holding her hand in both of his for a moment. She felt a blush rising to her cheeks.

"We miss her so much," he said quietly. His palms were hot and sweaty.

"Me too." Nell felt her lip tremble and tried not to tear up again.

He lowered his eyes and began to say something else but seemed to change his mind. He released her hand with a final squeeze and stepped past, speaking quietly to Bridget and Jake.

The Bascombs moved along to blend in with the crowd, and eventually, all the mourners went back to their cars and left for the reception being held at an old friend's home.

"We'll be along," Nell told David. "I'll ride with Bridget. Meet you there."

The two sisters strolled back to the parking lot, arm in arm.

"What now, Nell?" Bridget gave her arm a comforting squeeze.

Nell sighed, resigned to her future. "Back home to New Jersey, I guess."

"You… guess?"

"I have responsibilities, Bridget. I love my family. I need to go home and be a mom."

Bridget stopped and turned to face her. "But have you told David?"

"About what? There's nothing to tell. I told you, nothing happened with Adam that night." Nell looked her sister right in the eye so Bridget would see it was the truth. "We just talked. I was upset, and so was he. We're friends, that's all. Having an affair is not the kind of thing I do."

Bridget looked at Nell doubtfully but let it go.

Nell took Bridget's arm again. "Need some company for the ride back north? I could stay for a few days."

"Well… I already have some company." Bridget hooked her arm through Nell's as they walked toward the parking lot. "Jake just offered to drive me back to Hartland. I'm going to stay at Mom's place for a while. I can use her car."

"Did you tell Jake about the baby?"

"Darlin', I'm telling everybody about the baby nowadays," Bridget said, laughing. "What's the point in keeping that tired old secret anymore? He offered to help me look for her. I'd like nothing more than to find the girl, say I'm her momma, and invite her to Christmas dinner for the next fifty years."

Nell nodded. "From your lips to God's ear." She used one of their mother's favorite sayings.

Nell and Bridget drove away from the cemetery and left their parents behind, resting side by side under an oak tree. For the moment, the Reilly family would carry on in two separate worlds. The complete story of Mom's secret life was still a mystery, and Nell wondered whether she would ever learn the details. It drove her wild with curiosity to think about her mother planning and preparing for a dramatic life change then giving it all up for a part-time compromise.

Nell had thought about it again and again, especially in recent days when she was worrying about her own life. Her parents had seemed so comfortable together. They had held hands walking down the sidewalk, laughed at each other's jokes, kissed hello and good-bye, shared a bed, and went out for dinner on "date night" every Friday, just the two of them. As far as Nell knew, that had been their tradition right up until the time when Thomas became so disoriented it was hard for him to leave the house.

Why had she done it? What had happened between them?

CHAPTER 33

Bridget ~ 2014

A FEW WEEKS LATER, BRIDGET AND Jake put their bags in the back of Mom's white Ford and headed southwest into the Berkshires. He drove while she navigated, and she recognized various landmarks though it had been many years since she'd traveled that road. The smooth highway cut slow curves through the foothills, which gradually grew in stature to become graceful wooded mountains. As they neared the town of Stockbridge, Massachusetts, billboards advertising Jacob's Pillow and Tanglewood reminded them that the summer concert season was in full swing.

Soon after Mary's death, Nell and Bridget had gone through the contents of her safe deposit box at the bank. The only surprising thing they found there was a copy of Bridget's daughter's birth certificate, carefully preserved in a heavyweight brown envelope. It said the baby's name was Elizabeth Mary Reilly, and the father was listed as Coleman Montague Longworth. Bridget didn't remember ever having seen it before, but now the document was safely tucked inside her purse.

As they drove toward the place where it all started, she remembered everything as clearly as if it had just happened. Bridget came to the Berkshires with a high-school friend to work as a waitress at one of the big family resorts, where she met the boy who swept her off her feet and got her pregnant at age seventeen.

"His name was Coleman Montague Longworth the third, actually. His family called him Trey. From the French word for *three*." Bridget slid her eyes sideways with an expectant grin.

"No kidding?" Jake raised his eyebrows and whistled.

He had promised not to drink on the trip and to be on his best behavior. When Jake was sober, he was good company. But even his dark side didn't scare her—it felt familiar. They were both trying to rebound from the mistakes of the past, and it pulled them together. She could tell Jake missed Mom too, something else they had in common. Since Bridget had been living in the cottage alone, he and Adam had become her family in Vermont.

"Hush. It was his real name, poor thing. We called him Cole," Bridget said. "At first, I refused to tell anyone who the father was. Then I caved in and told my mother. It still makes my stomach hurt to think about that conversation."

"I'll bet. Ellie was a lot more conservative than people thought." Jake gave her a reassuring smile. "She never told us anything about this at all, you know. Your mother knew how to keep a secret."

Bridget remembered the soft look of sadness on Mom's face when she heard about the baby. That dark, enfolding gaze carried a message of inclusion, not criticism, as though all the women through the generations of the world were looking at Bridget in that moment with shared sorrow. The sorrow of impending loss.

She would forever be grateful for her mother's unwavering support, but it gave her a sense of guilt too. The stress of the situation must have added to the reasons why Mom wanted to get away from her life. The pregnancy was one more thing for her to worry about.

"I'm not surprised," Bridget said. "Nobody knew except the family. It was too shameful. There weren't a lot of choices in those days." She looked down at her hands, clasped together in her lap. "Mom wrote to Cole's parents, but they made it clear that marriage was not an option. When I decided to give the baby up for adoption, I thought it would close the door on that phase of my life and the whole disaster would just... go away."

"Weren't you pregnant all through your senior year in high school? That must have been rough." Jake reached over and gave her hands a squeeze.

"I had some extra credits, so I was able to graduate a semester early. At Christmas, I was four and a half months pregnant, but it didn't show much yet. Didn't tell anyone, not even my best friends. Then I went away and told everyone I was backpacking around Europe."

Bridget stared into the tree trunks that slid past as she looked out the passenger window, remembering. Their priest had recommended a facility, and Mom had helped her pack and move after the holidays. The drive west had been silent that snowy day. Stark black-and-white mountains loomed over them as their little car slid and slipped between the frigid slopes. She remembered it being like a voyage into a frozen hell with a white-out flurry blinding them as they fumbled into the driveway of the old estate that had been converted into a Catholic Charities home for unwed mothers.

She had signed herself in and lived there until the baby came in the spring. Bridget was allowed to hold her daughter for a few minutes in the delivery room at the local hospital. She took the little pink-faced flannel bundle that the nurse handed to her and looked into the infant's unfocused dark-blue eyes. They had put a pink stocking cap on the baby's head to keep her warm, but Bridget pulled it off. The little girl had a light fuzz of golden hair, the same color as hers. She cooed up at her mother, tiny pink lips turned up in an expressive curl. Then just before Bridget's heart began to break, the nurse took the baby away to the nursery.

She never saw her daughter again. It was better that way. Everyone said so.

The nurses showed her how to bind her breasts to help the milk production stop, and her resilient young body snapped back to its original shape in a month or so.

Life went on. *Really, life goes on*, Bridget had told herself.

Every so often, in those days, Bridget would wake up with mysterious tears on her cheeks and the vague memory of a small pink face in her dreams. That was rare, however, and it really was not until years later, when she was in her thirties and seriously trying to have a child with her second husband, that she began to be haunted by questions about her daughter. Where was she, and what did she look like? Was she smart, funny, artistic? What was her name? What were her adoptive parents like?

"Many years later," Bridget said quietly, "I found out I would probably never have any more children. It was the punishment I earned for giving her up."

"You were young. We all do stupid things when we're young. Some of us even keep on doing them when we're old." Jake looked at her sideways. "You're here now, kid. You stuck with it, and you're still trying. That counts for a lot."

Bridget had a plan for when they arrived at the hospital. She hoped to find out who had worked in the maternity ward at the time her child was born and try to track them down. *Somebody might remember something useful.* It was worth a try.

Jake pulled up to the Berkshire Medical Center and parked in the lot. He looked across at Bridget, who was hiding behind big sunglasses and felt a little sick to her stomach.

"You want some company, or shall I wait here?" he asked.

He was so kind to come all that way with her. He looked good, neatly dressed in slacks, a sport coat, and a clean white golf shirt. In general, his appearance and mood had taken an upturn lately. He'd mentioned going to AA meetings a few times since Mom died, and Bridget was encouraging him. His expression was calm and full of admiration when he looked at her. Spending time with a man who didn't want anything from her except honesty and friendship was a balm to her frazzled soul.

"You're wicked brave to dig up the past this way," Jake said. "It's honest to God one of the scariest things I ever heard of. You're my hero."

"And you're mine, kind sir. Convenient, isn't it?" Bridget took her sunglasses off and hugged Jake around the neck.

For the first time in many years, Bridget was thinking about staying single for a while—just being herself instead of some man's vision of the perfect mate. If she even knew what *herself* meant anymore. She hadn't been her true original self since high school. Most of her adult life had been spent transforming in order to impress some man, starting with Daddy, to whom she had been such a big disappointment.

Her father was taken by disease and death before they had a chance to forgive each other. Jake might be able to help Bridget forgive herself and Thomas both. He was filling a hole in her life at just the right time.

"I think I need to do this alone," she said, and he nodded.

Checking her purse one last time to make sure the birth certificate was still in there, she got out of the car and walked to the main entrance. After asking at the information desk, she followed directions to the human-resources office. It was lunchtime, and only one employee was sitting at her desk. The petite brunette was about Bridget's age, in her mid-forties, and looked up with a friendly smile when she entered the room.

"Hi." Bridget's voice quavered. "I'm… not sure if this is the right place."

The woman got up and came over to the counter. "Let's find out. What are you looking for? A job application?"

"No, actually, I wanted to ask about the people who worked here... around this date." Bridget inched the birth certificate forward.

The woman glanced down and saw what it was. Her expression subtly changed. "Are you looking for someone in particular?" Her voice was lower, confidential.

"Well," Bridget said, "pretty much anyone who might remember the birth of my daughter."

"Is there something wrong? A health issue?"

"Oh no, I don't think so, anyhow. It's not about that."

"Then... why are you asking?"

The two women looked at each other across the divider, and Bridget tried not to appear nervous. She relaxed her face and smiled in her most charming manner.

"I want to locate her and offer to meet. Even if she wants to see me now, we can't connect. I was hoping somebody might remember something that would help." Bridget reached out her hand in an unconscious imploring gesture. "I was... just seventeen."

The woman's eyes were sympathetic. "Unfortunately, I'm not allowed to give out information from the files without permission from my supervisor. She's not here right now. But... I can tell you what I happen to know, I suppose."

Bridget raised her head, alert.

The woman continued. "You see, my mother is a nurse, retired now. She worked here then, in the eighties."

"She did? In what department?" Bridget asked eagerly.

"In neonatal, actually. She took care of the newborns."

Bridget's heart leapt with hope. "Do you think she would talk to me?" She was breathless.

"These days, she's so bored she'll talk to anybody who comes to the door," the woman said, laughing. "The Fed Ex man, the newspaper boy, the exterminator—you name it."

Bridget laughed along with her. "You see, the records of my baby's adoption were lost," she started to explain.

"In the fire at Catholic Charities? Yes, you're not the first person to tell us that. A lot of adopted people are looking for their birth parents these days. Wanting to establish a genetic history to screen for potential diseases."

"Oh. I hadn't thought of that." Bridget realized that her daughter might be open to the idea of establishing contact for that reason if not for emotional ones. "So she may have been looking for me too."

The woman nodded. "And she would have run into the same roadblock."

"Could I speak to your mother today, do you think?" Bridget pulled out a pen and a little notepad from her purse. "What's her name and address? Can I have the phone number too?"

The woman wrote the information down. Bridget's pulse racing with excitement, she stumbled over her thanks and hurried back to the car. When she got back to the Jeep, she found Jake with the windows all rolled down and the driver's seat tipped back, dozing in the sun.

"Wake up," she cried happily. "We've got a hot lead."

Jake opened one eye. "Where to, fearless leader?"

She smiled at him with a determination she had never felt before. "325 Hawthorne Street, to see a woman who used to work in the nursery here."

"Aha. Sounds promising."

While he typed the address into the GPS, she dialed her cell phone. After a short conversation, she nodded to Jake. "Okay, she's home and willing to see me. Let's go."

Bridget wished she were driving so she could step down harder on the accelerator. She tried to be patient as Jake carefully pulled out of the parking lot. This was not the time to let her emotions take control. She was on her way to have the most important conversation of her life so far.

A woman in her late sixties answered the door of the little white house with green shutters. "Just call me Sandy," she said, laughing, when Bridget stumbled over her last name. She offered iced tea, and they sat in a pair of rocking chairs on the screened front porch.

Sandy remembered Bridget's baby very well and for good reason. "Believe me, it wasn't every day that a child to be adopted was picked up by a chauffeur-driven limousine with a private duty nurse and a gorgeous woman, like a model or a princess, dressed all in white silk. Not to mention a tennis bracelet of diamonds the size of chickpeas."

Bridget instantly knew the woman Sandy was describing had to be Cole's mother, Evelyn Longworth. Bridget had seen that bracelet many times when waiting on their table at dinner. It was hard to miss.

"Sweetest little golden-haired, blue-eyed girl I ever saw." Sandy patted Bridget's hand. "I always felt bad about taking her away from you."

"We thought it was the best thing at the time." Bridget felt her voice catch.

"Well, at least you know she went to a rich home where she'd be well taken care of."

"Yes, I'm sure she did. Her grandmother would see to that."

"That was her grandmother, then?" Sandy rocked and sipped her tea.

"Yes, I'm pretty sure." Bridget took a big swallow, trying to wash down her anger.

Sandy's worried look split into a wide smile. "Well, then, see? It all worked out fine after all. Funny how that happens sometimes."

Bridget's anger toward Cole and his family simmered over the next few days, expanding as it grew hotter. How dare they take the baby and not tell her? How dare they let her think, all those years, that the child had gone to strangers and been lost forever?

Bridget decided on the direct approach: she called Cole on the telephone. It wasn't hard to find him in the national white pages on the Internet. He was the only Coleman Montague Longworth listed, so his father must have died. Cole was now an attorney in West Palm Beach. She called his office number, having no desire to embarrass him at home.

When she gave her name to the secretary, she added, "An old friend from Stockbridge."

He picked right up.

"Bridget?" His voice was a little lower but still recognizable. "Is it really you?"

"Yes, it really is." She tried to keep her tone even and light.

"I have thought of you so many times over the years," he said enthusiastically, the way one might speak to an old friend. "How have you been?"

"I'm well, Cole. How are you doing, and your family?" She kept her tone polite but distant, surprised that he wasn't giving her the cold, aloof-aristocrat treatment. She had rehearsed for that but heard an unexpected warmth instead.

"My parents are both gone now, but Jack and my sisters are doing great," he said, hesitating slightly toward the end of the sentence.

"Sisters?" she said. "I only remember Martha, the one my age."

"I thought… I-I thought you knew," he stammered.

"You thought I knew what, Cole?"

"Mother said you knew all about it," he said with a panicky squeak. "She spoke to you, and you agreed it was for the best."

"Are you talking about… our daughter?" She held her breath and closed her eyes to wait for the answer.

"Of course I am. Lizzie. Elizabeth Mary Longworth, that is. We adopted her, Bridget. Mother raised her as my sister. Nobody knows who she… really is." His voice faded to a whisper.

Bridget felt her heart leap and soar like a lark in the sunshine.

Found at last.

Found and safe.

He rambled on, oblivious to the enormous dimensions of her silence at the other end of the connection. "She looks… like me, sort of, but with your hair and eyes. Like both of us, really. She's beautiful, Bridget. And smart and funny. You'd be proud, I think."

Bridget began to shake. She wanted to laugh and cry and scream at him, all at the same time. She tried to speak, but her voice cracked. Taking a deep breath, she clutched the telephone and steadied herself.

"I want to see her, Cole. Does she know who she is? She's twenty-eight. You must have told her by now, haven't you?"

"Well, not exactly. No, actually." His voice trailed off.

"What?" She wanted to jump through the phone and throttle him.

"Well, Mother always thought it was important not to make her feel insecure. We didn't want her to worry about being taken away or think she wasn't wanted." He sounded put upon, as though she were unfairly criticizing him.

Bridget tried to reason with him though she was still furious. "How could she worry about that if she knew what your parents went through to get her?"

"I mean, not wanted by... you, her mother. We didn't want her to know you had given her away. You did it willingly, you know. Nobody forced you." He shot the accusatory words at her like bullets, and they all hit the target dead center.

Bridget's eyes filled with tears. "I was so young, and it all happened so fast, and my father forced me. I've been looking for her for all these years, Cole." Her voice shook.

"Oh my God, Bridget." Cole's tone softened as he began to understand the truth of what had happened. "I'm so sorry. She was safe with me the whole time. I thought you knew where to find her. I figured you just weren't interested."

There was a moment's silence while Bridget closed her eyes and stopped herself from shouting into the phone. "Cole, I am *very* interested." She spat the clipped words out one at a time, each syllable loaded with venom.

"Okay, I get it, okay. I'm so sorry, Bridget." He sounded sincere, and knowing what she did of his mother, Bridget found it easy to believe the woman had lied to him.

She dropped her hostile attitude and reached out to start anew. "Really? Well, then, what can we arrange?"

They talked on amicably after that for nearly an hour, and Cole filled Bridget in on the status of his life and his family. He was married, with three kids. Two were off in college. Lizzie was engaged and living in Boston. She worked for a regional magazine, and her fiancé was in medical school at Harvard.

Cole reluctantly agreed to tell Lizzie the truth. "It seems like now is the time to try and set things right."

The only person who had kept them apart all these years, his mother, was dead and gone.

CHAPTER 34

Mary ~ April, 1968

MARY CLIMBED UP THE FRONT steps of Madigan General Hospital in Tacoma, Washington, a US Army evacuation hospital for troops wounded in Vietnam. At fourteen weeks pregnant, she had difficulty hauling herself toward the top, but she managed to do it without drawing attention to herself. So far, the baby didn't show, and nobody had mentioned it. But Mary felt the tightness at her waist and knew those days were numbered.

She spoke to the sergeant by the door. She returned his salute, and he pointed her toward a desk in the lobby, where a receptionist confirmed she was on the approved-visitors list for Lieutenant Commander Thomas Reilly, second floor south, room 283. She found the elevator and nervously smoothed the skirt of her dress uniform. Mary's civilian clothes were all back home at her parents' house. Now that her tour of duty was over and she was leaving the army, she'd have to buy some clothes fast. She'd come to see Thomas straightaway after landing in the US and hadn't had time for shopping.

Mary made her way to the room containing six curtained beds. Thomas lay in the one by the window with his left leg in a cast from foot to hip, raised up by a pulley device. His head was wrapped in bandages, one of which covered his left eye. Both hands were also bandaged, and the few parts of him that were still visible were marked by assorted cuts and bruises.

While she watched, he struggled to pick up a paper cup from his bedside table and fumbled, spilling water on himself and the bed. The cup went flying, and Thomas lay helpless, trying to pull the wet sheet off his body, unable to pick it up. He hung his head, and she saw his shoulders shake.

Mary stepped forward.

"Hello, Thomas." She lay her hand gently on his shoulder.

His right eye focused on her face, and a smile came slowly to his lips. "Mary? Is it you?"

"Yes, darling." She heard his voice, and a jolt of overwhelming love rushed through her. She thought of the last time she'd seen him, their engagement party at Honey's. The way they'd felt then, so hopeful and optimistic and with such a bright future, began to trickle into her memory like light finding its way through a crack in a wall.

"I can't believe it. It's really you, not a dream this time." He peered down at her left hand, where the diamond sparkled. "You're still wearing it. My ring."

Mary leaned forward to kiss him. "You bet I am. You didn't think you'd get away so easily, did you?" It was really Thomas, her Thomas. Under those bandages was the tall, handsome Irishman whom everyone loved, the man *she* loved. For so long, she'd thought of him as gone. To see him alive and healing seemed unreal. "It would take a lot more than getting shot down and captured by the Viet Cong to escape me," she said, teasing.

He laughed, but it obviously hurt him. She noticed his broken ribs were still taped. The report they'd sent said his eye was intact, just bandaged shut while the cornea healed. The poor man was a wreck.

Mary melted into her professional nursing personality and chatted with him, bustling around to change the sheets, bathe his hands and face, feed him some applesauce. She sat with him every day for a week, and they talked, or he slept and she consulted with the hospital staff about his condition and plan of care. Mary noticed that his flinch reflex was abnormally strong. He recoiled if she gestured suddenly as if she were about to hit him. His doctor told her they thought Thomas might have been tortured though he wouldn't talk about it.

The phrase *Post-Vietnam Syndrome* was being used to describe a condition he might have to contend with, as many veterans did. The nurses warned Mary to be prepared for major changes in his personality due to depression, inability to concentrate, insomnia, and nightmares. Hopefully, those difficulties would resolve over time. His injuries would take six months or more to heal, and then he'd need physical therapy to rebuild the muscles in his leg so he could walk.

The jolly, happy Thomas Reilly seemed to still be MIA. Instead, Mary saw a frightened, brave man who needed her love and compassion to help fight off his demons. His vulnerability spoke to her.

"Do you still want to marry me, Thomas?" she asked him quite seriously.

"Are you kidding?" His one eye opened wide. "It's what I've been staying alive for, like we said that night at Honey's. If you don't marry me now, I may as well go back to that camp and let them cut me into little pieces."

Mary recognized the fear in his voice and made her decision. "Never say such a thing! And of course I'll marry you. Just wanted to be sure you'll still have me."

"Can you wait for me, Mary, just a little longer? I've got this pesky broken leg... and a couple other little bumps..."

"No problem. I'll be ready to take over any nursing duties required as soon as the doctors think you're ready to come home. Then we can talk about planning our wedding, right?"

"I can't wait, and boy, do I mean that. Even with just one eye, you look good enough to eat, baby."

Mary laughed, then she looked down at her hands. "They say it will be a few months, Thomas. I'd better go home and live with my parents until then, don't you think? I'm not officially in the army anymore as of tomorrow, and I've nowhere to stay out here, no job."

"Yes, of course. That makes sense." He didn't sound too convinced. "Wish it weren't so far away."

Mary knew she had to persuade him to agree. "We can call, and write, and send photos."

"Sure we can. That'll be fine." He gave in, though his tone was wistful. "I sure do love you, Mary. Can't even tell you how much. I promise to get well real fast. It's the perfect motivation."

She leaned forward and kissed him gently on the mouth. In a flash, she thought of Jake, whose luxuriant moustache gave kissing a special frisson of danger. Then she brought herself back to that moment, to Thomas—the man she'd promised to marry, the man who said he loved her.

"If you're not out of this place in a few months, I'll come and get you," she teased, raising one eyebrow. "So have no fear. By the way, did you hear about my friend Charlotte and that guy Steve, the ones we used to go out with?" She tried for a casual, light tone as she prepared to fish for information.

"Nope, don't hear much gossip from this hospital bed, Mary."

She busied herself tidying the bedside table, pouring him another glass of water.

"Well," she said, "Charlotte was working out in one of the field hospitals and took pity on some soldier when she thought he was going to die. Turns out she got pregnant. So Steve stepped up and offered to marry her, adopt the child. Isn't that something? Guess he was always sweet on her." Mary chattered casually, making up the story as she went along to see how he would react.

Thomas snorted. "What an idiot. Pick up after some other GI's roll in the hay? So he's going to have to feed and clothe that brat for what, sixteen years? Hope he gets a hell of a lot of yard work out of him."

Mary turned to face him. "Really? You don't think it's an admirable and Christian thing to do? Think of the poor child." Her pulse began to pound faster as the discussion got heated.

"Mary, you can't be serious. I know you have a soft heart, dear one, but please don't tell me you've brought home a houseful of slant-eyed, blond-haired babies in your luggage. I want our own children, not somebody else's."

"But—" she sputtered, disappointment swelling over her as she realized she would never persuade him to take on the child in her belly as his own.

"I don't want to talk about it anymore, Mary. I know there are a lot of kids out there who need help, but let someone who can't have kids of their own adopt them. They'll be thrilled to do it. If you want to help, do some charity work to put couples together with unwanted babies. Catholic Charities does that kind of work, don't they?"

"Yes, they do." She stared into space, her mind racing through options and calculations.

"You should check into it, Mary. It'd be good for you, keep you busy while I'm recovering."

Mary watched his face while his good eye fell shut and he drifted off to sleep. Yes, it would definitely keep her busy for about six more months. And then something would have to be arranged.

She thought wistfully of Jake, her accomplice in pregnancy. When they were together, time stood still and the war went away for a while. When

Thomas was MIA, she had thought there would be a future for her and Jake after the war. Their connection was electric, shattering. But her lover, who'd carefully avoided using the word *love*, had apparently moved on with his life while she waited for her tour of duty to end. After his release from the hospital in Boston, he'd promptly married his former high-school sweetheart, Virginia.

Before telling Jake about the baby, Mary had wanted to find out how Thomas might react. Now she knew there was no way he would raise another man's child as she had hoped. She suspected Jake might respond well to news of a baby coming, but his wife would probably be another story.

The words Thomas had said were prophetic: "Let someone who can't have kids of their own adopt them." *Especially if the husband is the child's natural father. Why not?*

That way, Mary could have everything she wanted—a marriage to Thomas in Massachusetts and a safe haven for the baby with his or her father just a few hours away, as well as a chance to see Jake again and secretly visit her child. As long as Ginnie didn't object, it would work out beautifully. Mary would have to make her a best friend, a bosom buddy. She would earn Ginnie's trust. Then everything would be perfect forever after.

CHAPTER 35

Nell ~ 2014

As the summer slowly passed back at home in New Jersey, Nell drove the kids to day camp and sports, got David the special vitamins he wanted at the organic foods store, and vacuumed the pool every afternoon so it was spotless when he got home from work and did his laps. At night, she lay in the brass bed next to him and sweated while the window fan blew hot humid air across them. David thought it was wasteful to use air conditioning at night unless there was a major life-threatening heat wave.

Nell lay awake in the damp spot her head made on the pillow while she watched the way moonlight shone down through the skylight, remembering the long, snaky shadows of trees on the lawn in her mother's garden and the scent of lemons and turpentine. She longed for green that glowed like neon and the taste of clean air.

The overdeveloped world surrounding her buzzed constantly, day and night, with the faint sound of engines grinding, tires rolling, and sirens screaming. She hid her head under the pillow and covered her ears with her hands, but it was always there in the background.

Sometimes she snuck into the bathroom in the middle of the night to try and write poetry, but instead, she just wept. She didn't know why. It came over her like a pang of hunger or the urge to cough. Tears poured down her face, and she looked at herself in the mirror, wondering who that miserable woman was.

Nell didn't think David noticed her unhappiness. He was always so wrapped up in his work, his exercise regime, and in getting his dry-cleaning back promptly. She cooked him dinner every night and caressed his body where he liked to be touched, never saying a word about her true feelings.

Meanwhile, another life was in her thoughts. It hovered before her eyes when David told her about his day at work. Nothing had been the same since she'd returned from Vermont, nor would it ever be again.

She deeply regretted her anger toward Mom for wanting to leave her family and run away, because now Nell imagined doing the exact same thing.

Oh, Mom, I finally get it. Wherever you are now, please forgive me.

"I understand so much more now." Nell stood alone on the patio in New Jersey, talking to Bridget on the phone.

"Me too. I'm sorry I didn't have a chance to tell her. Living here in her house is so peaceful. Sometimes I feel like she's here with me."

"Don't you worry about your business or Eric?"

"My staff will handle it. Eric has made some kind of a deal with my lawyers to keep the house. He's buying me out as part of the divorce agreement."

"Did he call you? How do you know?" Nell shivered at the thought of him. He had always seemed like someone who might snap at any moment. And she'd never liked the way he looked at her rear end, either.

"My lawyer told me. Haven't heard from Eric and hope I never will." Bridget seemed unconcerned and changed the subject to the ongoing search for her daughter, which seemed to be her favorite topic at the moment—that and her deepening friendship with Jake Bascomb, a development Nell had seen coming from a mile away.

"It's such a relief to be around a real man. He's strong and kind and he treats me with respect. We're building a solid friendship. He's teaching me to sail. I'm having fun, and we're not even having sex." Bridget sounded happy.

"I'm glad for you, sweetie. You deserve it."

"I even like being a country girl. By the way, where do you order those warm silk long johns? I found a pair of cross-country skis in the basement."

Nell gathered from her sister's other shopping questions that she had transformed herself once again, this time from Donna Karan-Jimmy Choo-sexy-sophisticated into LL Bean-UGG boots-happy-relaxed.

On the long Columbus Day weekend in early October, David surprised everyone by agreeing to go camping with Ben, his buddies, and their fathers. Lauren was invited to spend the weekend with a friend. Nell decided it was a good chance to help Bridget clean out the cottage, so she got into her car alone to head north.

Crossing the Hudson River at New York City and cruising up I-91, Nell followed the signs to Vermont. The brilliant-orange hills of the Pioneer Valley became tall mountains with long stretches of farmland between the tidy homesteads. Hay was baled in giant yellow wheels that sat in the fields waiting to be collected and stored for the winter. Vegetable gardens featured scarecrows, pumpkins, and withered vines while ragged cornstalks stood like lonely sentries in the wasted rows.

The forest in northern New England was a rampage of reds. The mountains were dappled where stands of dark blue-green conifers were woven in amongst the bright oaks and maples. A riot of color and life decorated every view, a last hurrah before winter stripped the deciduous branches bare. The air had ripened to a translucent dusty rose, coating the landscape and its inhabitants and warming them with a flash of Indian summer. They'd hold the memory of that final burst of heat and color until the midwinter solstice, when the Yule log burned all night long and the light began to return.

Leaf-peeper traffic clogged the highway. Couples in the cars and at the rest stops pointed their cameras at the fall views and at each other. They were old and young, gay and straight, happy and not so happy. Some of them were arguing, some kissing. Jealous of them all, she realized it was because even the ones fighting weren't faking it.

The way she was.

Nell drove as fast as she dared. With every passing mile, her heart grew lighter. As she approached the Hartland town green that afternoon, signs proclaimed that citizens were celebrating their Fall Festival. Green-and-white striped tents with banners streaming in the breeze already dotted the periphery surrounding a grassy area kept clear for activities. A Farmers' Market was in full swing in the parking lot by the library.

Nell turned onto the road that led past J. Bascomb Antiques, but she frowned to see the barn doors were closed. She passed Jake's farmhouse and saw his old blue truck parked near the shed. It looked as though it had recently been washed. The front of the house had been painted, the lawn had been mowed, and the flowerbeds were filled with neatly trimmed shrubs and colorful mums. Either the man had totally transformed within a few months or Bridget had helped him tidy up the yard.

She turned right onto Lakeshore, where water gleamed through the trees like liquid fire. She pulled up to the cottage. Seeing Mom's white Ford through the open garage door, she parked behind it in the driveway. For the first time in months, she felt as if she had come home.

Nell got her suitcase out of the car and slammed the door shut. Excited barking filled the air as Winston and Lulubelle erupted from the front door. They were followed by Bridget with a smile on her face. Winston jumped up in a yipping frenzy when he recognized Nell, who took him into her arms. He covered her face with kisses.

"Welcome back." Bridget put her arms around them both.

"Thank God," Nell said wearily.

Rolling her sister's suitcase up the walkway, Bridget led Nell inside.

A little while later, they sat on the glider in Mom's garden, drinking wine before dinner. Bridget had been at work in the flower beds, and the fall colors were rich and mellow. A few russet leaves drifted down from the woods behind the vine-covered arbor, its withered foliage studded with ruby rose hips. Blackbirds and grackles grumbled over the seed heads on the sunflowers, their squawks and clucks like the voices of bickering old women.

"So tell me." Bridget made the swing sway. "What happened?"

"Nothing happened. Little stupid things that didn't bother me before are incredibly annoying now. It's so bizarre. Everything's the same, but everything is different."

"What are you going to do?" Bridget took Nell's hand in hers and laced their fingers together.

"I don't know. He treats me… like a servant. Maybe it's part of being a stay-at-home mother. Everyone gets so used to you being there they don't even see you anymore. I need something of my own. It's how Mom must have felt."

"Are you going to file for divorce?"

"No way. I still love David. I just don't love… me, the way I am with him right now." Nell was verbalizing it for the first time. "Anyhow, if I asked David for a divorce, I'd never see my kids again." It was a strange role reversal for Nell to be talking to her sister about ending a marriage, even hypothetically. She was usually the counselor, and Bridget was the one in trouble.

"Oh. Yes. I remember now. His college roommate is a divorce attorney in New York, right?"

"David's buddy would hire a fleet of detectives, who would immediately find out everything I ever did wrong or even thought about, and I'd never have a chance. I can see it now. Attempted concealing of assets, psychic infidelity, faking orgasms, sneaking off to write inflammatory poetry in the middle of the night... I'll be the unfit mother who is always late to pick up her kids after school. People will sniff my breath to see if I've been drinking in the daytime." Bridget laughed at all this, but Nell moaned. "Anyhow, I don't want to get divorced. It's not about that. I just can't seem to get it together like I used to. I don't know what's wrong with me."

"So what will you do?"

"I wish I could stay up here and have them all come to visit when the kids aren't in school. But that's a dream, I know." Nell pulled her hand away and rubbed her arms, hunching her shoulders into a defensive pose. "He'd have to *want* me to leave. And feel guilty about it. Then I'd have the upper hand."

"Never. Not David Williams, all-American apple-pie boy. He'd croak first." Bridget giggled.

"Stop teasing," Nell said. "You have to help me. Let's brainstorm. All suggestions considered, no matter how wild. Maybe we'll come up with something I can use." Nell drained her glass and set it on the little table. She tucked one leg under her and sat at attention, turned toward Bridget.

"Okay, so, you want him to get bored with you or suddenly become irritated by your personal habits or something like that, right?"

"Exactly. I need to drive him crazy. Then he won't want me around all the time." Nell looked at her sister expectantly, hoping for a brilliant idea. If anyone knew how to manipulate a man, Bridget did.

Bridget sipped her wine and rocked thoughtfully. "But not so badly that he refuses to give you any money or challenges your authority. Hmmm.

The obvious thing is to withhold sex. Have you tried that?" She grinned and poked Nell in the ribs.

"It just makes us both grouchy, and he thinks I'm mad at him, so he hassles me even worse to find out what's wrong."

They swung in silence for a few minutes.

"Born again?" Bridget said.

"Too Southern. I couldn't pull it off."

"New-Age Wiccan health-food freak?"

"Possibly. It might work. Especially if I turn vegan. The food alone would totally flip him out."

They burst out laughing, bumping shoulders.

"God forbid David Williams should ever have to go without his *filet*," Nell remarked in a wry tone.

"You mean *Goddess* forbid, don't you honey?"

They burst out laughing again.

"I could tell him I'm secretly an alien."

"Or a former call girl."

"Or that I didn't really graduate from Vassar but went to Mercer County Community College."

"Oh my Goddess! Anything but that." Bridget pretended to be appalled.

"We'll think of something." Nell spoke with more confidence. "I just know it. I'm already annoying the hell out of him by only doing the laundry once a week. And sometimes I let it sit around on the dining room table for a few hours after I fold it. Things like that drive him up a wall."

"Baby sister." Bridget hugged her closer. "Don't you worry. It will all work out for the best. And Mom would be proud of you."

"Would she? I don't know, Bridget. I think I still love him. I really can't tell." Nell rubbed the spot near her temple where the migraines usually started, wincing as her fingers found the tender heart of the pain.

"Love is a mystery," her sister intoned, trying to make her laugh.

Nell spoke in a timid voice, a little ashamed. "Maybe I just want to be selfish and I'm looking for a good excuse."

Bridget pointed at Nell. "That is the wisest thing you've said all day."

"Maybe I want someone to blame for being unhappy, and David is handy?"

"You're getting warmer..." Bridget leaned toward her, eyes teasing.

"Maybe I should actually *do* something about it instead of just complaining?"

"Bingo. You got it." Bridget hugged her and kissed her on the cheek.

"Maybe I'll look for a job. Or apply to grad school. Hmm…"

They rocked. Nell had a sudden vision of Ginnie and Mom sitting in the swing and talking like this. The moment was an echo in history, a sliver of time reflected over and over in a hall of mirrors. As though she and Bridget were the current initiates in a much deeper tradition and Nell was being sheltered and comforted by a long chain of supportive women.

Nell breathed in, tasted the earthy sweetness. Her body relaxed, and her temple stopped twitching. She turned toward her sister. "And what's the latest with your big news? Have you and Cole agreed on a place and time for the meeting?"

"I'm not sure he told her yet. He's 'working his way toward it,' as he said. Called me last week. I think he's embarrassed. She looks up to him, and he doesn't want to lose that."

"He let it happen. I don't buy all that blaming it on his parents."

"I know, Nell, but we're going to let that go." Bridget sounded determined. "We're giving the guy a break because he was just a kid, like me, and now he's sorry, like me. Also, I don't want to piss him off."

"Okay, okay. I get it. Well, I'm glad things are moving along at least."

"I've waited almost thirty years," Bridget said. "I can be patient a little while longer."

They swung together, each lost in her thoughts, watching the evening shadows gather in the forest and spill onto the lawn.

Nell heard Adam's truck approaching when it turned onto Lakeshore. She looked at Bridget, and they smiled. They listened to the truck door creak and slam and watched to the left of the cottage where the path came around from the front yard. Adam appeared a minute later, striding toward them across the grass, carrying bags and packages in his arms. He grinned, threw everything down on the ground, and scooped Nell up out of the glider, smothering her in a bear hug.

She squealed in mock terror as she clung to him. "Adam! You're squishing me!"

"It's so good to see you, woman!" He released her and picked up a bouquet of white roses.

"For you, Mrs. Williams." Adam presented them to Nell, who smiled and buried her nose in the head-spinning scent.

Then he picked up the box of Godiva chocolates, tied with a blue ribbon. "And for you, Ms. Reilly." He presented it to Bridget.

She looked at him with approval and shot him a wicked wink. "Yum. You darling man."

"And this is for all of us." He picked up the bag of wine bottles and held it aloft.

The sisters cheered and held up their empty glasses.

The three of them trooped inside to cook dinner and celebrate Nell's homecoming.

Later that night, after Bridget and Jake had gone over to his house to watch their favorite show on cable TV, Nell and Adam once again sat in the lawn chairs at the end of the dock across the street from the cottage. The night was dark and magical. The black sky above the lake cupped a bowlful of stars topped by a white quarter moon that looked like a sly, half-turned face. The image was reflected below in the water, smooth and glassy. Lights blinked far across the lake. No other human beings were within sight or sound—it was their own private preserve. The cry of a loon sounded in the distance, sad and spooky.

"This is wonderful," Nell whispered. "I so missed this. Nature with a capital N."

Adam looked at her profile. She turned to meet his eyes.

"And I missed you, Adam." She reached out and gave his hand a squeeze. "I don't have many friends in New Jersey, people I can really talk to."

He grasped her hand tightly then let it go and cleared his throat. "How are things at home?"

"Same as always. The kids are great. Doing well in school, sports, ballet, etcetera. They are truly great kids, you know. Never a bad attitude. Even my teenager, Ben. I'm lucky."

"It's not all luck. You can take some credit too."

"Thank you. It's unusual to hear a compliment like that." Nell hadn't experienced a sense of pride in quite a while, maybe because she didn't really approve of herself at the moment. But always trying to hit the highest possible mark was so stressful. She didn't really want to know how she measured up anymore. She just wanted to go with her instincts, be spontaneous. "I put a lot of energy into my kids. Every day."

"I'm sure you do." He nodded.

They sat and looked at the sky for a moment.

"So, how are you and David… doing?" He stared across the lake.

"David and I are doing fine. It's me who is not doing so fine."

"What's going on?"

"Things have changed." She didn't know how to explain it, the sense of being a stranger in her own life.

"In what way?"

Nell took a deep breath and closed her eyes as she let it out. "I'm lazy and flawed now. Can't live up to my own expectations anymore." It hurt a little to admit the truth, but like ripping off a Band-Aid, it was easiest done briskly.

Adam turned to face her. "Changed for the better, I'd say. You were too uptight, Nell. You needed to chill out."

"Oh, really? Is that a compliment, or a poorly disguised insult?" She scowled, not expecting criticism, but he was still smiling at her.

"I'll always approve of you, Nell. Especially when you're not perfect. You know, like the rest of us humans." He leaned back and joined his hands behind his head, watching for her response.

She couldn't help noticing his strong arms, brown from a summer of working outside. She had once seen him lift a dining chair up over his head with one hand just as easily as she might lift an umbrella. He was smart and well educated too. Adam could have been a lawyer, a doctor, a corporate executive. But he'd chosen something less glamorous. He did manual labor and had created his own business instead of selling his intellect the way David and her father had done. Adam had chosen what made him happy, and he wasn't worried about impressing anyone.

He was an inspiration. Nell wanted to choose what made her happy too.

She looked up, and they both smiled. Her thoughts seemed to have merged with his like two halves of a whole. It was a blissful sensation she had only experienced before with her sister.

There was a tightness in Nell's throat as an idea hit her: she needed to find her own place in the world, a place where she wasn't just somebody's wife or somebody's mother. She could do something that fulfilled her spiritually and intellectually. She didn't have to run away from her husband and her family to make it happen. She needed to redefine herself and move on to the next stage.

Just as Mary Reilly had done when she created a second life.

Nell still couldn't guess why Mom decided to handle the details the way she did, but she'd finally forgiven her mother. In this secret place, all three Reilly women had found the gateway to change, each in her own way.

CHAPTER 36

Bridget ~ 2014

JAKE STOOD IN THE SHADOWS behind a thick pine tree, watching the cottage again. Bridget saw him there when she brought the dogs out for one last pee after Nell had already gone upstairs. Winston and Lulu didn't even bother to bark at him. They were used to Jake lurking around in the woods. It had been happening every few weeks since the first night Bridget came to Hartland.

At first, Bridget had been scared, then intrigued. Now she suspected she knew what was going on. He had a pattern. Something happened, it reminded him of the bad old days, and he started drinking. Then he hung around, watching Mary's house as though the ghosts inside might come out and confront him.

Sometimes she couldn't figure out what had set him off, but that night, Bridget could guess. Soon as she told him Nell was coming up for the weekend, he started looking funny. His eyes got that wild, terrorized expression. Nell had always disliked him and not without good reason, since it was Jake's negligence that had led to their mother's final illness. But Bridget couldn't hold a grudge. There were too many counts against her for her own bad behavior. Jake was like family to her at that point, and she wanted to help.

She would bet her last dollar there was a bottle in his hand. She thought she saw the moonlight glint off glass when he raised it to his lips.

Bridget brought the dogs back inside, settled them down, and turned out the lights. Then she crept back outside and slipped into the woods. *Damned if this is going to go on any longer.* It was time for Jake to confront his devils, and Bridget would be standing beside him when he did.

She approached him silently from behind and stopped to watch before making a move. Jake reached into his jeans pocket to pull out a pint bottle of transparent liquor, almost empty, unscrewing the cap and taking a long swig. The breeze brought her the scent of gin. He looked to already be deep in a drunken fog. He hadn't answered his cell since early in the morning, and no one had been at the farmhouse all day. The back door had been left standing open.

He'd probably been wandering around the neighborhood and watching Mom's house all day. She could see that his face and arms were covered with scrapes and bruises from banging into things and getting caught in the brambles. He slowly worked his way around the house, making his way through the woods until he was in front of the den then crouched there and peered into the window.

Jake tried to take another swig of gin, but the bottle was apparently empty. He shook it, then he cursed and threw the bottle into the woods, propelling it with all his strength. It smashed into a rock, shattering. He lunged forward and ran straight into a tree limb, hitting his head with a resounding thunk. Reeling back in shock, he blinked and tried to focus, groping around.

Just as Bridget stepped forward to offer help, he ran. She followed cautiously, trying not to trip on vines and rocks in the spotty darkness.

Wheeling around, he crashed through the woods, knocking into trees and ripping through the bushes. A flash of moonlight revealed that his skin was bleeding from multiple scratches and there was a deep gash on his forehead. Black shadows patterned the ground with confusing bars and splotches, transforming the familiar landscape into a frightening maze as Bridget tried to follow him. He seemed disoriented, confused.

Just like he's lost in his life. Unable to move toward the future or let go of the past and incapable of understanding the present.

When Jake finally passed the giant maple tree and came out into his own backyard, his clothing was ripped and he was limping badly, but he didn't seem to notice. Bridget saw him stumble up onto his back porch, yank open the screen door, and burst into the kitchen. His foot caught on the threshold, and he tripped, going down hard like a tall tree falling. His head hit the floor with a bang.

She rushed inside and found him passed out on the kitchen floor.

Worried about a concussion, she reached for her mobile phone to call an ambulance. Then he roused, tried to get up onto his hands and knees, and vomited. He was dead drunk and smelled terrible.

"Bridg-ah?" he slurred, squinting at her with watery eyes, his mouth dripping blood and vomit. Then he passed out again.

She cleaned up the kitchen floor by mopping around him while he lay there, moving in and out of consciousness. Every time he woke up, he was surprised to see her. She brewed strong coffee and made him drink some. He started ranting incomprehensibly, and then a while later, he roused and crawled into the bathroom. After watching him try to stand in front of the sink and then collapse, she helped him get up again and balance. He turned on the cold water and washed his face then looked up at the mirror with yellow, bloodshot eyes. An ugly wound crossed his forehead, his hair hung down in greasy strands, and he hadn't shaved in a day or two.

Jake was a mess. His life was a mess. Bridget could tell he was thinking it.

Then he turned his head and stared at the double-edged razor on the side of the sink. Bridget remembered the dark moments when she had considered suicide, when she'd thought about how peaceful it would be when the pain stopped. She appreciated the allure and thought she knew where they stood now. The landscape was familiar. It looked to her as though Jake had hit rock bottom.

What happened next had to be managed carefully. Having been in therapy on and off since high school and being an expert at how to survive self-loathing, Bridget decided to go with her gut.

Bridget picked up the razor, unscrewed it, and removed the blade. She held it in one hand and turned up her other wrist. Seconds passed, as she stood unmoving in the dirty bathroom. He watched her, confusion and panic on his battered face.

"What do you say, Jake? Shall we be losers together? Is it time to check out of this shitty hotel we call life?" The sly smile and demonic glint in her eyes was calculated to scare the crap out of him. It seemed to work.

Jake's eyes widened as he tried to decide what to do. He reached over toward her, then a sob welled up and escaped his throat. He grabbed her hand and flung the razor blade across the room. It bounced off the ceramic-tile wall and rattled to the floor.

Then Jake hung his head and cried, deep sobs shuddering through his tall frame as the sorrow and desperation ripped out of him. She held him while he slipped down to sit on the toilet lid and held his face in his hands. Jake had surrendered but not without a struggle.

As she watched the pain pass through him like a burning wave of fire, he mumbled through his fingers. "My whole life," he gasped. "It's total shit. I had so much, and now it's all gone. I can't just… forget."

"Nobody can," Bridget said. "Life isn't like that. The best we can do is learn to forgive ourselves."

They sat on the bathroom floor and leaned against the wall. She told him her theory that life was an unmanageable, unknowable force that flowed along according to its own nature. There was no point in trying to make predictions even if you did manage to catch a glimpse of what was going on behind the scenes.

"So the only smart thing to do is enjoy the good times while they're here. And know the bad ones are just around the corner. For every up, there's a down. But for every down, there's an up that's coming right along as well. It's kind of like the stock market."

When that idea got through to him, something in Jake's state of mind seemed to shift. "You know, I'm not a religious man," he said, "but it now occurs to me that there really is something bigger than me and you. It's not just random. There is a kind of framework behind all this."

Oddly enough, that seemed to make him feel better. He smiled.

"Maybe if we let life take its course instead of fighting so hard to change things all the time, it will help us face the future," Bridget said.

Inch by inch, Jake was able to creep forward. It was working for Bridget. The past few months had taught her she could change without an alpha male to tell her who to become. She was turning into herself like the lowly caterpillar that emerged from its chrysalis with radiant wings and a whole new attitude.

Jake reached over and turned on the shower. She went to work on the kitchen a bit more while he stripped off his filthy clothes and stood under the hot spray, letting it pound on him for a long time. Then the water stopped, and Bridget heard him pull back the shower curtain to step out of the tub.

His eyes already looked clearer and more focused when she came back into the steamy room to hand him a fresh cup of coffee. Standing by the sink with a towel wrapped around his waist, he opened the medicine cabinet. He smoothed on some shaving gel, put a new blade in the razor, and used it on his beard.

As Bridget watched, she thought that life still had something good to offer Jake after all those years. Maybe it needed to happen all on its own— no matter what he had done and what he thought he deserved.

It seemed Jake had finally admitted that his only option was to wait and see. Maybe Bridget needed to do the same thing.

CHAPTER 37

Mary ~ 1969

GINNIE CHANGED THE BABY'S DIAPER in the ladies' bathroom at the church and kept one hand on him while she put the wipes back into the diaper bag. She tossed the dirty diaper into the trash can. It was across the room, but she made the shot with her first try.

Mary laughed. "Looks like you're getting the hang of it."

"I sure am. This guy poops every hour of every day, so I get plenty of practice. These new disposable diapers are the greatest." Ginnie gazed at the baby with a goofy smile on her face. "He is such a doll. I didn't know I could love anyone this much. Never thought I'd get to have this wonderful experience."

"I'm so glad, Ginnie. All I ever wanted was for everyone to be happy." Mary put her arms around Virginia, and they stood for a moment, hugging, while Adam kicked his feet and blew bubbles with his spit.

"Shall we go up? They're waiting for us." Ginnie adjusted the antique white-lace gown to cover the baby's legs. She tucked a little white blanket around him and adjusted her coat. "Thanks again for bringing the christening dress. It's just perfect." She smiled at Mary in the bathroom mirror.

"Ginnie, I'm so grateful to you for asking me to come today. I can't even begin to say. You are a generous, lovely person." Mary's eyes clouded with tears. "Oh gosh, now I'm going to cry again." They both laughed, and Ginnie bounced the baby while Mary blotted under her eyes with a tissue.

"We're lucky the timing and everything else turned out like it did," Ginnie said. "This little guy is going to have the best home on earth. He's absolutely perfect, and I'm thrilled to be his mama."

"He's a lucky boy."

"Yes, he gets to have two mamas who both love him."

"And he looks just like his daddy, who loves him too." Mary met Ginnie's eyes and saw her struggling with apprehension. She put out her hand to hold Ginnie's arm. "It's in the past, in another world. It should never have happened, but maybe it was for a reason. Things are completely different now."

"I know. I believe you, Mary."

"You're a good woman, Ginnie. And you'll be a great mom to our boy."

They went up the stairs and outside to where Jake and both sets of grandparents were waiting with the pastor, who had just named the baby Adam Patrick Bascomb. Everyone smiled when the two women came through the door and into the wintry landscape. Ginnie wrapped the blankets around Adam a bit tighter.

"Reverend," Jake said, passing him the camera, "would you snap a few shots for us?"

"Why don't you stand in the middle?" Ginnie said as she passed the baby to Mary, who moved between Jake and his wife. They all lined up on the neatly shoveled sidewalk in front of the church.

Mary nuzzled Adam's sweet little head and breathed the hypnotic scent of baby pheromones. Tears came to her eyes, but she quickly blinked them away. When the pastor counted to three, she raised her head and smiled.

"He's a lucky boy," she said again, "to have you for parents."

Jake smiled for the second photo and glanced down at her. "He's lucky to have all of us. Right, Virginia?"

"We all love him." Ginnie put her arm around Mary's shoulders. "And we have that important thing in common. We're a family."

Everyone smiled together and didn't blink for the third photo. It seemed like a good omen.

Back at the farmhouse afterward, while Ginnie put the baby to bed, Mary and Jake sat in the parlor, drinking whiskey neat as they had in the old days. They listened to the wood fire snap.

"How are you doing, sweet thing?"

"I'm okay. Emotional day. Gave up my baby in front of God. What would you expect?" Mary stretched her neck, and it crunched. Being around

Adam all day had been a sweet joy and sheer torture. She had struggled to manage her conflicted emotions about letting him go, one moment feeling grateful for the wonderful home he would have and, the next, wanting to snatch him up and run away.

"Hard for me to say, since I'm on the receiving end this time." He leaned forward and threw on another log. Sparks exploded and snapped.

"I don't know if we've done the right thing or what will happen next. I do know that I'm an unmarried woman and my son needs his father. What we did was the obvious answer." Mary took a sip of whiskey and, on second thought, took another. "So why do I feel so shitty? Am I just being selfish?" It was far too late to back out. She knew she should stop torturing herself and trust in the future. It would all work out for the best, and Thomas was counting on her.

"How are the big wedding plans coming along?" Jake's voice sounded gruff as though he needed to clear his throat.

"Thomas is still at the hospital out in Tacoma. It will be a while before we set the date. He's doing well, though, physically. The broken bones are knitting. They just need some time. The psychological trauma takes longer to heal, as you know."

Jake stared into the fire. "Yeah, we all see spooks at night for a while."

"I still do sometimes. Those poor boys…"

"Their voices in the back of the truck while we were driving to the hospital. I still hear them." Jake turned to look at her.

"Oh yes. Their voices. Begging me to save them, to love them." Mary remembered the boys in her wards at night, calling out for their mothers and their wives.

"Does your fiancé know what a lucky man he is, Ellie?"

"Knows he's lucky enough to come back from the dead." She raised one eyebrow and smiled. "And that's pretty damn lucky."

"True, true." Jake knocked back the last of his whiskey and reached for the bottle. "Do you love him? Glad you decided to stand by your promise to him?"

Mary turned and stared at him, her eyes fierce. "I do love him, Jake. You know I do. That's never been a secret. And you also know that by the time I found out about the baby coming, it was too late for most options."

She lowered her voice, conscious of Ginnie's presence upstairs. "You ran right off and got married."

"I did not run right off." He frowned and jabbed the logs with the poker, sending sparks flying up the chimney.

"Okay, you strolled off in a leisurely fashion. Do you like that better? Just want to point out that you were married three weeks later."

"Ellie, I figured no means no. You said, 'Thomas is back, and I'm promised to him.' Ginnie and I were an item back before Saigon—you know that." He lowered his voice, glancing toward the stairs. "I was wounded, flipped out, on doctor drugs. She loves me, and I couldn't be alone. If I'd have known there was a snowball's chance for us to be a family..." He took Mary's hand and held it. "But you told me you were staying with him." His eyes went blank, then a spark of anger flared.

"Good lord, Jake, my missing fiancé had just reappeared after a horrendous experience. He thought we were still going to get married. How was I supposed to spring it on him right off the bat that while he was dead, I was having a passionate affair with you instead of crying into my pillow every night?"

He looked down and rubbed the back of his head with his hand. "Guess I see your point."

Their eyes met, and Mary shook her head.

"Well, here we are. What's done is done," she said. "It's right that our son should grow up with two parents who love him unconditionally. In fact, he will have three. I could never offer Adam that, even if I told Thomas the truth and he agreed to take the boy in. For that matter, our wedding day may never come. I have to allow for that possibility as well. We can't predict the future. Anything could happen." Mary sighed and reached for Jake's hand to give it a squeeze. "Sorry I sounded so grouchy. It was really a lovely day. I enjoyed meeting your parents."

"They like you too. Said you'll be a wonderful godmother."

"And indeed I will. I'll be here for every birthday with a proper godmother gift. Something educational. I promise never to bring him a puppy or a squirt gun. Scout's honor."

"You'd better not." He sent her a threatening glance.

They watched the fire for a while and drank their whiskey.

"Did we do the right thing, Jake?" Mary sniffed the aromatic wood smoke and felt the whiskey softening her tension. Upstairs, Adam let out a brief cry, quickly soothed. Mary curled up in the chair and tucked her feet underneath her.

"Sweet thing, the way things worked out, we didn't have much choice."

"This way, everyone can be happy, right?" She needed his assurance, his compliance.

Jake patted her on the shoulder. "I know how important that is to you. Don't worry."

"We'll be friends forever, Jake."

"Yes. And it will be our secret, just the three of us." Jake squeezed her hand and smiled.

CHAPTER 38

Nell ~ 2014

WHILE BRIDGET WAS STILL ASLEEP the next morning, Nell made coffee and wandered into the living room. She was still in her bathrobe and considered lying down on the couch. *How self-indulgent. That would never be allowed at home in New Jersey. Far too many early-morning chores to do.*

But the new Nell kind of liked the idea. She put her mug on the coffee table.

This sofa was more formal and stiff than the comfy one in the TV room, so she and Bridget never sat on it. The morning sun streamed in through the side windows, and Nell could see the lake gleaming across the street, so she tucked a needlepoint pillow under her head and stretched out on her side.

Bridget had been going through some boxes and had left them on the floor. There was a big white one under the coffee table. Nell stared at it as her eyes fluttered shut.

She opened them again. That must be the box containing Dad's uniform, the one Bridget had told her about. A photo of Mom and Dad's engagement party was in there. Curious, Nell reached out and snagged the box, pulling it toward her across the carpet.

She found the photo and gently touched the crumbling rose tucked into the uniform lapel. She pulled the jacket out of the box and held it up. Ben might want it. The jacket looked as though it would fit him in a few years.

Nell stood up and slipped into the garment. Being surrounded by the fabric was like an embrace. It was enormous on her, the sleeves hanging down past her fingertips. The smooth lining felt cold at first, then it started to reflect back her body heat. The threads touching her had also touched his body many times. The very essence of her father was in that coat. She closed her eyes and tried to get a feeling of him, but the image wouldn't focus. She sniffed the cuff and caught a hint of cedar.

She explored the pockets. They felt cavernous to her small hands, but she slid her fingers all the way down to the bottom. There was something slippery and metallic in one of them and what felt like an envelope in the other. She pulled out a chain with something dangling from it: Dad's dog tags. There was his name.

Nell's throat tightened as she thought of her father flying off to battle, putting himself in harm's way for his country. Luckily, he had come home. Many others had not. And Mom had been waiting for him. How thrilling it must have been when they finally saw each other again. *What a spectacular love story.*

Then Nell remembered the envelope in the other pocket and took it out. The cream-colored paper looked old, discolored along the edges. The envelope was sealed and stamped, ready to be mailed. It was addressed to Thomas Reilly at their home in Amherst, written in Mom's handwriting with a blue ballpoint pen, and the return address was 27 Lakeshore Drive, Hartland, VT.

Nell's pulse beat faster as she stared at it.

Both of them were dead, so what harm could it do for her to intrude? All the answers she had been searching for might be contained inside. There was no way she could resist. Nell ripped the envelope open.

The one-page letter was scrawled in her mother's handwriting. It was dated *August 28, 1992.* Mom must have written it when she'd first moved into the cottage.

Dear Thomas,

I'm sure this isn't a complete surprise. Things between us have not been good for a long time. The girls are both away at school now, so I have decided to live on my own. Hopefully, we can continue to have a cordial relationship for their sake.

When the telephone is installed, I'll send you my new number. My address is on the envelope.

~Mary

Nell sat on the couch with the letter in her hand. She felt as if she was dreaming. It was what she'd suspected all along, but seeing it spelled out like that was still a shocker.

Her suspicions had proven true. Mom was leaving Daddy. That was why she came up to Vermont and bought this cottage. Their fairy-tale romance hadn't turned out so well after all.

Mom was going to leave her life behind, just as Nell had daydreamed about doing. Granted, she and Bridget had been in college then, but still, Mom had been ready to break up the family. And she never said a word about it to her daughters. Ever.

Nell wiped her tears on the sleeve of Daddy's jacket. Mom had never mailed the letter. And obviously, she never left him. What had stopped her from going through with it?

Maybe she couldn't bear to leave her family. She thought the girls still needed their mother. It was certainly the truth. That was just a couple of years after Bridget got pregnant and Daddy had such a fit. Bridget had miraculously made it through a few semesters at Wellesley and was running wild all over Boston with men she'd met in bars. Nell was a nervous freshman at Vassar in Poughkeepsie, shy and insecure, living away from home for the first time and uncomfortable in the elite socialite environment.

That was also when Thomas began to show the first symptoms of Alzheimer's. Maybe Adam was right. Maybe Mom had noticed it before anyone else and knew what was to come.

"Do I smell coffee? Thanks for letting the dogs out." Bridget came into the room, wearing flannel sleep pants and a Ben & Jerry's T-shirt. Her look had definitely changed since moving to Vermont. "No offense, Nell, but that jacket is a little too long for you. It looks great over the bathrobe, though."

"Read this. It was in the pocket." Nell handed her the letter.

While Bridget read, Nell took off the jacket and folded it carefully.

"It was still sealed in the envelope," Nell said. "Never sent."

"So he didn't know she was leaving?"

"It was another of Mom's secrets. She kept it forever, even from him." Wearily, Nell laid the jacket back in the box and closed the lid. "All this is getting to be too much for me, Bridget. I can't feel okay with it. Did we ever really know our mother at all? Who was she, anyhow?"

Bridget put the letter on the coffee table, shaking her head in agreement. "My brain absolutely cannot cope without caffeine. I'll be right back." She took a step toward the kitchen and hooked her foot on the white box, flipping it over. A fold of tissue paper fell out along with something white and lacey.

"What's that?" Bridget pointed.

Nell knelt down and pulled on the paper. A small gown of soft white lawn and fine lace, embellished with narrow white ribbons and seed pearls, slowly emerged from where it had been hidden under the tissue at the bottom of the box. She held it up. "It looks like a christening dress, doesn't it? Haven't seen this before. The kids both used mine, so this must be yours. Isn't it pretty?"

Bridget squinted. "No, I have mine too. It's the antique one passed down by the Reilly clan to the firstborn child. Came to me from Dad. Wishful thinking, I guess, but Mom gave it to me when she moved to Maplewood."

"This dress looks old." Nell touched the delicate embroidery with a gentle fingertip. "See how the fabric is discolored? I think it's the one Mom got from Grandma, the Sullivan christening gown. She showed a picture of some baby wearing it to me once. I wondered what happened to it."

Bridget shrugged. "Must be. Now, getting coffee." She wandered off toward the kitchen.

Nell sat and examined the sweet little ruffled collar and cuffs. Then a lightning bolt of realization struck her, and she ran to retrieve Mom's photo album from the den. She flipped quickly through to the end and pulled out several loose prints from where they were tucked inside the back cover. Then she sorted through them until she found the image she'd remembered.

A group of people were standing on the sidewalk in front of a church. There was snow on the ground. The photo had been shot in bright sunlight, and black shadows made splotches on their faces. Nell had glanced at it before and tossed it aside. Now she looked more closely because in the middle was a young woman holding a baby who wore a long white dress. By squinting and holding the photo up to the light from the window, Nell recognized the ruffles and embroidery she had just been admiring. It was the same gown. She flipped the print over, but there was no date stamped on the back.

Nell looked more carefully at the young woman. She was slender and petite, and she wore a stylish gray suit and matching wide-brimmed hat that obscured most of her face with the dark shadow it cast. Standing next to her were another young woman with masses of curly hair and a tall young man with short dark hair, a moustache, and a handsome white smile. Four older people were arranged on either side of this trio.

The kitchen door slammed, and Winston and Lulu came racing into the living room to demand Nell's attention. She heard voices in the kitchen, threw the photo down on the coffee table, grabbed her empty cup, and went to see what was happening.

Bridget and Adam stood at the counter, filling two mugs with coffee.

"Howdy, neighbor. Please, make yourself right at home," Nell said, smiling.

"Already have. Want a refill?" He filled her mug too. "Your dogs showed up at Dad's door this morning, begging. They said you're starving them to death, and I can see it's true. You should be ashamed."

Lulu and Winston had both buried their heads in their breakfast bowls of kibble enhanced with leftover chicken soup.

"Nell, make those yummy pancakes you do, the fluffy ones with whipped egg whites. Please? Pretty please?" Bridget yawned and collapsed into a chair at the kitchen table. "I need carbs and sugar to help my poor brain process all these new family secrets. I hardly recognize us anymore."

"New?" Adam started to sit down across from Bridget, but Nell stopped him.

"Hey. Shoes off. No mud on my newly washed floor, please. We're leaving our shoes at the door from now on. It's the new rule."

"Yes, master."

"Nell is mean on clean, Adam. Better watch out because she will seriously hurt you if you disobey."

He left his sneakers on the mat by the door and padded back to the table in his socks. "What did you mean, 'new' secrets?"

Bridget told him about finding the letter, and Nell made pancakes. She served three plates and delivered them to the table along with a jug of maple syrup. As she was getting the silverware, Bridget told him about the christening gown, and that reminded Nell. She went into the living room and brought back the photo, tossing it onto the kitchen table. Bridget and Adam were already devouring their food, but they both glanced over at the picture.

Adam swallowed and leaned in for a closer look. "Hey, that's my parents. And me. Where'd you get this?" He wiped his hands on his napkin and picked the print up, holding it carefully by the corners.

Nell stared at him, mesmerized, as her mind raced. "It was in Mom's den. That is the christening gown we found today."

"This baby is you?" Bridget was very still, but she and Nell exchanged a gaze of deep knowing, shared intuition.

Adam pointed. "That's my Grandpa James Bascomb and Grandma Caroline here on this side, and over here are my mother's parents, Earle and Catherine Westerly. All deceased, unfortunately. In the middle, of course, are my parents and Ellie, holding me. Never understood why they make boys wear a dress to get christened. Doesn't that seem weird to you?"

Nell reached out her hand to get his attention. "Adam, you're saying that our mother was your godmother? You've known her since you were born?"

"Um… yeah, I guess so. I mean, I knew her when I was a kid. I don't remember many details. And I never saw this picture before." He put the photo down on the table between them. "But Ellie was definitely around. I sort of remember her being at a couple of my birthday parties too. I think she might have brought me a puppy, my old dog Shep. And a Super Soaker 5000 water gun, I remember that. Then she was here more and lived in this house." He frowned, thinking.

Nell and Bridget exchanged glances again.

"Okay," Bridget said as she stood up, getting the coffeepot to pour everyone a refill. "So when Mom bought this house and moved here, she already knew your family. She had friends in the neighborhood. That makes sense."

Nell nodded. "Yes, it explains why she chose this town. But your christening was a long time ago, Adam. It would have been back around the time when our father came home from Vietnam, 1969. Was Jake in the military?"

Adam nodded. "Yes indeed. Sergeant Jake Bascomb. He was an

ambulance driver with a medevac team, '67 to '68. They gave him a bronze star. His truck got blown up, and he was hurt pretty bad."

"That's got to be it, then. Mom and Jake must have known each other in Saigon. Maybe she was his nurse." Bridget pointed at Nell and wagged her finger. "I told you there was a man at the heart of all this mystery."

Adam leaned back in his chair, stretching out his long legs and crossing his feet at the ankles. He sipped his coffee. Nell noticed, not for the first time, that he wore one blue sock and one dark green. He needed someone to pair his socks for him.

Just like Ben and Grandad too, Mom's father.

"Nice color coordination," she said deliberately, various wild scenarios spinning in her brain. "In a hurry with the laundry?"

Adam actually blushed. "Oh, sorry. I get it wrong sometimes." He frowned.

"Don't worry, it happens to my son Ben all the time. I pair his socks for him when I do the laundry. It's no big deal. Our grandfather had the same thing."

Bridget looked at him oddly. "Adam, you're colorblind?"

"Just for certain colors. Blue and green are the worst."

"Anyone else in your family ever have that?" Nell asked him softly.

"No, I don't think so. Why?"

Nell put her hand on his. "Because colorblindness is hereditary. My grandfather had it, so my mother was a carrier. She passed it to me. I carried it and passed it to Ben."

"You mean...?"

Bridget took her cue from Nell and continued the explanation, excitement growing. "It skips the women and only shows up in the men. We know Mom had the gene because it came out in Ben. If she'd had a son, he would probably have been colorblind too."

"Like you." Nell raised one eyebrow.

The three of them sat there and stared at one another for a good long moment.

"That's crazy," Adam burst out in a loud voice and scowled, pushing his chair back from the table. "You're saying Ellie might have been my mother? That my parents adopted me? You're out of your mind."

"Adam, why else would she have dressed you up in the Sullivan family christening gown and then kept it packed away with her other secrets in the living-room cupboard? Why else would she have continued sneaking up here for all these years? To go to your birthday parties?" Nell thought it through, adding up the evidence.

"What's your middle name, Adam?" Bridget looked over at Nell.

"Patrick. Why?"

Now Nell thought she knew for sure. "My mother's brother, who died when he was three, was named Patrick Gerard Sullivan. I'd bet every mutual fund my husband owns that you were named after him."

"Hey there, bro." Bridget clapped him on the shoulder, grinning at his frozen expression.

"Maybe this is why we've been such great friends from the start," Nell said, putting her hand on his arm. "I have to say that being with you is a lot like being with *her*." She nodded toward her sister, who laughed. Nell thought about how lucky it was that she'd recognized that Adam belonged in her life and his comfort and advice were there to support her.

"Look, just because my socks don't match and Ellie was at my christening, let's not assume I'm your mother's illegitimate love child," Adam said, standing up to pace the floor. "I am the spitting image of my dad, in case you've forgotten. How do you explain that?"

Bridget looked at Nell then gazed at Adam thoughtfully. "Probably because he is, indeed, your dad. In the absence of blood tests, there's only one way to find out, you know."

"What? Oh, no. You're not thinking…" He raised his hands as though warding off evil.

Nell got up and went into the hallway. "I'm going to get dressed and go over there to ask Jake. Anybody else coming?"

Jake made no effort to hide the truth. When he started talking, his face relaxed into an easy smile, and he spoke in a calm, natural tone. He seemed relieved that the story was finally coming to light.

"A few weeks after we got married, Ginnie developed an enormous fibroid tumor and ended up having a hysterectomy. When Ellie told me of her plan to have the baby adopted, I knew Virginia and I would never have children. It seemed best for everyone if we took the baby. Ginnie was thrilled, and Ellie could check in on Adam, be a part of his life. It was a wonderful gift for all of us."

Nell sat next to Adam, her arm around his shoulders. He was calm, perhaps too calm. The news had to be even harder for him to process than for her, and at the moment, she felt confused as hell.

"I'm sorry if it hurts you to find this out now, son," said Jake, his eyes worried. "We all wanted what was best for you."

Adam leaned forward and clasped Jake's hand in both of his. "I got to have all three of you as parents. I've always felt very loved."

"As you were, son."

"What about our father?" Bridget asked. "Did he know about this?"

Jake shook his head. "Not a word. Ellie wanted it that way. She lived up to her promises, that woman, and she knew how much Thomas needed her. I was even stupider in those days, and I forgot to tell her how much I loved her. Then I got shipped out, we lost touch for a while, and then it was too late. But when she gave Adam to me and Ginnie, she changed our lives forever, and we could never do enough to pay her back."

There was a pause while they all absorbed what had been said. The kettle whistled, and Bridget got up to make tea. She opened cupboards and assembled mugs and spoons with the confidence of someone who knew her way around the space.

"So… now my dream girls turn out to be two annoying kid sisters?" Adam said it with mock dismay, winking when he looked at Nell and Bridget. They returned his grin.

"I always figured it wasn't my secret to tell," Jake said. "Maybe I was wrong, but that's why I never said anything. It was up to Ellie."

Bridget spoke up. "Explain about you and Mom. How did you know each other?"

So Jake told them the story of war and terror, blood and death. He told them about the moments of peace he had shared with Mary. She'd worn a diamond engagement ring during the war and was determined to honor it afterward, so he hadn't pressed the matter. He knew a nice girl who loved him, so he settled down with her. He never expected to see Mary again.

When they all finished talking, it was getting dark outside. Then, like every other family in Hartland, they turned on the lights in the kitchen and started to cook dinner.

Later that night, Nell sat alone in her mother's living room and thought about the events of the day. Amazing, yet not so surprising. The truth had been coming together since she'd first discovered the cottage—a trail of secrets, leading to the biggest secret of all.

And there she was in Mom's hideaway, sitting next to a box of her mother's most important mementos. It had been Nell's destiny to stumble across them.

A ripple in time had curled up and then shaken itself out like a rumpled blanket, and a clean smooth future lay ahead. No longer wrapped in layers of faded memories and tucked away on the deepest shelves of the past where they might never be found, Mary Reilly's secrets had been released.

Nell put her mother's keepsakes back into the white box, replaced the lid, and slid it onto the bottom shelf of the corner cupboard. She closed the cabinet door firmly and heard it click.

CHAPTER 39

Bridget ~ 2015

BRIDGET LIVED QUIETLY IN HER mother's cottage for the next year, overseeing a few renovations and updating the décor but keeping it essentially a rustic country home. The Fall Festival weekend came again, and the town green filled up with striped tents, scarecrows, and the scent of fresh-baked pumpkin pie.

On Friday afternoon, before Nell and her family were due in town, Jake offered her another sailing lesson. Thrilled to control the big boat, Bridget loved to fly across the water, whipped by the wind and spray.

"Heading out onto the lake," he said casually, looking away even though he knew she was eager for another lesson. He was blatantly teasing. "Want to come?"

"If you'll let me skipper."

He snorted. "That will be the day." It was gruff, but a little smile emerged from under his shaggy moustache, and they drove to the town beach in Jake's old King Cab pickup with the windows all rolled down and the hot afternoon sun bouncing up off the black pavement. It shimmered ahead of them in the road like a ghost.

Jake parked in the lot next to the docks. He grabbed a cap and sweatshirt for each of them out of the backseat, then Bridget stood still and let him patiently dress her, his shirt absurdly too big. The adjustable cap was a better fit. She turned it around with the bill in the back and put on her big Dolce & Gabbana sunglasses, striking a model's pose to make him laugh.

Jake instructed Bridget as she stood at the tiller while he cast off from the dock, and they motored the old wooden sailboat slowly away from the pier. He came to stand beside her as they chugged past a few moored boats and out into the lake.

The crisp, cool breeze was in her face, and she breathed in the aromatic scent of the pines, her spirits lifting as they always did out on the water. When they were clear of the harbor and other traffic, Jake shut off the motor and raised both sails, and soon they were racing along the eastern side with the wind whipping the cap right off Bridget's head. She laughed as it flew up and away behind them, and her long hair streamed out like Botticelli's Venus gone mad.

Energized and free, with the spray-filled air rushing by, Bridge was transfixed by sensations. The boat made it nearly all the way to the far end of the lake in one long port tack, and then Jake watched while she carefully turned the wheel and came about with the wind on her right for the starboard tack.

Looking at him pointedly, Bridget yelled, "Coming about" just before she turned. The heavy boom swung across the deck as the mainsail shifted from one side to the other. Jake had taught her to do this just as she would yell, "Fore" at the golf course before hitting the ball.

Bridget looked down into the dark water and thought of Ginnie, floating like a naiad with her white eyes glowing and pale limbs splayed. Finding a person in that deep water would be impossible—somebody drifting, unconscious, down toward the faraway bottom with its thick, confusing grasses, the air bubbling out of her lungs, the life spark quenched. *It's a miracle they weren't all three drowned.* If there was one thing she understood, it was guilt. But maybe the days of remorse were over both for her and for Jake.

Life was coming about onto a new tack.

Living without a man in her bed at the moment was actually okay. Sex was great, but love was better, and Bridget had decided to wait for the real thing. She liked having her own space, and time to think about where her life would go next. She and the Bascombs went back and forth between the two houses and shared a lot of meals.

She wondered what Jake saw when he looked at her so lovingly. Was it just a memory of a younger version of her mother? He already knew Bridget better than most other people on Earth and seemed to still be fond of her despite it, unlike her ex-husband Eric, who had used her private confessions as a weapon and mocked her. He had signed the divorce papers without a fuss, though, and it was all over fast.

And the next day, she would meet her daughter for the first time since Cole's parents took her away. Bridget's new life was sailing along at a very nice clip.

⌇

Early on Saturday morning, Bridget slipped out the back door of Jake's farmhouse, where she had just dropped off a homemade cinnamon coffee cake for the volunteers who were meeting there before the charity auction. She walked home on the path through the woods, picking her way through the speckled morning light. The air felt fresh and smelled like new-mown grass. Falling leaves zigzagged lazily under the trees.

She wrapped her cardigan sweater tighter around her waist, took a deep breath, and tasted the air. She came through the arbor into the garden and quietly let herself into the fragrant kitchen, where a pot already steamed in the coffeemaker. A second coffee cake waited on the wooden cutting board.

Bridget rummaged in the fridge, which was packed full of leftovers from recent family meals. She managed not to think about meeting her daughter that day for a good thirty seconds while she looked for eggs.

Quiet in the house was a precious thing these days, so she tried not to wake everyone up. She made breakfast, chewed calmly, washed the frying pan and utensils, rinsed her dishes, and put them in the new dishwasher.

Then before she could start getting nervous again, she went upstairs to look for Nell.

CHAPTER 40

Nell ~ 2015

THE SCENT OF FRESH COFFEE trickled into Nell's dream, and she opened her eyes just as David was putting a warm mug into her hand.

"Oh. Mmmm… yes," she mumbled, sitting up and sipping. The sheet slipped off her bare shoulders and fell to her waist. She saw him watching with obvious interest and let him have a nice long look then pulled the covers back up. "Oops." She flirted, smiling, and carefully lifted the full mug to her lips again.

In the broad light of day, she was a tiny bit embarrassed by the memory of things they had done the previous night in Mom's old bedroom. It seemed kind of weird with most of Mom's clothes still hanging in the closet. But it had been exciting too. They were getting along so much better.

Because something amazing had happened. On New Year's Eve, lying in bed together and watching Times Square on television as the ball dropped at midnight, David had made a shocking confession.

"I love you, Nell, but… I want to make a change in our marriage."

"What?" She couldn't believe her ears. Immediately assuming he meant a divorce, her stunned mind went totally blank, and she stopped breathing.

Her mouth fell open with surprise, and he hurried to add, "I feel so isolated from the family, Nell. My job is incredibly stressful, and it's wearing me down. At this rate, I'll soon be an old man. Don't want these years with the kids to pass me by. Soon enough, they'll be off to college." He blinked, his face innocent and excited, gazing at her like a puppy hoping for a reward.

Nell inhaled, closed her mouth, and slowly gathered her wits. Not what she had thought. Not a disaster. *Breathe, just breathe.* How dare he scare her like that? She glared, not sure whether to kiss him or kick him. "What are you talking about?"

He sat up in bed and talked, waving his hands and turning all the way around to face her. "I want to divide up our responsibilities differently, to share the parenting. My New Year's resolution is to find a new job. Maybe telecommuting or consulting work. Might go back to teaching. You know, something less intense."

Nell thought about David being at home all day, telling her what to do, leaving her no time to herself, and a surge of anxiety welled up inside her. "But... I need a change too, David. I need to stop spending all my energy helping everyone else, and—"

"This way, you would have much less responsibility for the family and more free time for yourself. I know you gave up a lot to stay home with the kids, Nell. It's not too late to get it back. We've saved enough to earn less if we move someplace that isn't so expensive. Maybe up to New England, in the country. What do you think?"

Nell thought this all sounded fabulous. She had somehow managed to get what she wanted without even having to ask for it. David seemed totally sincere and was more like the man she'd married than the irritable corporate clone she'd been living with for the past ten years. She felt a fragile tendril of hope start to grow inside her, and it had strengthened every day since.

They put their house on the market and almost immediately got a good cash offer. David gave his notice at work, and suddenly, they were a team, working together side by side to find a new home for their family. The dynamic between them changed. David volunteered to do things that Nell dreaded, like cleaning the pool and weeding the flowerbeds. They talked a lot more, discussing the future.

"We need to spend more time together, Nell." David held her hand across the table at the restaurant where they'd been going for date night lately. "I want our relationship to be like it used to be."

"I do too, sort of."

"What does that mean?" His brow furrowed, and his eyes widened.

"There are things I want to change too. I've been thinking about it. Now is the perfect time since all our routines are shifting."

And so she told him about her fantasy of having time alone with just her thoughts for company and maybe trying to write. It all came out, and to her surprise, he was not upset. Nor did he try to manage a solution for her. Instead, he gazed at her with love and kissed her hand.

"I support you, Nell. Whatever you decide to do. You're the greatest."

"Really?" That was the best reaction he could possibly have given her. Why hadn't she said all that before? Maybe things would have changed sooner. Or maybe not. He would have had to be ready too.

"Absolutely." He smiled warmly. "I'm grateful that you stuck with me on my fifteen-year paid vacation in Hell, but now I've realized my mistake, and it's your turn. Go for it!"

Since then, David had found a job teaching business management at Northeastern University in Boston. He would only have classes three days a week and got the whole summer off. They moved to Sherborn, Massachusetts. It was quiet, rural, small-town America with top-rated public schools.

Nell had written a poem nearly every day since then, sent off a few submissions, and signed up to attend a writer's conference. She couldn't decide whether to apply to graduate school or look for a job. What she really wanted to do was write. One of her poems had been published in a small journal. When her copy of the magazine arrived in the mail, it was like seeing her babies for the first time. A piece of her mind had gone out into the world, and now it had a life of its own.

Nell's family was back in Hartland for the Fall Festival and to enjoy the lake one last time before cold weather set in. David and the kids were heading back to Sherborn afterwards, but Nell wanted to stay on for a while. Bridget had promised not to interrupt when she was writing.

David watched her sip the coffee he'd brought then sat on the edge of the queen-sized bed that now occupied the spot by the garden window. "What's your plan for today?" He stroked her arm, leaning over to kiss her.

"I'm going to bring Lauren and Bridget over to the festival."

"See you at the town green, then. Ben and I are helping Adam bring some furniture to the auction. We're going to hang with him and Jake, do man stuff for a while." He was wearing a plaid flannel shirt and jeans and had made himself at home in the mellow country atmosphere.

"Cool. I'm glad you're friends with my brother." Nell smiled, remembering how different from each other she used to think the two men were.

David stood to leave but paused. "He's really a great guy, Nell. I like him a lot."

"Not much like your old competitive corporate buddies, is he?" Nell laughed and tried not to spill her coffee.

"Yeah, but even though he's a country boy, he's not a hick. He's a successful entrepreneur." David kept his eye on the sheet tucked under her arms, which was slipping again. "Hey, I'm not afraid to get my hands dirty, either. By the way, the guys are talking about going camping together sometime soon. Adam's going to help me and Ben get geared up."

"Great, we can have a girls' gathering here with Bridget."

"Perfect." He leaned over to kiss her again then turned to go. "Love you," he said from the doorway and smiled. Nell thought she hadn't seen him so happy in years. She heard him clatter down the stairs and collect Ben from the den, where he'd slept on the couch.

It's this place. Something about the air and the pure light and the brilliant colors. The wild got into a person, and a new spirit emerged. First Mom, then Nell and Bridget, and now David.

The back door slammed, and soon the smell of toasted bread wafted up the stairs. Bridget was home.

Nell put her coffee on the bedside table and stretched. She lay and daydreamed, reveling in her newfound sense of infinite possibilities. She heard the door to the front bedroom open, just as Bridget reached the second-floor landing. Eavesdropping was impossible to avoid.

"Good morning, missy."

"Don't call me that." Lauren sounded grouchy.

"Good morning, beautiful princess. Is that better?"

"Yes. Morning, Auntie B."

"Come in here," Nell called. "Both of you." She put on her robe and tied the belt.

Lauren and Bridget appeared in the doorway, looking sheepish.

"Good morning, Mommy," they said in chorus. Bridget grinned.

"Get over here right now. You are both in such big trouble." Nell frowned and pointed down at the bed.

Giggling madly, Lauren and Bridget raced across the room and leapt onto the bed. A pillow fight erupted then a tickle attack, then all three of them lay piled together looking out the bedside window into the back garden.

Sheer lace curtains fluttered, and lemony morning sunlight dappled the white sheets. Bridget pulled the top one over their heads like a tent. They peered out through the opening made by her hands. Lauren's orange-and-white tiger cat, Pumpkin, was chasing butterflies in the flowerbed. Nell pointed then made the *shush* sign with a finger to her lips.

"Meow," she said, perfectly imitating a cat. Pumpkin jumped up and whipped around, looking suspiciously toward the house. All three of them burst out laughing.

"Meow," Lauren and Bridget said. "Meow."

"Time to get dressed, little kitties."

Nell, Bridget, and Lauren drove into town and parked on a side street near Adam's apartment. The festivities were in full swing, and the whole town seemed to be there. Nell saw her friend the librarian and waved to some of the nurses from the hospital. Kids were playing games and racing around. People visited the vendors' booths and placed bids on items at the open-air auction. An old-fashioned barbershop quartet wearing red-and-white-striped jackets was singing in front of the fountain. Two huge Belgian draft horses hitched to a hay wagon were standing at the curb, waiting for the next load of passengers.

"Let's go over there." Bridget pointed at an empty bench and clutched Nell by the arm.

"Okay, don't cut off my circulation. Look, there's Adam." Nell waved. He was carrying a pair of lamps up onto the stage to be auctioned.

Adam saw them and smiled. A couple of attractive mid-thirties women standing nearby looked to see whom he was smiling at. They frowned when they saw Nell and Bridget sitting in the shade of a big red maple. The women put their heads together and whispered behind their hands.

Bridget looked at her watch and then scanned the crowd.

"Be calm. I'm sure you'll do great." Nell took Bridget's hand and gave it a squeeze. "She's lucky to have you. So am I. I've always known that too."

"Thanks." Bridget took a deep breath.

She jumped to her feet. "I'm going to take a walk around, see if they're lost in the crowd."

"Can I go hang out with Daddy over there?" Lauren said, pointing toward the auction stage, where David and Ben were helping.

"Okay, I'll wait here." Nell watched her go, enjoying the comfortable vantage point.

Local produce and goods were for sale, and there was every kind of food imaginable. The smell of cinnamon, maple, and grilled sausages filled the air. A few minutes later, Nell noticed a silver-haired man in an expensive-looking beige jacket and gray slacks. He was walking with a young woman with long blond hair who looked strikingly familiar.

Just then Bridget turned from the booth, where she'd been examining handmade quilts, and she saw the couple too. Her face flushed with excitement and a yearning, wistful expression. Stepping forward, she waved. The man looked at her. He touched the girl on the arm and pointed.

Lizzie turned, and Nell thought how alike they were, mother and daughter, as they stood facing each other across the lawn. Profiles identical, the same hair. The girl was younger, taller, and slimmer, but the Reilly genes were obvious. She was another child of the clan.

The two approached each other and spoke. Bridget looked nervous, and the girl's body language was stiff. Then Bridget reached out as the girl swayed toward her. She leaned forward and kissed her on the cheek, scanning her face as though memorizing it. Then she looked over at her sister and laughed when she saw Nell was watching.

"My daughter." Bridget mouthed the words. Her smile was radiant, and she gestured excitedly. She pointed out Nell to Lizzie, who waved and smiled.

Nell waved back and stayed put, giving them time. She sat on the bench and watched Hartland doing what it did best. In front of the fountain, benches were filled with mothers with baby strollers and backpacks. Dads followed toddlers as they waddled along the sidewalks chasing toys, pigeons, and each other. Grandparents sat in lawn chairs under the trees, guarding blankets where babies slumbered. People laughed, patted each other on the back, and hugged.

They know the secret. What we're all trying to discover. A simple idea but so elusive.

Once, Nell would have said that people ought to constantly struggle to evolve and improve themselves, to achieve bigger and better successes. Her life had been a series of hurdles and challenges, many of which were impossible to attain. But in Hartland, she had discovered a new attitude. And it had made all the difference.

Life is short. Be happy. That was it, the nutshell version.

Nell smiled, and endorphins rushed into her bloodstream as her body responded to the facial expression. She felt a subtle shift in consciousness. She had taken control of her reality, and it had changed. She was happy. All because by coming here and finding out how her mother had dealt with regret, a veil had been lifted.

There were no more secrets to keep.

AUTHOR'S NOTE

There is a real place called Hartland, Vermont. I have borrowed the name and surrounding landscape for this story, but the town and its inhabitants are totally imaginary.

ABOUT THE AUTHOR

Gail Cleare has written for newspapers, magazines, and Fortune 100 companies. Her advertising agency worked for the co-creators of the Teenage Mutant Ninja Turtles, and she was Leonardo's date for the premiere of the second movie. She got to wear a black silk evening gown and sparkly shoes, and ride in the Turtle Mobile.

When she worked for AOL, Gail wrote a cooking column about chocolate and read Tarot cards live online. Her fine art photography is held in private collections across the US.

Gail lives on an 18th century farm in Massachusetts with her family and dogs, cats, chickens, black bears, blue herons, rushing streams and wide, windy skies. She writes fiction full time now, sitting by a view of woodlands and pastures.

20988910R00152